BUT NOW I SEE

BUT NOW I SEE

John A. Brothers, Jr.

iUniverse, Inc.
New York   Bloomington

But Now I See

Copyright © 2008 by John A. Brothers, Jr.

iUniverse books may be ordered through booksellers or by contacting:

iUniverse
1663 Liberty Drive
Bloomington, IN 47403
www.iuniverse.com
1-800-Authors (1-800-288-4677)

ISBN: 978-0-595-53324-4 (pbk)
ISBN: 978-1-4401-0707-8 (cloth)
ISBN: 978-0-595-63379-1 (ebk)

Printed in the United States of America

Library of Congress Control Number: 2008940906

iUniverse rev. date: 11/11/08

For the second time they called the man who had been blind, and they said to him, "Give the glory to God! We know that the one you say healed you is a sinner."
He answered,
"I do not know whether he is a sinner or not.
One thing I do know:
I was blind, but now I see."

John 9: 24-25

WILL McKENZIE

I pronounced the blessing, the service ended, and "Joy to the World" belted forth from the enormous pipe organ. I loved Christmas Eve Communion. Tonight's service pleased me, but I felt my fatigue as I walked to the door. Outside, the tower bell rang twelve midnight, announcing Christmas Day to the New Orleans neighborhood.

"Merry Christmas, Reverend McKenzie," little Amy murmured, resting her head on her father's shoulder as he carried her out. "Merry Christmas to you too, Amy." I gently rubbed her soft cheek with the back of my first two fingers. I was surprised to see her since most children came to the early service. "Have a good one, Will," her father said as they left.

An usher rushed up, jumping between the exiting members. "A woman just came in who's real upset, hysterical. She's in a pew near the back of the church. Can you come take care of her?" My heart sank. Christmas could be a rough time for people who were lonely or depressed, and I wondered if that might not be her case.

She was sitting alone, sobbing so hard her shoulders twitched with each spasmodic gasp of air. Her lowered head made it difficult to see her face, but I recognized her -- Alice Hendricks of a wealthy, socially prominent family. I put my hand on her shoulder, calmly calling her name. As our eyes met, she lowered her head again and tried to stop her convulsive sobbing.

I sat down beside her in the pew. Her hands were clenched into fists, and she blurted, "He broke my heart; so I broke his." She sobbed some more. "How could he? On Christmas Eve." She still breathed in

1

spasms, although not crying as hard now. I thought I smelled bourbon on her breath. Taking a Kleenex from her purse, she wiped her eyes, rubbed at the mascara running down her cheeks, and blew her nose. She looked directly at me and repeated, "He broke my heart; so I broke his." Her repeated words bothered me, and I suspected that the story of an affair was about to unfold.

Several folks had gathered around us, so I led Alice into the church parlor. She slumped into a wingback chair as I closed the door. When I pulled up a chair, I noticed her coat had fallen open revealing her white blouse heavily spattered with blood. My senses sharpened. I felt my neck tense. I also noticed her hands were spotted with dried blood. "Good Lord," I thought; "She and Stan must have really gotten into it."

When I looked at her bloody blouse again, I felt my own blood drain from my face. In my mind I saw an image from the past of black hair lying in a pool of blood …like it just happened … then a child's limp arm spattered with browning blood. Shaking my head, I regained control of myself and focused on Alice. She didn't seem to notice my distraction. Rather, she looked at me with angry eyes and started telling me what had happened.

She repeated through gritted teeth, "How could he? The cheating liar. That same woman. I knew it all along. He often had perfume on his shirt when he got home from work. I could believe a random hug from the switchboard operator. That's what he claimed the first time. But three times with the same perfume?" She shifted in her chair, blew her nose, and then continued. "There were evenings when he claimed to be meeting a colleague's plane. I knew he'd met that slut instead. I even traced his phone calls to her when he traveled out of town. Again and again. The whore. Young, ambitious, and pushing to be dean of the law school. She couldn't care less."

Alice grabbed a Kleenex from the box on the table and wiped her eyes. "Stan finally admitted to having the affair. He swore she meant nothing to him and that he'd never see her again. Said she'd caught him in a weak moment." Alice took a deep breath and exhaled. "Weak moment my ass. He knew what he was doing."

Her anger increased and her crying stopped. "I dropped the kids off at mother's tonight; we planned to pick them up early in the morning. Stan had gone to his office Christmas party, and we were supposed to meet here at church. He didn't show and didn't show." She paused and sobbed several more times. "When the service got started, I decided to go to that party to get him. I was furious by then. The guests were horrified when I barged in to find Stan. I figured he would probably be drunk or something. When I swung open the door to the kitchen, I found them going at it. He was all over her. One hand in her blouse and the other on her rear." Alice paused and lowered her head, covering her face with her bloodstained hands. "O God. Forgive me. Forgive me." She sobbed uncontrollably once again.

Three very loud raps on the door startled me. "Police! Open up," came the shouted command. As I opened the door, I found myself facing a policeman with a drawn gun in his hand. "Police!" he repeated. "Is Alice Hendricks in here?"

"Yes she is," I replied as I swung the door open wide. "Can you put that gun away?"

The officer was all business, ignoring my request. A policewoman with a rifle quickly followed him in. Alice remained silent and lowered her head into her hands. The male officer asked her to stand, told her she was under arrest for murder, then read her rights to her. His partner handcuffed Alice's wrists behind her as she stood silently, staring into the parlor's cold, dark fireplace. The policewoman took Alice's arm and asked her to go with them. Alice balked for a second, looking panicked. "My God, what will happen to me?" she blurted out. "The kids, what about the kids?" She looked at me with pleading eyes.

As the policewoman led Alice out of the parlor, her partner turned to me and blew a lungful of air through barely open lips. "Killed her husband with a kitchen knife. Straight through the heart. Twice." I winced as the officer shook his head and continued. "That's what they say, anyway." He followed Alice and the policewoman out, and I went right behind them.

On our way to the squad car, the policeman told me several party guests had seen Alice leave the kitchen with the knife in her hand. Others saw her drop the knife on the front lawn before she left in her yellow PT Cruiser. The officers heard the radio dispatch and easily spotted her car near the church.

I felt useless as they put Alice into the cramped back seat of the police car and radioed in their report. "Can I ride with her?" I asked the officer.

"Sorry, Reverend. Against regulations. Besides, no one's going to be able to see her for a while. Why don't you check on her children? Someone said they were with the grandparents."

I nodded, and then looked at Alice in the back seat of the patrol car. I wanted to tell her something, but I didn't know what. The police radio squawked loudly, the back door to the police car was locked, and Alice stared at her feet. The policewoman turned on the blue dome-light, no siren thank God, and drove off.

I watched the car disappear around the corner. A handful of lingering church members murmured to one another, and then drifted to their cars. One man, however, kept asking me questions. I didn't know him, but visitors at the Christmas Eve service were not unusual. Then he pulled a small notepad out of his pocket as he followed me to my car.

"I'd appreciate your not following me," I told him. "I'm going to tell her parents, and that's not an appropriate place for the media." He asked me several more questions and finally backed off when I didn't answer him.

My thoughts turned to Andy and June, who were now about five and seven. Their father dead, their mother on her way to jail, and Christmas made the entire situation even worse. What on earth could I say to them? Who would raise them? Alice's parents were certainly too old. Stan had only a father in Atlanta, so that wouldn't work. Who will tell Stan's father? I pushed that question out of my mind, figuring it was a police problem, not mine. I wondered if the press would get to him first.

Then I wondered how to tell Alice's parents. Faye and John Benson were long-time, active members of the church. Their house was less than two miles away, but I dreaded going there. They were undoubtedly already asleep. Maybe the news could wait until morning when Alice might be able to call them herself, or maybe a police officer would call them, or perhaps an attorney. As unpleasant as the prospect felt, I realized they needed to know tonight, and I seemed to be the one who would have to tell them. I took several deep breaths and then drove toward their house.

I was not surprised to find the house pitch dark. I hesitated again. Forcing myself out of the car, I closed the door very quietly for fear of waking up someone. The neighbors? I felt like if I kept quiet long enough the horror would all go away, but it didn't. With a sinking feeling in the pit of my stomach, I walked up the steps to their front door.

Is this how those Marine officers felt when they had to inform a family that their son or husband or father had died in combat? I only wrote letters that their widows might read weeks or maybe months later. Nobody told me to write those letters. I had to. So many men -- well over half my platoon. Thirteen guys whose names still come to me in the night. Jefferson, the first to die -- blown apart because I ordered us to advance. The horror continued. My men.

I paused at the Benson's front door. Damn Vietnam. Damn tonight. Damn this killing business.

With more resignation than courage, I rang the doorbell. The ring echoed in a house that didn't yet know it was hollow.

+++++

Arriving home at last, I hoisted myself out of the car. Earlier I had called Carol on my way to Faye and John's home, waking her up, as I knew I would. I told her something had happened to one of our members and promised to tell her the details when I got home.

Carol was asleep on the sofa when I entered the family room. She had hung our stockings, complete with the traditional navel orange bulging in the toe. No one ever ate the orange. Carol had also set out the one special present we'd purchased for David. Santa Claus remained alive and well in our house, we joked, even though David was fifteen. On the fireplace hearth sat a Coke bottle, a ritual we had continued for several generations. My parents used to give me a cold coke and a bottle opener to place on the hearth for Santa. When I came downstairs on Christmas morning the bottle was always opened and empty. As I started to question Santa Claus, the empty Coke bottle kept me believing one more year. I've put a Coke out ever since. I smiled at the memories that bottle brought as I admired the readied hearth.

I sat down on the rug beside Carol who was still sound asleep. The drama and sadness of the evening had drained me. Besides, it was already past two-thirty. I knew I would have a hard time in the morning pushing aside all that had happened in order to make our Christmas a happy one. Still, that became my hope.

Carol looked beautiful asleep on the sofa. She lay half curled up, a hand under her head. Sitting on the floor beside her, I adored her and smiled warmly. She had drooled just a little on the light green pillow, but she still looked almost angelic. Carol was just a little taller than five foot two, and like the old song said, she had eyes of blue. David, whose picture was on the end table, had her cheeks and nose. Our frustrated hope of having more children ran through my head, and I felt that twinge of sadness surface again. Be thankful for David, a late child, I reminded myself. I leaned over and kissed Carol on the cheek. She blinked awake, yawned, then mumbled, "What happened?"

I told her the story as quickly as I could, but she wanted to know all the details. I went through the sad saga, including Faye's fainting spell when I told her the news and John's smashing the table-picture of his unfaithful son-in-law.

"I offered to go over again tomorrow, well…today. They wanted to tell the kids by themselves, but they also wanted me to be there shortly afterwards. I urged them to have Christmas for the kids before telling them. Was that a good idea or not?" I looked to Carol for a response, and she nodded affirmatively. "Anyway, I hope they don't call too early. I also hope David's true to his habits and sleeps in."

Carol nodded again. I yawned deeply and then helped her up off the sofa. I could tell she mulled a lot of questions in her mind as we wandered back to the waiting bed. Just before Carol crawled in again, she caught me off guard by asking, "What does God do with someone like Alice?"

I thought for a second, then replied, "Forgives her, I guess. Whether the state will do the same is the question."

She probably didn't hear my reply. She was already asleep again.

Sleep came more slowly for me.

+++++

The shrill ring of the bedside phone ended our Christmas morning's sleep. Carol sat up on the side of the bed. "Merry Christmas," she answered in a sarcastic tone. Then came a series of, "Yes. Yes. I don't know. No," and then she hung up. "Well, the word is out. It obviously made the paper." She rolled out of the warm bed, put on her fleece robe, and headed to the front door. She always got the morning paper as soon as she woke up.

Carol returned, reading the headlines aloud as she walked. The front page shouted "Christmas Eve Slaughter" in bold, inch-high letters. A picture in full color of Stan Hendricks lying face down on the blood-filled kitchen floor appeared under the headline.

" I sure hope their children don't see this," Carol exclaimed. "What trashy journalism." Carol walked over to the bed, still reading out loud. Our phone rang again.

"Yes, Lilly, that's right. No, I haven't had a chance to finish reading the article yet; Will hasn't either. We just got the paper out of the driveway. No, he got home just a few hours ago, so he isn't completely awake yet." She paused. "Well, it *is* only six-fifteen on Christmas morning," Carol snipped. She could be very blunt, yet most people liked that about her. She was straightforward and trustworthy, and you knew where you stood.

I felt guilty that I wasn't already shaved, showered, dressed, and ready to handle all incoming demands. After all these years I still fell into the parish-guilt routine. I always expected myself to be on top of things, which I never quite managed. I wanted to be ready to contend with whatever arose, which often I wasn't. I felt like I was back in Vietnam with a platoon looking to me for direction and survival. I pushed off the ridiculous comparison. Or was it? My feelings right now were much the same as then, with one big difference: I loved being a minister, but I hated Vietnam.

When the phone rang again, Carol flipped on the answering machine, turning the volume down as low as it would go. After the sixth call, she unplugged the phone completely.

"It says here," she continued reading from the paper, "Rev. William McKenzie offered Alice Hendricks sanctuary in the church. He finally turned her over to the police after sheltering her in the parlor."

"Offered her sanctuary! Sheltering her!" I gulped in disbelief. "Good Lord, what else does the paper say? Did I hide the knife too?"

Carol continued to read the article out loud. The story quickly became sketchy and trailed off to a close. It didn't continue past the front page. She handed me the paper when she'd finished reading. As I looked at the bloody picture, I commented, "Everything you ever wanted to know about family-dynamics-gone-awry spread front and center in full living color."

On the right side of the front page was an article featured the Toys for Tots program scheduled at the Jefferson Civic Center at ten. On the left was a news story about twenty-five more deaths in the Middle East. We've gotten totally numb to those killings, I thought. I looked again in disbelief at the photograph of Stan's bloody body. Twenty-five killings were a long way away; one killing was right here. That made the difference in our attention, I thought. Both articles, nevertheless, featured dead humans.

I automatically rubbed the tear off my right cheek with my index finger and wiped it on my robe. It was too early for that to start. Usually about mid-morning that eye, and only that eye, watered up, and the tearing would continue unpredictably throughout the day. I'd gotten used to wiping the tears away, usually without thinking. I'd given up finding a cause or a cure. I had come to accept this quirk as a part of my life. The tear was benign enough, but annoying. Something worse could plague me, I told myself after the last doctor threw up his hands.

"I'm going to talk to Malcolm about this picture," I told Carol. "I find it highly offensive. Perhaps he didn't have a chance to sign off on it due to the holiday, but that's no excuse. It's all geared to sensationalism." Carol agreed with a clipped "yep."

I respected the *Times-Picayune* as one of the state's oldest newspapers. For two generations it'd been the flagship publication of Louisiana. However, when the current generation of the Ellison family took over, things changed. The new publisher, Malcolm Ellison, allowed, probably even encouraged, an appeal to the sensational. He's one of my flock.

I felt my anger increase, partly at the newspaper coverage, partly at Alice's impulsive stabbing, partly at Stan's unfaithfulness, and partly because of those early morning phone calls that kept coming. Even now I heard a muted voice identify himself as a reporter, leaving his number for me to call back. Good luck.

"Good thing you didn't answer the phone," Carol declared. "I can see the follow-up article now," she smirked. "High-Steeple Preacher Curses Out Truth-Seeking Reporter on Christmas Day." Smiling wryly, she walked over and kissed me. She understands me pretty well, I thought.

"No comments in that article from the District Attorney, I noticed. I bet Alice won't be arraigned until sometime next week because of the holidays, and until then she'll be confined to central lockup."

"What's with the phone calls?" interrupted David, who stood in our bedroom door in his boxer shorts and t-shirt.

"A mess, that's what." I replied, pointing to the newspaper on the bed. "I'll let your mother catch you up on what's happening while I get some coffee going."

"I'll be damned!" David blurted out when he saw the headlines. "Stan Hendricks! Shit! He helped with baseball last year. Murdered." Carol and I winced at his language, but neither of us called him down. David picked up the paper as we all went into the kitchen.

"Well, Dad, now that you're involved in this murder, are you going to explain how God fits into all this? I mean both Mr. and Mrs. Hendricks are Christians, aren't they?"

David knew how to ask the questions I hated to see coming. But before I could answer, his thoughts had already moved on. "Talk about hypocrites. How could they call themselves Christians and do stuff like this?" He didn't wait for an answer to that question either. "Will you have to go to the trial? Will you have to tell what happened while she was at the church?" This time he did pause for an answer.

"I don't know," I responded. "My hunch is that the trial won't start for months. The whole prospect makes me none too happy. I dread the thought that the trial might drag on for months." Killings had a way of doing that, I found myself thinking.

"Let's finish getting dressed," Carol suggested. "Maybe we can have a somewhat normal Christmas for a while. I'll fix us some breakfast, and then let's open the presents."

David announced that he was going back to bed.

So much for Carol's attempt to bring order to the morning's chaos. I'd noticed she'd been watching me carefully, but trying not to get caught doing it. I knew what that was about.

"You're afraid this murder will cause me to have flashbacks, aren't you?"

She sighed. "That had crossed my mind."

"Well, so far so good." I paused. "Strange memories did hit me while I talked with Alice, and more came shortly afterwards. But I've managed to keep things under control; it's going to stay that way. I feel sure of it." Grabbing the coffee pot, I poured us both a cup.

Carol sliced a bagel in half with a sharp butcher knife and popped both halves in the toaster. She put the knife on the counter and spun it. That struck me as strange, but I didn't say anything.

+++++

"Faye called to say they told the children "a bit of what happened," I told Carol and David. "They didn't want me to come by now, but asked me to be on stand-by. I am always on stand-by, right?" I sipped some of my coffee. "They were worried sick about Alice and were particularly upset they couldn't see her. However, they were certainly not concerned about Stan. Their angry feelings toward him had surfaced last night, and they expressed even more anger on the phone this morning. They knew things had been sour between Alice and Stan for a long time. Seems a lot of people knew that."

I pushed the telephone further back on the desk, and my thoughts continued to flow. Children aren't stupid. Andy and June had to know something was very wrong. It just wasn't right for both their parents to be gone on Christmas Day. It just wasn't right to have to stay indoors all day on Christmas either. Furthermore, I'm also sure Faye and John couldn't effectively hide their own feelings from the kids, no matter how hard they tried. Kids know when something is wrong.

I thought about how hard we try to protect the ones we love, trying to shield them from things we can't control or contain. Above all, I think we try to shield our loved ones from death. We say it's because we love them, but if we talk about death with our four or six-year-old, we have to come to terms with death ourselves.

"Have faith; it will all work out for the good" is a platitude I hear people use to comfort themselves at times like this. Tell that to a Holocaust victim. Tell that to a mother of four who has just heard her doctor use the word cancer. Tell that to a soldier oozing blood while bullets and shrapnel still heat the air. Tell that to a mother who's behind bars for a murder she's not entirely sorry she committed.

Faith can help us live in an imperfect world, but having faith certainly won't make things right. We may need God's help to get through the mire, but the mire's still there. Always has been, always will be.

Meanwhile, where's the peace of Christmas today? This particular Christmas felt like a facade of peace mocked by anguish and death. This Christmas was staged against the backdrop of blood, highlighted by a rage that had lashed out without restraint when a desperate cry within screamed, "kill or be killed." Alice reached that point last night. We've all been there at some time in our lives, or we soon will be, but the shadow Alice's actions cast over Christmas became long, dark, and enveloping.

+++++

After opening the presents, we had a late Christmas dinner complete with turkey, dressing, and cranberry sauce. Then we drifted into the family room where David flipped channels on the television looking for the latest news. We had deliberately left the TV off all morning, but now we let the media pull us back to the unavoidable reality happening within our community and our church.

One channel showed a sharply dressed young woman with perfect teeth standing in front of our church. "A little after midnight last night, Alice Hendricks was arrested in this church where she talked with her minister following the brutal murder of her husband only blocks away. Sources say she had planned to meet her husband for the midnight service, but when he didn't show …."

I quickly tuned her out. I figured she was just doing her job and would soon join her boyfriend or husband for Christmas. They would probably talk about the story, what she felt while gathering the information, how she came across on TV, and what her boss might say about her coverage. Everybody's got an angle.

I wondered what mine was. Sometimes I thought I knew; at other times I hadn't a clue. The ministry allowed very little time to think about angles, only time to react to needs. Most of the time I simply responded to those in need, aiming to be caring and helpful. In the Marines, I learned to evaluate strategies and make plans before an assault, because once the shells started flying you only had time to react. The same had been true in this large parish.

Our answering machine clicked on with another incoming call. The counter showed sixteen messages. This time I listened because I recognized the voice of Peter Bernard, the Clerk of our Session at church. As the head of our governing body, Peter could be my best ally; he could also be my most acrid critic. He was always honest and straightforward, and you never had to guess where he stood. But he could be blunt and abrasive. In some ways Peter and Carol were a lot alike -- except that Carol was loveable and Peter wasn't. I wondered for the twentieth time what the difference was.

Peter wished us a merry Christmas and then got to his point. "I'm calling, Will, to urge you to stay out of this Hendricks affair. We don't want you or the church to get entangled in some sort of legal mess. Not that I don't trust you, but lawyers and reporters can make mincemeat out of even the most alert witness. We'll talk some more about this later. Meanwhile, don't say anything to the news or to attorneys. I hope you all have a great Christmas." The machine clicked off.

I deleted the message. "I'm glad I didn't pick up," I said. Carol looked away from the TV; David was playing a new game on the computer. "Peter chaps me at times, even though he means well. Say, exactly how long do you think we should we leave this phone on the "monitoring" mode? We can't keep this holding pattern forever."

Carol shrugged. "Whatever," she replied and headed for the kitchen.

While the aroma of fresh brewed coffee drifted from the kitchen, Carol started clipping the lead article from the paper. She had been keeping a scrapbook about me since we arrived in New Orleans almost ten years ago and was now on her second volume. I watched as she routinely looked on the backside of the article to see what she had destroyed.

"Look at this." She held the clipping up for me to see. Behind the picture of Stan's bloody body was an ad, in equally brilliant color, from the First Baptist Church. "Keep Christ in Your Christmas" was its message. But the manger scene had been sliced in half.

+++++

The day after Christmas I went to the French Quarter for coffee. I pushed back in my chair and stirred in a spoonful of sugar into my café au lait brewed with chicory and hot milk. Then I and fired up my laptop. Several weeks had passed since I had e-mailed James, and weeks could be a long time not to be in touch with my Vietnam buddy. I still can't believe he left New Orleans. Eating red beans and rice every Monday at Ye Olde College Inn had been an important time together ever since we met here after the war. His move to Paris really put a kink in our relationship. We had gone through every skirmish together and had come to rely on each other like twins.

James married a girl from Vietnam, Lanna, whom he managed to get to the States. But when she died from breast cancer last year, he moved to Paris to start a new life. I think being an African-American was another factor pushing him out of New Orleans, even though he'd become a well-known pediatrician and taught at the med school. Before he left he took Carol and me out to dinner, using some excuse or other, and when dessert was finished he told us he was leaving in the morning. "Starting over." Just like that. Gone.

I really miss him. James understands me better than anyone else in the world. There's a lot of acceptance from James, so there's very little need for forgiveness.

Bright sunshine offset the damp chill of the New Orleans winter as I sat on the fern-filled patio typing a longer e-mail than I had originally envisioned. A clump of banana trees had been cut to the waist for the winter, and the wonderful fragrance of a sweet olive tree came and went with the gentle breeze. There had not yet been a hard freeze, so everything remained green. The patio was still lush … and peaceful.

It was a small patio, secluded, and encased by brick walls. Lush ivy covered one wall with prolific foliage. This patio was one of many retreats tucked generously throughout the Quarter. Each patio was different; each had its own ambiance, and each created miles of separation from the noisy hassle of the street. All shared the common marks of French heritage resplendent in the Vieux Carre. This patio had been a regular coffee spot for James and me. It was home.

"*James,*" I typed, "*I wonder if I'm starting to lose my faith. Or maybe I'm starting to find a deeper faith.*" After a pause I typed, "*I guess the answer would depend on who you asked.*" I took a deep breath and stared at the banana trees. They were already starting to grow back.

"Who defines faith anyway? A believer? A group of insiders we call the church? Or an outsider? What is the true faith anyway? I know such questions are not on your top ten list, but they are pretty important if you're a Presbyterian minister. For yours truly, the Reverend Lieutenant William Blake McKenzie ... at your service Sir ... sorting out what constitutes a valid faith has become a quest, a journey. You would probably call my odyssey a moving target, right?" I sipped more coffee. I was surprised when a small mouse ran out of, and then back into, the base of the banana trees. I guess it is an open patio, I thought, as I turned back to my e-mail.

"I always thought I stood pretty much in the mainstream of protestant religious belief. Lately I'm not so sure. Jesus can't be the only way to forgiveness and life. No one knows what I'm thinking, so no one's ready to run me out of town on a rail or burn me at the stake. I don't know where all this is taking me and I wish I did. Oh well, I'm floundering, James — particularly when it comes to the whole subject of forgiveness, who gets it and how. Anyway, let me hear news from you. Later. Will."

I clicked the 'send' button and sat back. E-mail's okay, but it's not the same as face to face. I drank some more coffee and stared vacantly at the vine-covered wall.

+++++

The church calendar read "December 29th -- "Thomas à Becket Day." There's a day for everything, I guess, but I did remember the story of Thomas à Becket, the martyred Archbishop of Canterbury. In college I had read T.S.Eliot's play, "Murder in the Cathedral." Eliot's words describing Becket's temptations came to mind:

"The last temptation is the greatest treason:
To do the right deed for the wrong reason."

I opened the file on my desk and glanced absently at the stack of papers in it, thinking that we ministers do a lot of good, but not always for the right reason. I had scribbled two names on a note entitled "hospital visits," and I planned to go by Memorial Hospital after lunch to see them. I visit people in the hospital all the time. I'm effective at it, I do it well, and I thoroughly enjoy doing it. Do I always go to that bedside because I genuinely care about the person who is sick? Usually ... but not always. Sometimes I go simply because it's part of my job. I also often receive praise for such visits, and that can be a great ego trip. So my actions are usually a mixture of conflicting motivations, never totally pure.

I think ministers see people as they really are. I've certainly found that to be true. You name it; I've seen it. I see people in hope, and I see them in despair. I see the good and the evil and the in-between, often all in the same person, often all at the same time. I feel like it's a real privilege to be allowed into the lives of my people, and I treasure it.

But some people put me on a pedestal, and I don't like that. They assume I'm closer to God than they are. The resulting behaviors can get ridiculous. I still get amused when someone apologizes for cursing in my presence. It's like I'm too holy to hear a four-letter word. They're usually the same people who think I have a direct pipeline to God. To them, my prayers are more effective, and they think I have an inside scoop on the truth. Such people can be a pain in the neck, and their attitude creates distance between us. Who knows, maybe it's distance they want. Some people get uncomfortable if their minister gets too close to them.

I checked my calendar, noticing that I was having a meeting with Fred later today; he's a real friend. Sometimes I struggle to figure out who is a real friend and who is simply being nice to me because I'm a minister. When I first became a minister, I was often taken in by someone's kindness or attention. I would start thinking of him or her as someone with whom I could get close and trust in a special way, only to discover I was just a figurehead to them. I can usually tell the difference now, but every so often I still misjudge someone's motivation and get hurt as a result. Still, I'd rather be overly trusting than overly cautious. I had enough of the mistrust in Vietnam.

I thought of the many roles I play in the lives of my members, and sometimes those roles conflict with each other. I helped one couple keep their marriage together, and I knew a lot about them as a result. I soon felt their coolness when we were in the same room. One day the husband angrily told me how much he resented my public reference to the difficulties he and his wife had experienced. To this moment I have no idea what he was talking about.

Some people think I don't do anything all week. Paid to do nothing except speak on Sundays. This perception is aggravated, I'm convinced, because I don't go around bragging about how many hospital visits

I had made each day or how many counseling appointments I kept. While everyone wants his or her conversations with me to be held in strict confidentiality, silence about my pastoral work leads some people to think I don't do much. Other people think I'm sheltered and naive. Most television shows often depict the minister as a pansy who could never survive the rough and tumble real world.

I thought about a deacon in my church who sees me as naïve. He was among a group of church members we had over for supper one evening. I saw him heading into my study, as many people had done that evening, so I followed him and stood silently at my study's door. He examined my display of Marine pictures and memorabilia. After a few moments he shook his head and mumbled out loud, "I'll be damned."

When he turned around, he was embarrassed to see me standing there.

He apologized for cursing.

So it goes.

GRITS GRAVOIS

Jimmy pointed to our welcome mat in the front hall and carefully read it out loud: "Welcome to the Gravois home." Then he turned to me and asked, "Why do people call you Grits, Grandpa Gravois?"

"Grits became my nickname when I did my psychiatric residency, Jimmy. Roger Gravois is my real name, of course. Some friends gave me the name Grits when they heard I came from the South where they serve a lot of that Southern ice cream. I liked the name, so I've kept it. I bet you don't know too many people called Grits."

"Grits. That's silly. I like Grandpa Gravois better."

"You can keep calling me Grandpa Gravois, Jimmy. Look! Your friend Bobby from next door is here." Jimmy turned and ran out the back door, which slammed loudly behind him.

My daughter smiled and poured three cups of hot tea. Gail, my wife, had been reading the newspaper. The headline stated, 'Christmas Eve Murderer Pleads Temporary Insanity.'

"Anything new, honey?" I asked.

Gail put the paper down and took a sip of tea, flinching when the hot liquid touched her lips. "Well, yeah. Alice plans to plead not guilty by reason of temporary insanity. Besides that, a judge has denied her bail, so she'll remain in jail until the trial."

"Why no bail?" I asked.

"Seems she called her sister in Canada and a guard heard her say that as soon as she got out of jail she would take the kids and move up to Quebec to live with her." Gail raised her eyebrows. "The judge concluded she was a high-risk prisoner who might flee. So he ruled that she would stay in jail until the trial is over."

Martha gasped, "But what about her children?"

Gail blew on her tea to cool it off. "The judge has given temporary custody to Alice's parents. Both kids adore them, but Faye and John are no spring chicks, so I think it'll be difficult on everybody. The whole thing is so sad."

Martha commented, "Daddy, you've done a lot of these cases. Do you think they'll ask you to do the psychiatric evaluation?"

"I doubt it. Too many conflicts of interest. Alice is in my church school class, and Stan used to be part of a tennis group I belonged to some time back."

Gail put her tea down on the kitchen table. "Still too hot." She stirred her tea to cool it off. "Alice is pleading not guilty by reason of insanity. Isn't that going to be difficult to prove, Grits? "

I sighed. "It could get real messy. Innocent by reason of temporary insanity is a very complex plea. Besides, this is a city where being crazy is a matter of choice and style." I chuckled as I thought about Mardi Gras. "The jury selection will be crucial, of course. I bet the trial becomes a circus as well as a nightmare before it's all over."

"Do you think Will is going to get pulled into the middle of this?" Gail asked.

"I have no clue how the attorneys will look at his involvement. Alice undoubtedly confessed to him, but then she's not contesting that she stabbed Stan. The temporary insanity plea is what complicates the matter. They might ask Will what her state of mind was when he talked with her that evening." I paused and thought for a moment. "Will has a good head on his shoulders, but he may need some good legal advice if they call him as a witness."

I looked out the window where I could see Jimmy and Bobby playing. "Boy, when I think about all the things Will has to deal with. His experiences have got to cover the waterfront. I think we are very fortunate to have a man like him as our minister." I paused to sip the herbal tea. "He sure has endeared himself to a lot of families by being there for them when they hit a bump in the road. His sense of timing is amazing." Gail and Martha nodded in agreement. "I also think his sermons are an interesting balance, they stir up just enough guilt to make people want to accept Jesus and contain just enough folksy lore to help them feel good about themselves."

"What do you mean 'stirring up guilt,'" Gail challenged, glaring at me.

"It's an unconscious formula most preachers fall into," I answered. "They do a little blaming, a little scolding, and a little illustrating how we've fallen short. That makes us feel guilty. Then the preacher offers Jesus as the solution to the guilt. We Presbyterians are more subtle about it than some denominations, but it's usually still there in some form or another. If you really want to see that pattern in action, check out one of those TV evangelists."

"You are such a cynic, Grits," Gail objected, slapping the paper down on the table. "I think Will's sermons are good messages that are very helpful. I don't feel guilty when I hear his sermons. I like them."

"There you go again defending Will," I retorted in a ribbing tone. Gail didn't find it funny at all, and I noticed that Martha remained silent, but she usually does when the subject of religion comes up.

"I was actually saying how good a minister Will is, not how bad. How on earth he remembers as many names as he does is beyond me. That part of his brain's well developed. I wish mine were half as good. And he really seems to care about his people."

"I got a nice note from him on my birthday," Martha injected with a big smile. "It made me feel special. I was impressed." She nodded in affirmation of herself. "For a while I wondered why he had picked me out. Then I heard that he writes birthday notes every morning, mailing them to arrive on the proper day. Amazing."

"I'm impressed too," I said. "He thinks about me at least once a year, whether he wants to or not." I chuckled. "Do your math. With about fourteen hundred members that's an average of about four notes a day; that's a lot."

"You know," I continued, "it worries me that Will doesn't seem to get much relief from the constant burdens he carries. Brian does what he can, but when people are hurting they usually want to see the head honcho, not the associate. Ministers are like doctors, nurses, schoolteachers, and social workers; they're in constant danger of burnout. I did a study on the subject about three years ago." I noticed Martha rolling her eyes, but I continued anyway.

"I asked our denomination headquarters to notify me every time someone left the ministry for another occupation. You'd be amazed how many there are every year. I contacted each of them on the phone and asked them several questions. The huge majority of dropouts were victims of burnout. Very few of them took a regular day off, very few had outside interests, and they usually burned the candle at both ends. The danger of burnout is real for ministers, and Will is no exception.

"I keep telling him to forget the church on a regular basis. You believe in God, I kid him, so turn the church over to God for at least two days a week. Trouble is, Will feels guilty saying "no" to anyone, so he ends up working far too many hours every week. If you ask him about it, he'll tell you he loves his work. Mark my word; his pace is eventually going to take its toll.

Martha had stopped listening and was staring off into space. Gail had picked up her teacup again and sipped very loudly. I got the hint and dropped the subject.

I looked at my watch. Gail and I needed to shower and dress for the party tonight. I turned to my daughter and asked, "Martha, do you and Jim have anywhere to go tonight? I think it's a myth that everybody goes to a party on New Year's Eve. Why else would such huge crowds gather in the French Quarter to welcome in the New Year?"

"Actually we do, Daddy," Martha smiled. "I need to take Jimmy home, get him fed and settled, then go get the sitter. Jim's working on a big case and won't be home until after supper. Talk about someone heading toward burn-out." She walked to the back door and called out, "Jimmy come on in. It's time to go home."

"Aw Momma," came the familiar reply.

+++++

"Miriam's house is the one with the white Volvo out front," Gail indicated as I turned onto Magnolia Street. "It looks like a lot of people have already arrived. What is her daughter's name again?"

"Ashley." I responded, and then reflected for a moment. "I think it's really neat that a divorcee with a young daughter gives a party tonight. I'd say that's looking after their own needs in a healthy way."

"Yes, Doctor Gravois," Gail snipped. "Miriam is an earth mother anyway. It doesn't surprise me she can take care of herself and her daughter." She paused. "Ashley must be twelve now, not any older I don't think." I nodded.

Ashley greeted us with a broad smile. Ten or twelve people milled about in the family room and kitchen. A TV in the corner of the family room showed Times Square packed with people. It was 10:25 our time, an hour earlier than New York, but our local station was broadcasting the New York event in a delayed manner to correspond with our central time zone. What a mind-game. "I hope I won't get too sleepy by midnight," I whispered to Gail. She nodded, and as though she'd been prompted, she yawned.

We found Miriam tending to the drinks and nibbles in the kitchen. I kissed her on the cheek and expressed our appreciation at having been invited. I quickly realized she was about to get stuck serving drinks all evening, so I offered to take over for her. Miriam accepted my offer and pointed to a green pitcher, indicating that it was non-alcoholic. "For the kids and anyone else who wants it. Also plenty of sodas in the fridge." She dried her hands on a dishtowel and started mingling with her guests.

Miriam's smile radiated warmth, and she showed a deep interest in people. She was very attractive in spite of her chunky figure. I wondered again about her background. She moved to New Orleans as a single mom about ten years ago when Ashley was still in diapers. I had no idea what her life had been before then, but she and Ashley have always been active in our church.

I had finished surveying the drink options when Carol McKenzie arrived. Our eyes met, and she immediately waved at me. Soon she made her way into the kitchen.

"Hello, Grits. Is it true that psychiatrists are frustrated bartenders?" she asked, smiling broadly as she kissed me on the cheek. "Well, doctor, make mine a gin and tonic, if you will."

"Sure," I replied. "I didn't see Will come in with you. Nothing wrong, I hope."

"No. He stopped by the hospital to see Janie Quince, who was brought in by the rescue squad. They think she has appendicitis. He promised to be along shortly."

Carol stirred her drink with her finger. "Will's hoping to have a totally free New Year's Day tomorrow, so he's seeing her tonight. A free day surely would be nice!"

I thought about how spoiled I had become in my psychiatric practice. My patients arrived and departed on schedule. I took no appointments at night or on weekends or holidays. Phone calls at two o'clock in the morning from desperate patients who were about to commit suicide just didn't happen very often, and daily hospital rounds had become rare since health insurance companies had drastically limited in-patient care. I had become an hourly worker laboring from nine to five, and that wasn't all bad.

But a minister … well, that's a whole different world. When people are in need they want a personal contact from their minister as soon as possible. Will had told me that the telephone was increasingly accepted for pastoral support, and a lot of people preferred to come to his office rather than have him come to their home. I'm sure those two trends saved him a lot of time and energy. Still, the overall expectations for pastoral support have got to be heavy.

"Not much down time is there?" I asked Carol who had already turned to greet another friend and didn't hear me. She wasn't in the mood to talk to her bartender tonight, I guessed. Neat woman, and a nice, slim figure too.

Ashley and a friend circulated among the guests with trays of hors d'oeuvres. They seemed to enjoy being hostesses. When I offered them a soda, Ashley indicated with an air of professionalism that they were working right now but would have one as soon as they passed the trays to everyone once.

That's exactly what I was counting on with my bartending job … except for the champagne cooling in the back of the refrigerator. I'd also help Miriam with that when the clock approached twelve.

Soon Will appeared in the front hallway. I heard him say Janie is due out of the recovery room in an hour or so, and Jack would spend the night in her room. "They'll be fine," Will concluded in a reassuring voice. Everyone who heard Will's report seems interested and relieved. He then paused to talk to Ashley and her friend.

Will's associate minister Brian Dawson and his wife Blanche arrived almost immediately after Will. They were an attractive couple and were readily included in social events by members of the church.

Brian, however, almost immediately left Blanche, made a beeline for Lisa Steen and gave her a big hug. They began talking by themselves. Lisa's husband Tony was watching the TV, and Blanche stood by herself for a moment. I was bothered by Brian's actions. I'd seen him be overly attentive to Lisa on other occasions, and she was your classic histrionic personality– wearing a too-tight outfit hugging her incredibly firm, shapely body which she flaunted freely. Brian seemed to like it ... a little too much, in my judgment. I also noticed that Lisa kept looking over Brian's shoulder at Will.

Blanche, on the other hand, was quiet but radiant. She wore a bright blue maternity dress and had that rosy-cheeked look of warmth and health that exuded from expectant mothers during the middle and later months of pregnancy. Her sparkling, dark brown eyes and short, chestnut hair added to her beauty. Brian finally came over to my drink station, bid me a cordial hello, and asked for a beer and a coke.

As he headed back to Blanche with the drinks, Sally and Martin LaRue joined them. Sally was also pregnant, just about as far along as Blanche. Sally was also dressed in blue, so they both laughed as they compared dresses.

Sally and Blanche each had one hand on their stomachs, outlining their pregnancies as they talked. Then Sally turned and stood side by side with Blanche, comparing their bulging middles with her free hand. Blanche was so shy she stood mute and turned beet red.

"It's hard to say who's bigger," Sally pronounced in too loud a voice. "But I think I've got you beat on the topside of things." She followed her declaration with a raucous laugh. Blanche lowered her head in embarrassment and stepped back a little.

"Well, let's see who arrives first at Tulane Hospital," Sally concluded. She grabbed Martin's arm and they walked over to the TV set. Times Square was very crowded and the noise level had heightened. Only about ten minutes to go.

I caught sight of Will out of the corner of my eye. He had turned away from the party and walked toward the back door. He looked ashen. I noticed his brow was damp with sweat. I walked over to him, fearing he might not be well.

"Anything wrong, Will?" I asked quietly but firmly. "You don't look so hot."

"Sorry, Grits," he replied equally quietly, breathing deeply. There was a moment of silence, and then Will stared out the backdoor window. "I watched two pregnant women in Vietnam stand side by side like Blanche and Sally just did. They were in a market place.

Seconds later one of them stepped on a land mine." He took another deep breath. "Have you ever seen a pregnant woman blown open? It was not a pretty sight."

"God, what a horrible memory, Will," I whispered as I squeezed his shoulder with my hand.

"Sorry. I'm all right. Really, I'm okay." He looked at me trying to convince himself. After another moment he turned again to face the roomful of people and forced a smile. I stayed with him as he moved toward Carol, who was in the middle of the crowd.

Miriam proclaimed, "Time to get out the champagne! We've got plastic champagne glasses in the box over there, Grits. If we use those, we can toast in the New Year, then go outside to watch the fireworks over the Mississippi River."

I remembered that in New Orleans it's legal to drink in public if you use a plastic cup. Glass was illegal; the booze was not. Glass could break and cut someone. Safety first, you know, no matter how drunk you might get. New Orleans.

Meanwhile, I noticed that Lisa Steen had left her husband in front of the television and was navigating toward us. The glasses of champagne were passed from hand to hand, and almost everyone had been served. The two girls had sparkling grape juice. Everyone began counting: "ten, nine, eight, seven … three, two, one!"

"Happy New Year!"

Noisemakers appeared from nowhere as everyone welcomed the beginning of the New Year.

Quick as a wink, Lisa stepped up to Will, took his face in both her hands, and planted a huge kiss directly on his mouth, beating Carol to the draw.

Will stood there stunned.

Carol's jaw dropped.

Lisa innocently slid back to Tony and kissed him on the cheek as he drank his champagne from a plastic glass.

WILL McKENZIE

"This is the day we honor the Circumcision of Christ," Father Ellis O'Neill declared as he and I settled into soft chairs in our family room. Carol remained within earshot in the kitchen, and I felt a bit embarrassed by what Ellis had just announced, even though Carol was a nurse. " It's always on New Year's Day," he continued. He smiled broadly as he told me about this piece of church lore. "I bet you all don't celebrate that, do you."

"No we don't. I'm sure not many people in my church have given it much thought."

Ellis laughed. He and I got together often, and always on New Year's afternoon, a tradition we started the first year I moved back to New Orleans from Dallas. Ellis and I were classmates at Tulane and hung out together a lot back then. That was years before he decided to go into the priesthood and even more years before I decided to go to seminary. Ellis called me on the day we moved back to town, welcoming me home, and we picked up our friendship where it left off during college.

"We usually don't do anything much with Christ's circumcision either," Ellis admitted. "But I plan to work it into my homily tonight."

"I hesitate to ask how," I wondered aloud with a broad smile. "At least you don't have to give titles to your homilies the way we do with our sermons. If you did, what would you call this one?"

"I have no idea. Well, maybe something like "Forgotten Suffering ." The day is supposed to remind us that Jesus began his life in suffering just as he ended his life suffering. But infant circumcision is also a time of suffering we don't remember. That's the slant I intend to take on it."

Ellis took a sip of his bourbon. I had just purchased a new bottle, the special stock we kept for his visits. "The suffering we've been through," he continued. "The suffering we've caused. Often we don't want to remember it. Sometimes we simply don't."

I found myself nervously fingering my key ring. I used the same key ring in Vietnam. I looked at that ring, genuinely wishing I wouldn't remember the suffering I had seen; the suffering I had experienced; and, worst of all, the suffering I had caused.

I saw myself back in Vietnam feeling very proud, having just tossed a grenade with amazing accuracy into a second story window from which a sniper had just shot and killed a South Vietnamese policeman. Following the grenade's explosion, I rushed up the stairs to check out the results. The sniper lay dead in a pool of blood, and I remember saying "Bingo!" out loud. Then to my horror I saw the second body -- a little boy. Maybe six or eight, lying in his own pool of blood, missing his right shoulder and half of his face. I dropped to my knees, covered my face with both hands and sobbed until a buddy came up to check on me.

"How do you just let go and forget some horrible things?" I asked Ellis. "I wish we could pick and choose what to remember and what to forget. That'd be nice. That would be a relief."

Ellis wrinkled his brow. "I think it has to do with forgiveness. Forgiveness for ourselves and forgiveness of others. Without forgiveness, we'll never let go of pain. We've got to turn it all over to God."

"Ellis, don't pull the God stuff on me, okay? That's just too simple." His glib words irritated me. "Doesn't anything you've done ever keep haunting you?"

"I guess so," he replied, wrinkling his brow again. "But I still think Jesus doesn't want us to dwell on suffering. We need to move on, that's all." He paused and looked carefully at me. "If you can, that is." He finished his glass of bourbon as he studied my face. "I've got to go. This New Year's Day service is one of our most popular special services. Always brings out a big crowd. I guess everyone wants a fresh start." Ellis laughed as he headed toward the door.

I picked up my key ring off the table and put it in my pocket … out of sight … but not out of mind.

"Carol, can you imagine me preaching a sermon about Jesus' circumcision? Our folks would really love that one."

"I bet," Carol laughed in reply.

"A bizarre thought entered my head. "You know how churches all across Europe claim to possess an authentic piece of the cross. Well, I wonder if there's a church tucked somewhere in Europe that…. Naaaah …"

"You're bad," Carol said trying to hold back a smirk.

+++++

"I'm going to the *The Times Picayune* at three this afternoon to talk with Malcolm about his paper's handling of the Hendricks murder," I told Carol as I started out the door. "It was bad enough they ran the half-page picture of Stan's bloody body on the kitchen floor, but they referred to Alice as 'The Christmas Eve Heart Breaker,' 'The Passion Killer,' and 'The Woman Who Killed Christmas.' Come on. Get real. I find it offensive." I paused. "Carol, I'm sorry I won't be free in time to get David."

Carol sighed and shrugged her shoulders in a bit of disgust. She had asked me if I could pick up David from school, so she could go to a garden shop across town. I realized anew the truth in her accusations that the church seemed to come first in my life. I felt caught. I wanted to be supportive of Carol and David, yet I also wanted to be responsible to my profession. I just didn't want to put myself under a deadline while talking with Malcolm.

Malcolm, the paper's editor, had been an Elder and was now the chair of our education committee. Last year he taught a church school class for senior highs. I hoped to encourage him to aim for a higher standard of reporting. Surely Carol could understand the importance of that.

+++++

It was one of those rare winter days in New Orleans when the sun was shining, the humidity remained low, and the temperature held steady in the high fifties, so I decided to walk to Malcolm's office. I tried to slow down and relax as I walked up the Avenue. A streetcar approached, and I recognized a church member looking out of one of the windows. We waved at each other as her trolley rumbled past.

The newspaper had its own building not far from the heart of the business district. It was located beside the old city hall, a grand, marble-columned building now used to host receptions for special city guests. I had been to Malcolm's office before, so I knew to go to the sixth floor and walk through the busy pressroom. The afternoon edition was about to go to press, and you could feel the pressure mount. At the end of a long aisle bordered by desks, I entered the glass double doors that sheltered his office. One door had his name painted in black on the glass: Malcolm T. Ellison, IV. Impressive.

Kate, his secretary had to be handpicked. I had no trouble remembering her. She had legs that could turn the pope's head, and she beamed with a smile that could disarm a suicide bomber. I had also seen her hide Malcolm like a Maginot Line commander. She directed her bright smile at me as I approached and buzzed Malcolm, announcing my presence by name. I was very surprised that she remembered me; I was impressed, and flattered.

Soon Malcolm invited me into his plushly furnished office. I always did like overstuffed leather chairs, and we each settled into one after greeting each other. I wondered what it must be like to be the fourth generation to run a newspaper. Part of me envied him. Yet I was also glad that I didn't have the kind of unrelenting pressures of daily deadlines he faced.

After some casual conversation about the forthcoming Super Bowl in the Superdome, Malcolm turned to business. "Well, Will, what's on your mind?" he asked. He wore a vested suit with his coat unbuttoned, exposing the chain to his Phi Beta Kappa key. A watch in one vest pocket was linked by a gold chain to the coveted emblem of brilliance in the other vest pocket. Those who knew, knew; those who didn't know, didn't matter.

I shared my concerns about the 'lack of dignity' that had characterized the paper's coverage of the Hendricks's murder, about the "poor taste' and 'yellow journalism" it reflected. He smiled at my choice of terms. He assured me that his editorial staff had talked specifically about the bloodstained picture and subsequent headlines.

They were keenly aware, he assured me, of the public's "comfort zone," as he called it. He told me they all agreed the stories and pictures fell within the tolerance zone of the readers. He cited increased sales and lack of complaints as evidence backing his decision. He told me I was the first to register an objection to the picture, and I found that hard to believe, but maybe it was so. Our conversation was getting testy and uncomfortable.

I dared to suggest he was "determining ethics by Gallup Poll." He quickly took exception to that 'inaccurate concept' and dismissed it, but he offered no reason for concluding otherwise. I also suggested that a good newspaper shouldn't play to the sadistic side of human nature. He pushed off that comment too. I began to realize I was getting nowhere. I also began to feel that Malcolm considered me a minnow compared to the sharks he normally dealt with. I was terribly frustrated and a bit offended by him.

Throughout our conversation he sat with his leg crossed above the knee, dangling his black wing-tipped shoe. He removed his wire-rimmed glasses with one hand and rubbed his hazel eyes with the other hand. He carefully put his glasses back on using both hands, having first blown the dust off the lens. He spoke with quiet authority, backing his paper all the way. He didn't budge an inch.

Soon he was thanking me for coming and gently leading me to the door. "You'll have to excuse me, Will. It's time to put this edition to bed. Good of you to come by. By the way, my daughter's really looking forward to being in that children's musical you're putting on. That kind of thing means a lot to the kids and their parents. Keep up the good work, Will. Give my best to Carol." He closed his door behind me.

I quickly found myself back in Kate's office, staring pointlessly at a great pair of legs. I was irate and frustrated and knew that my visit had been in vain. I tried to forgive him and move on, but it was not easy.

Suddenly a loudspeaker blared: "Fifteen minutes. Fifteen minutes." I felt the tension mount throughout the office. I went to the elevators and pushed the down button. I stared at a sign saying "National" which hung over a nearby desk. This had to be the place where the national stories were written, sorted out, and edited. A middle-aged woman at that desk seemed glued to one computer monitor while typing notes into another computer. Out of curiosity I moved closer. One computer did word processing. The other was logged on to CNN news.

She realized I had seen her monitors and put her index finger to her pursed lips. "Shhhh…" she gestured and smiled sheepishly.

+++++

I stopped at a drugstore on my way back to the church to buy some aspirin. I found them and went to the cash register at the pharmacy where Mary worked. After exchanging hellos, Mary motioned me to lean closer over the counter. She barely nodded toward the folding chairs where people could wait for prescriptions. A middle-aged man sat there, dressed in sharp-looking casual clothes.

Mary leaned forward and whispered in my ear, "It's the band-aid man." She nodded her head a second time in his direction. "He comes in about every two weeks. Just watch him for a few minutes. Hang around."

The man sat with his penny loafers firmly planted on the floor. He was perhaps in his early fifties, had a head-full of handsome, black hair, complemented by a cleanly shaven face, but his eyes were filled with anxiety and a look of panic filled his face.

Five boxes of band-aids sat in the chair next to him. A stack of band-aid wrappings piled up on the floor between his feet. One by one he carefully opened a band-aid and put it on the palm of his right hand. His palm was covered with large band-aids, small band-aids, and medium band-aids. You couldn't see any skin anywhere on the palm of his hand. I wondered what terrible wound or infection he must have under those bandages. I wondered why he didn't buy gauze to wrap up his hand. That would be a lot easier and probably a lot cheaper.

He turned his hand over, palm down, and looked at it. I could see the back of his hand clearly, and it looked perfectly normal to me. One by one, with practiced haste, he opened more band-aids and carefully put them on the top of his hand. Soon no exposed skin could be seen. He inspected his work very carefully, slowly turning his hand over and over several times. He added one more band-aid on the palm side. Then he sighed an audible sigh of relief.

The anxiety vanished from his face. His eyes reflected a newfound calm. He gathered up his trash, and threw everything into the nearby trashcan. He buttoned his shirtsleeve, which had been folded back on his arm and walked to the front door of the store. He was now calm and serene.

I shook my head in disbelief.

"Every couple of weeks it's the same thing." Mary rolled her eyes. She spoke in a whisper. "When he first started coming in, I tried to sell him a bigger bandage, but he wouldn't hear of it. Then I noticed there wasn't a thing wrong with his hands. I've never seen anything wrong with his hands. But he sure is nervous when he takes the old band-aids off. We call him 'the band-aid man.'" As Mary turned to help another customer, I waved goodbye. "Goodbye Rev. McKenzie," Mary said.

"Band-aids," I mused. "Reverend McKenzie," I mused some more, saying that titled name out loud in a whisper. I wiped a tear from my right eye with my crooked index finger, pushed the door open, and walked out.

PETER BERNARD

Mr. Mallroy greeted me as I tried the door to the church boardroom. "Let me unlock that for you, Mr. Bernard. I know our Clerk of Session needs to get everything set up jus right for the meeting."

"How are you, Mr. Mallroy?" I asked.

"Jus fine, Mr. Bernard," came his automatic response.

Our sextant looked particularly old this evening. He had always been thin, but he seemed to have dropped more weight lately, and his hair was now completely white. I wondered if he wore it cropped short in order to look younger. He turned on the lights and adjusted the Venetian blinds to keep the streetlight from shining directly at the head table. "Thank you," I said as I entered the room and put my files on the table. "What is that I smell, Mr. Mallroy? Smells like good cooking to me."

"That's my eggplant Creole stuffed with shrimp. My supper," he beamed with pride. "The Missus's a mighty good cook. You name it; she can do it right. Mii-tee good."

"Well, where are you cooking it? We're a long way from the kitchen." I hoped he hadn't started bringing a hot plate to this part of the church. That's the last thing our insurance company needed to hear.

"I always puts my lunch on top of the hot water heater, Mr. Bernard. Keeps it nice and hot and ready to eat. The Missus wraps it in aluminum foil 'fo I leave home." Mr. Mallroy smiled broadly. "You want to try some? I can get some now if you'd like to try some. Sure is good."

"No thank you," I declined, even though I hadn't yet eaten supper and the aroma really did smell delicious. On the other hand, the thought of food in aluminum foil on top of the water heater was a major turn-off. The water heater stood in a closet in the hallway, and I wondered how old that water heater had to be to lose enough heat to keep Mr. Mallroy's supper hot. One more thing to deal with, I thought. An old water heater. Speaking about old. "How long you been with us here at church, Mr. Mallroy?" I asked.

"Twenty-three years next month. I started jus after we moved to the city from New Iberia. I worked for the el'mentary school down there for over 25 years. Then my mother died. After that, the Missus and I decided to come to the city for a change. Been here ever since. Not a bad place to live, New Orleans."

"Well, how old are you now?" I wondered out loud, hoping he wouldn't know or care enough about employee relations to call me out of bounds for asking such a question.

"Don't rightly know, Mr. Bernard. I don't think my age is any of my business. It's the Lord's business, not mine. I let Him worry about that." He beamed with assurance, nodding as he talked.

I pondered his unique answer, wondering if it were a dodge or really the way he felt. Still, Mr. Mallroy doesn't keep the church very clean anymore, and we'll never be able to retire him unless we can document his age. I did some investigating last spring when Mr. Mallroy told us he couldn't push the lawnmower anymore. I never did find out his legal age. There were no birth certificates issued in the swampland when he was born. We ended up buying him a ride-on mower to care for very little grass.

"I'll close up after y'all finish. I'll lock it up good. You all have a good meeting." Mr. Mallroy faded into the hallway and disappeared around the corner.

The elders, both men and women, started arriving for the monthly meeting. Most had seen each other at worship this morning, but the talk continued fresh and lively.

"Hello, Peter," one greeted me … "How're you doing, Peter?" greeted another … "Good to see you, Peter." … "Make the meeting a short one!" The elders spoke to me one by one as they took their seats.

As Clerk of the Session, I always sat at the head table where Will joins me to conduct the meeting. I'm the Clerk and take the minutes, but he's the Moderator. I've been Clerk for ten years now, and I've served on the Session for over twenty. The job has become old and tedious, and I wanted to be replaced.

As I looked about the room, I realized most of the elders were relative newcomers on the Session. I used to think new blood was a good thing, infusing fresh ideas. More recently I realized the constant turnover of new leaders enabled Will McKenzie to control what happened. Those who were shy on experience looked to him for direction and wisdom and how to vote when a controversial item came up. Will pretty much called the shots and got exactly what he wanted. The Session used to be composed of "wise old heads," as my father used to call them. No more. A lot of young blood now. Will, as a result, controlled what happened and got exactly what he wanted.

Will's dominance got started when he suggested who should serve on the nominating committee. In just a few years, that committee became Will's handpicked group. Soon only people Will wanted on the Session were elected. If an Elder bucked Will on too many issues, that Elder wouldn't be re-nominated for another term. I'd seen it happen.

That kind of stuff went on in our government, but here in the church it happened more smoothly, more subtly, and in many ways more viciously, because it was wrapped in a package of righteousness that no one finds easy to criticize. No one in the church wants to accuse someone else in the church of being power hungry or manipulative. Certainly no one wanted openly to accuse the minister of such things.

I wish everyone would stop kidding themselves. Besides, ministers shouldn't have that kind of power. Ministers should serve the church, not have the church serve them. Will's politics frustrated me and made me furious. Not that I haven't put my best licks in. I'll keep kicking too, but in the church you also had to be careful how you kicked. Even rebellion had to display the label of goodness and godliness.

I looked at my watch and it was time to start, but Will hadn't arrived yet. Actually, I think it's high time we get a different preacher. Will's sermons are all right, but he needs to talk about sin more often. That would bring people to their knees. Lord knows I have told him to study that church in Los Angeles; they're on TV. Their minister can make you eager to rededicate yourself to the Lord. I bet Will has yet to watch their broadcast.

Will arrived and sat down. He nodded a polite hello to me, and then addressed the group. "We have a quorum present, so let's begin. We'll begin with a devotional followed by our study of great Presbyterian doctrines. Then we'll move on to the business before us."

I found myself wondering what subject Will would talk about tonight. Last month he talked about the Virgin Mary, in keeping with Christmas. That was really dull. I hoped his devotional would be better tonight.

"Original sin is a belief Presbyterians have held throughout the generations," Will began.

Oh boy, here we go, I thought. This could get real heavy, real fast.

"Original sin means that beginning with the fall of Adam and Eve all humans have been enmeshed in sinfulness. John Calvin, one of the key figures in the Reformation, talked about the 'total depravity' of man. He believed we couldn't do any good using only our own power. Original sin keeps pulling us down."

Will's droned on, and my mind drifted back to my youth when Rev. Waters served as our minister. He was a grand old man, a caring pastor. I was really impressed that he came to see me in the hospital when I had my tonsils taken out. I was only a kid.

"So that's why we all need a savior," I heard Will say, and I watched him close his Bible. After a prayer, we discussed a few routine items. Then the property committee raised an issue that already had some of the Elders buzzing. A local AIDS support group wanted to use our parlor for a meeting every Thursday evening. Wesley Marshall presented the request, moving its adoption. You could feel the tension rise in the room. There was a brief silence, then the Session's liberal, Sam Tennin, seconded the motion, and the debate started.

The discussion went back and forth. We should show our concern. We should put our foot down on "outside groups." We should reach out in compassion. We should distance ourselves from such people. One man voiced his fear that the disease would be spread to other people who use that room. That led Dr. Wells into a five-minute lecture on how the disease was transmitted and how it wasn't. I think most people assumed the doctor favored letting them use the room, but many missed the doctor's nod of agreement when Mabel Johnson asserted that homosexuality violated God's will, that the Bible condemned it, and that most people with AIDS were homosexual. Mabel went on to say she never wanted to be in the same room with any "homo," male or female. By that point she had taken to finger wagging.

Drew Hudson cleared his throat to speak. Drew was a highly respected attorney, and no one thought twice about the fact he had remained a bachelor. He turned to Mabel. "Well do you want to leave the room, or do you want me to leave?" You could have heard a pin drop. "Or is it all right if we both stay?" he added.

Will interrupted the tense exchange, "Let's all remember Jesus' words to the woman caught in adultery: 'Let the one without sin cast the first stone.' Remember, we are all sinners, just like we talked about in our devotional." Mabel calmed down a bit, not wanting to take on both Drew and Will.

But Will's comments didn't settle well with Drew. He spoke with calm but forceful deliberation. "That woman had committed adultery and Christ forgave her, but there's no real analogy. Being homosexual is not a sin. Sexual orientation is a matter of nature, and being homosexual doesn't mean someone has done anything wrong. I plan to vote in favor of the motion, and I call for the question."

No one else seemed eager to speak, so Will put the motion to a vote. The proposal passed on a voice vote with only a handful of 'nays.'

Drew stood up again and in his calm, strong voice announced, "I want you all to know I am straight, not homosexual. But what if I were homosexual? Would some of you have been eager to stone me? What if someone else in this room is gay or lesbian? What about him or her? Think about this tonight as we continue to meet together." He gently touched Mabel on the shoulder and sat back down.

"Well," Will said, "maybe we've all learned a lesson tonight." His remark had a good effect of bringing closure to the issue. A brief period of shifting in chairs and coughing followed. Then Will called upon the worship committee to make its report.

As Clerk of Session, I'd seen many issues aired over the years, but I felt sad following the debate about the use of the parlor. Why was that even a problem? A murderer had used the parlor recently and no one batted an eye. Will tries too hard to hold things together, I thought. I wondered if he would ever learn that he's going to make some people unhappy no matter what position he takes on various issues. He may as well be true to himself and take his chances. He tried to be the peacemaker tonight like the peace-making middle child he is. Sometimes I wished he had more guts. But then at other times I thought he was too pushy. The two didn't go together, yet somehow they did. I shook my head in confusion.

Following the committee reports, we usually moved with lightening speed through "old business," "new business," and on to adjournment. But tonight during "new business" another issue was raised. I couldn't believe it. I was fatigued and ready to go home, and I knew others were too.

Jimmy Roberts spoke. "Since we're speaking our mind tonight, I've got something on my heart I just have to lift up for our consideration." His pencil thin moustache always made him look like he came from another country. Spain perhaps. It just didn't look American to me.

"There's a young single lady," Jimmy continued, "who's on the slate of people nominated to be a new Elder. Mary Beth Stewart is her name, and she's pregnant. I think she became pregnant by in-vitro fertilization. I heard she wanted to stay single but also wanted to have a child. Now I just don't think we need that kind of example parading in front of our children. Certainly not as an Elder."

Jimmy acted like the earlier discussion had never taken place. He acted like what he talked about was a whole different matter, which in some ways it was and in other ways it wasn't. But Will cut the discussion short, thank goodness. "Jimmy, we'll have to take that up at another time. It's too late tonight." I noticed Jimmy was frustrated and silent. "Is there a motion to adjourn?" Will asked. Several elders obliged. I must admit I'd heard about Claudette's plans. I knew her to be a fine woman, but I shook my head at the hardships that were ahead for her and her child. As we adjourned, Will sought out Jimmy before he left the room.

As everybody left, the social chatter picked up again. This time much of the buzz centered on tomorrow's basketball game between Tulane and LSU. I closed my writing pad and stood up to go home. I made a mental note to call Will to arrange a meeting with him about tonight's issues. I found the evening frustrating. It really was time for me to step down as Clerk … and for Will to move on as the minister.

GRITS GRAVOIS

I cleared my throat and read to our Sunday School class, "The chief end of man is to glorify God and to enjoy him forever." I looked up. "Does anybody know where that comes from?"

"I do, Grits," Henry Marshall piped up. "I got a dollar for memorizing the Catechism as a kid, and that's the first question." He chuckled. "I spent the money on comic books."

"That's right," I continued. "It's the first question in the Westminster Shorter Catechism. You'll have to forgive the gender-biased verbiage. They weren't exactly gender sensitive back in 1647. Well, what do you think of that idea?" I scanned the class hoping for a reaction. "Anyone?"

Our class, "The Muddlers," had been going for about eight years. We got our name when one member made some reference to "muddling through life." It stuck. We're even listed in the Sunday bulletin as "The Muddlers." It's a good group of people, a great variety of ages, and a diversity of points of view. Will is my co-teacher, sort of. He says he doesn't have time to prepare for the lesson, but he still comes regularly and contributes now and then.

Maggie started to speak. "I like the action verb 'enjoy.'" She paused briefly. "We Presbyterians don't emphasize joy enough. We're too uptight. To me that's what it's all about -- spreading God's joy."

Thomas Gaubert countered. "How can you glorify God and fully enjoy God if you're dying from starvation or dodging bullets? I think those of us in America look at things through rose-colored glasses. I wonder how someone in the Middle East would hear those words as they gather the remains of a family member killed by a car bomb. Or what about all those starving people in Africa. What about the millions in Africa dying from AIDS? Or two people in our own church who are dying of cancer? Do you think they can glorify and enjoy God?"

"Maybe they can," Maggie retorted. "They can have the peace of God in their hearts, and that can help them face the cancer, or the hunger. Matthew Ronald is a great inspiration for all of us, even though he's dying of cancer." She spoke with conviction, and some nodded as she spoke of Matthew.

However, Thomas wasn't to be silenced. "Matthew might glorify God in the way he deals with his cancer, but it's hard to imagine his joy is very full when the pain takes over. Besides, millions of people are dying who have never heard about Jesus or God."

As the teacher, I felt the need to step in. So far, Will remained silent, so I ventured, "Maybe it's our challenge to help create conditions that could make joy possible. Maybe the burden of proof is on our privileged shoulders. Helping the world is one way we can glorify God. I like Maggie's idea about spreading the joy. We can do that in a variety of ways. A bowl of rice would sure be an important way to spread God's joy to someone who is starving."

"There you go on your liberal do-good track again, Grits," Thomas challenged. "We can't feed the entire world."

"It's been proven that we can," I asserted.

"That's a bunch of hogwash, Grits," Henry Allen blurted out. "That's ridiculous."

"Maybe we can't save them all, but we can save some," Mildred pleaded.

At this juncture Will chimed in. "If we turn from our sins and turn to Jesus, God will forgive us and bring us joy regardless of our circumstances." I glanced around the class and a lot of people started looking at their feet. Will's words were strong and dogmatic, but I could feel a depression beneath his words, and that bothered me.

Thomas went ballistic at Will's 'sermonette,' as he called it. He pointed again to the mass of hurting humanity in other parts of the world. Those words, in turn, launched Will into emphasizing our responsibility to bring Jesus Christ to the world. I could feel the atmosphere in the class become tense. Many were growing impatient with both Thomas and Will. People were shifting in their chairs and coughing nervously.

Thomas seemed comfortable with his own anger, so the psychiatrist in me wasn't worried about him. But Will worried me. I sensed a lot of self-doubt slithering around underneath the dogma he articulated. I felt his lack of joy. It sounded like he wanted to believe what he propounded, but couldn't really swallow it, so he spoke with a strong emphasis in hopes of convincing himself. This wasn't the first time I had detected such inner conflicts within Will. Being a psychiatrist had its drawbacks for me at times.

The church-school bell ended the discussion, and the class started to break up before the bell stopped ringing. Everyone smiled at each other as they left. Everyone except Thomas, who still wanted to keep arguing. Several people thanked me for the lesson. Several shook Will's hand. Whatever else Presbyterians are, first and foremost they are polite.

I watched Will walk toward his study to get ready for the worship service. A little boy about five years old came running up to him in the hall. "Give me five, Reverend McKenzie!" the tyke shouted as he held out his hand. Will bent over and they slapped hands. Then they both went beaming in their separate directions. I found the encounter very warming … and starkly different from the class.

"Well, I guess we muddled through again, didn't we." I mumbled to an empty room as I turned out the lights and left.

THOMAS GAUBERT

"Thanks for saving me a place, honey." I slipped into the pew beside Ann. "I ended up getting into a hot discussion again today. I guess I'll never learn." Ann put her hand on my thigh. Her affectionate touch meant more to me than a thousand words of reassurance. I kissed her quietly on the cheek. The organ started playing softly.

Ann handed me a page from a magazine. "Here's an article on a recent genome project Miriam clipped for you. She said it appeared in *Time* magazine this week. Who knows, maybe one of these days with all the help friends give you, you'll grow up to be a real live geneticist, huh?" She chuckled. I folded the page without looking at it, tucking it into my coat pocket. Ann smiled her tolerant smile and started to read her worship bulletin. "Oh, good," she whispered, "the children's choir is singing today. They're so cute."

"And I can usually understand the words, too," I added.

I looked at the stained glass window above the chancel. I love this church. I can remember sitting next to my mom and dad in just about in this same location in the pews. When I got bored I would count the stones across the top wall of the choir loft. I had trouble counting them without using my finger as a pointer. When I did, my mom would pull my arm down, causing me to lose count.

I also remembered stroking the fur coat of the woman in front of me. She never noticed, and my parents didn't stop me from doing that. Some Sundays she wore little fox furs around her shoulders. The fox's mouth was actually a spring clip that "bit" the tail of the next fox. Several were strung in a row to form the shawl. I never knew how

41

many foxes were biting each other, but I sure enjoyed playing with those furry little animals. One Sunday, when I didn't reassemble the foxes correctly, her fur shawl fell into three pieces when she stood to sing a hymn. She looked straight back at me, and I was mortified.

I really didn't mind sitting through worship as a kid, except for the 'long prayer' when you were supposed to keep your eyes closed. I used to peek and count those stones. My mother would open her eyes and close them again, showing me what I was supposed to do. I never did figure out how she knew when to open her eyes to see that my eyes were open.

"What are you thinking?" Ann whispered. "You seem to be in a daze."

"Do you know they still put moth balls in the urinals in the men's room here, just like they did when I was a kid? Must have been passed on from janitor to janitor to janitor," I whispered back.

"God!" Ann stuttered. "Sorry I asked," She tried hard to hold back a giggle.

Brian stood up to start our worship service. I like Brian. He's a bit younger than Will and doesn't have as much experience, but he seems to be honest and straightforward. He doesn't preach often, but when he does he always uses current illustrations. I've never heard of some of the bands he refers to, but a lot of the teenagers nod when he mentions them.

I took a hymnbook from the pew rack and found the first hymn. Good choice of hymns today, I thought. Thank goodness. I've got to remember to compliment Will on his selection so he'll keep picking the good ones.

"Would you believe we're singing this hymn again?" Ann complained in a loud stage whisper. The man in front of us turned his head back toward her to register his disapproval of her talking. I wondered how I could register my disapproval of his disapproval while also disagreeing with Ann.

When we got to the sermon, I braced myself for one of Will's straight-laced messages because his title was "Repentance and Obedience." I dreaded where he might go with that subject. I also wondered how many thousands of sermons had been preached on repentance and obedience. Will was actually a good orator and kept me awake. Yet there was something about his blue-lipped Presbyterian approach that didn't ring true lately. I didn't know whether it was me, or Will, or both. Perhaps I felt a disconnect that didn't exist. Who knows?

Before I knew it we were singing the last hymn. "Take care, Reverend," I said to Will on the way out. He made some comment about how he appreciated my contribution in the class this morning. Sure he did.

+++++

"There didn't seem to be much joy in Will's sermon this morning," I ventured as Ann passed me the creamed corn casserole. I took a large helping. "I love this stuff. You haven't served it in a while."

"Good for a cold winter day," she commented. "Yeah, Will did seem kind of heavy today. He has been lately. Have you noticed?"

" Not too bad, but still too judgmental." I paused and looked up from my plate. "Pass the ham one more time please. This is a great lunch, Ann." I helped myself to another slice. "You know our conversation reminds me of my encounter with Ralph Finkle."

"Who?"

"Didn't I ever tell you about that?" Ann wagged her head. "Well, Ralph worked in the stem-cell-harvesting lab. One day three or four years ago he saw a book on my desk that we were studying in "The Muddlers." That started us talking about religion. As we talked, Ralph indicated that he had never read anything in the Bible, so I promised to get him a copy. Matter of fact, I stopped by the church on my way home that day and swiped a Bible from the pew rack." Ann looked at me over her glasses. "I put it to good use, okay? Com'on." I paused. "Anyway, I gave the bible to Ralph the next day."

"I quickly forgot about it. Then Christmas came along, which brought on another religious discussion. I asked Ralph if he had ever read any of the Bible I gave him. He started reading it, he said, but added that he quit about halfway through. Then Ralph looked at me for several seconds and added, "You know, your God is a real son of a bitch."

"He never made it to the New Testament. All he read about in the first helf was an angry God. I don't think he ever opened the Bible again. Anyway, Ralph Finkle sure made me think.

"But you know, some people like that hellfire and brimstone stuff. I guess it satisfies their need to be punished." I paused and thought for a moment. "You know, when you get right down to it, love doesn't sell very well. Threats and warnings of punishment sell. How-to programs sell well too. The bookstores are filled with spiritual self-help books. You know, 'How to find salvation in three easy steps you can do in ten minutes in the privacy of your own bathroom.' That'll sell. Manipulation by guilt still sells. Fear sells too -- don't be left behind. And on it goes. Nope. Love and forgiveness just don't sell very well."

Ann stood, picked up her empty plate, and headed to the kitchen.

WILL McKENZIE

The back wall of the elevator was a mirror. I was alone, so I tried to comb my hair with my fingers. It didn't work very well. However, I did straighten the colorful silk tie Carol gave me for Christmas. She had James shop for the tie in Paris, and it was pretty fancy.

I was pleased to see that my stomach was relatively flat. I hadn't lost my entire Marine conditioning. I also wasn't in as good a shape as I'd like to be, but finding a regular time to get exercise remained difficult. Nevertheless, I jogged when I could, usually on the Avenue in the late afternoon. As I looked in the mirror, I promised myself to go jogging later today.

The elevator door opened onto the second floor, which was actually the bank's lobby located above the parking deck. I hoped to do my banking without running into Lisa Steen. She comes on to anything in pants. The fact that I'm a minister makes me an even more attractive target to her. I was still embarrassed about her New Year's Eve's kiss. I guess I should have been flattered, but it felt terribly awkward. Hopefully there would be another bank officer who could let me into my lock box. All I wanted to do was to get our passports in order to renew them for a potential trip to London this summer.

I spotted a young banker and walked briskly in his direction with my lock box key in hand. Lisa saw me, jumped up from her desk, and all but ran across the lobby toward me. You would have thought I was her long lost brother; or you might have thought something else just as easily.

"Will McKenzie, how are you?" she asked in far too loud a voice while still yards away. "What a wonderful service we had yesterday. I particularly liked your sermon. It really hit home. Good to see Carol too. Was that a dress she picked up at the Episcopal bazaar? I could swear I saw one there just like it." She pumped her hips a couple of times, then asked, "What can this friendly officer at the Bank of New Orleans do for you today?" Her white blouse flopped flimsily, revealing glimpses of her lacy, low-cut bra. I tried not to get caught looking.

"I need to get into my safe deposit box, Lisa. I'm in a bit of a rush, so if you could speed me along I'd appreciate it. Box number 326." I felt myself blush when she brushed up against me to get the key I held out for her. How did she manage to do that?

"Let's go see if your little key fits our box, okay?" She unlocked the door to the room of safety deposit boxes.

"All I have to do is to pull out our passports. I won't need to use one of the private rooms."

"No problem. Let's see, 326. Why you're right here just below waist level. How convenient you are." She bent over to unlock the box, giving me a wonderful eyeful of her breasts. She pulled the box far enough out of the slot so I could open it. "There," she proclaimed, making a point of looking away from the box as I opened it. I found our passports with ease, put them in my coat pocket, and closed the box. Lisa locked the box, taking both keys out of their slots.

She curled her finger into my key ring and held it out toward me. Then she started talking about Tony's new boss. I listened politely for a moment, and then reached for my keys. As I tried to claim them, she pulled her finger and my keys closer to her breasts, preventing me from taking them. Then she started relating another saga of the unreasonable things being expected of Tony at work.

I became eager to get out of this little room where I was alone with her. I kept saying I had to go, and she kept choosing not to listen. I finally decided to leave without my keys, hoping she would follow. Then I realized we were locked in, and only her key would open the glass door separating us from the lobby. What a terrible design this vault had. Surely it violated fire regulations. Finally I leaned up against the wall next to the door and firmly insisted, "Lisa ... unlock this door."

"Why of course," she replied, sounding insulted. Her hip bumped into mine as she pulled the door open. I still didn't have my keys. I turned back to get them one more time, and this time she didn't pull her hand back.

However, just before I took the ring she dropped it and quickly leaned over to pick it up, apologized profusely, and feebly attempted to keep her blouse from falling wide open. She picked up the keys and straightened up very slowly, prolonging my view of her luscious curves. I enjoyed the enticing moment and tried hard to register no emotion whatever. I avoided eye contact with Lisa as I left.

"Say hello to Carol for me. Bye, Will."

+++++

I tossed our passports on the kitchen table as I headed to the refrigerator. Carol glanced at the passports and asked, "Well, did you see much of Lisa today? I haven't run into her since New Year's Eve."

"Yeah, she was there in all her glory," I commented, hoping to brush off the whole thing as quickly as possible. Even though Carol and I have no secrets, I wasn't eager to detail the scene. I felt embarrassed, looking back, at how much I had enjoyed the incident. "She sends her best," I added, trying to gloss over the subject.

"That's nice. I bet she found a way to flaunt herself before you left."

"You might say that."

"I thought so." Carol fell silent. She remained silent throughout dinner.

As she slid back from the dining room table, she looked at me and calmly commented, "I hope you enjoyed it ... whatever it was."

+++++

"My marriage is great, James, don't get me wrong," I typed into the computer. "But I do wish Carol weren't so jealous of Lisa. You remember her, I'm sure -- the bombshell of Central Presbyterian."

I looked out of my office window, delighted to have a free hour due to a cancelled appointment. It gave me time to catch up on personal e-mail.

"*Things with Carol are fine, really, in spite of incidents like the bank vault peep show I just described. But Carol gets uptight about those kinds of things. She's never accused me of anything, but I wish I could erase that twinge of doubt from her mind.*" I paused in my typing, wondering how James might respond. I remembered Lanna's wrath when James smiled too broadly at her female oncologist.

"*And yes, I enjoyed Lisa's flirting. Who wouldn't? Flirtation can be fun, up to a point. But anything more? No way! I am baffled why novels and television make illicit sex sound so wonderful. Ultimately it never is. I've counseled scores of people who've tried to unsnarl affairs. Sure an affair can stir up excitement, always a bunch of hype, and plenty of adrenalin gets pumping. Trying to hide the affair often becomes an exciting challenge. But the thrill soon wears off as inevitable complications set in. Most affairs usually get pretty messy before they're over, and hearing about peoples' affairs gets boring after the first dozen or so. Believe me, a sure antidote for the temptation to have an affair is to start counseling people who have had one.*

"*Even so, I know the public record is filled with clergy and therapists who've gotten into sexual trouble with someone they were counseling. It's probably only one in ten thousand, yet you sure hear about them quickly. When it involves a minister or a therapist, the press is eager to print the story; it's headline material. When it's a tug boat pilot or a used car salesman, they wouldn't waste the ink.*"

I paused and looked out the window of my study. The bright sunlight made the day look warmer than it really was. I returned to my e-mail to James.

"*Some affairs happen simply because of body heat, but most ongoing affairs happen because a needy person finds a good listener. 'She listens to me.' 'He really pays attention to what I'm feeling.' I hear those kinds of comments all the time.*

"*Ninety percent of the time the spouse discovers the affair. Actually, the culprit wants the spouse to know. He'll leave a receipt from the local Holiday Inn on his dresser when he claimed to be in San Francisco. She'll place a long distance call to the other man while her husband's out of town, knowing full well he pays the phone bills. And these are smart people. One woman stashed all of her lover's letters in the glove compartment of her car where her husband kept the tire pressure gauge. Months passed before he checked the tires, but eventually he did.*

"*Affairs are always angry things, James, and the one having the affair wants the spouse to know exactly how angry he or she is. The angry messages run something like: 'If only you had listened more compassionately, this wouldn't have happened. If only you had taken my needs more seriously. If only you had spent more time with me. If only ....' Trouble is, the damage has usually spread like a cancer by the time the fling is discovered. Sometimes the marriage survives; sometimes it doesn't.*

"*And you know what else? I'm not sure going to a counselor has anything to do with whether the marriage survives or not. I believe that the commitment factor is what determines whether they stay together or split. That's my theory. Some couples have a strong sense of commitment; some don't. People with a high level of commitment in general also value commitment in their marriage.*

"*Of course staying together isn't always a good thing. I've seen couples stay together when they were destroying each other and genuinely needed to split.*

"*Yeah, Lisa's sexy all right. And yeah, I enjoyed the incident in the bank. But there's a whale of a difference between window-shopping and shoplifting. 'Nuf for now, James. I'll send this off to cyber-land.*"

+++++

Sundays arrived with relentless regularity. I looked out at the congregation during the first hymn, and Carol's eyes met mine. She smiled supportively, which gave me a boost of confidence, particularly since today's sermon hadn't developed as well as I had wanted. If there hadn't been two funerals this week, and if there hadn't been five people in the hospitals, and if Brian hadn't been away all week at a seminar, and if David's teacher hadn't called us in for a conference, and if my father hadn't fallen again … well … then … then my sermon this morning might be better… maybe.

When the service ended, I went to the main door to greet people. The doors were massive and gothic, and half of the huge door remained closed and locked. The open side was wide, but a bottleneck always occurred getting out.

Today's jam-up got particularly bad and the exit line all but slowed to a stop. I noticed Mr. Mallroy standing to one side in the narthex, so I caught his attention and motioned him to come over. I asked him if he would unlock the other door. He pulled a ring of keys off his belt, unlocked the door at the top and at the bottom, and then swung wide the second half of the exit.

A floodgate had been opened. People were no longer crowded or pushed. Many exited in a second line that went out faster because they didn't pause to shake my hand. In a few minutes the crowd dispersed.

When everyone had left, I thanked Mr. Mallroy again. He smiled the broadest smile I have ever seen him smile. "Dr. McKenzie, opening the other half of that door was a great idea. I sure wish somebody would tell me to do that every Sunday."

I had trouble not bursting out laughing, but I managed. He wandered on back toward the church offices.

As I started to re-enter the church, a shot rang out.

I swung around, crouched, facing the street, and quickly checked out the area. I realized I had grabbed for a weapon I didn't have.

A Leidenheimer French Bread truck turned the corner and backfired again.

I exhaled loudly, and stood up straight, hoping no one had seen me crouch. There was no one around.

I sighed … and was sweating.

+++++

"What do you mean they're not going to let Alice attend the funeral?"

"All I know is the funeral home called saying Alice Hendricks wouldn't be in attendance at her husband's funeral today." Marie added, "I figure that if she hated him enough to run a butcher knife through his heart, she might not want to attend his funeral. If I were in her shoes, I think I'd still hate his guts."

"He had it coming. Is that it?" Marie didn't respond. 'Cold-hearted, razor-toting woman' ran through my mind as I looked at Marie. I rarely saw this side of her, and it took me by surprise.

About that time a man dressed in black knocked on the doorsill of Marie's office. He moved overly cautiously and had an overly polite a demeanor. He must to be with the funeral home, I thought.

"Reverend McKenzie, may I have a word with you? I'm Harold Brown from Dorset Funeral Home." Yep. I looked at my watch; there were still twenty-five minutes before the service would start. "Sure, come on in." I gestured to a chair as I closed my study door behind us. He chose to stand.

"As it turns out," he began, "Mrs. Hendricks will be in attendance at the service after all. Her attorney made a last minute plea to the judge, who granted her permission. She's also wearing her own clothes rather than the State's bright orange jump suit. However, she must remain handcuffed and under a deputy's surveillance at all times. Right now she's in a patrol car parked outside the side door. What shall I tell them to do?" He paused obediently.

"The children are already in the church parlor," I said, thinking out loud. "Alice's parents are there as well, as is Stan's father, a widower who flew in this morning from Atlanta." I paused to think. "Tell the police to hold Alice in the car while I go to the parlor and sort out how we're going to handle this. I'm sure the children will want their mother with them. I'm equally sure Stan's father doesn't want anything to do with Alice. Meet me back here in my office in a few minutes."

He nodded and left. I had to walk past Marie on my way out. She had become nervous by now, pointlessly shifting papers on her desk. What happened to that tough-talking woman of a minute ago? She literally wrung her hands as she watched me go down the hall.

As expected, Stan's father didn't want to sit near Alice during the service or wait in the small parlor with her either. Only then did I realize that this parlor was where I had talked with Alice on Christmas Eve. I wondered if anyone else made that connection.

I developed a plan. Stan's father would go to a room on the other side of the sanctuary to wait. He would enter the church on the opposite side from the children and Alice's parents and sit in the pew on the other side of the center aisle. The casket had already been placed in the middle of the church in front of the communion table. I would conduct the service using a portable mike while standing behind the casket. That way there would be no preferred side during the service, although the side with the children and Alice would undoubtedly be the focus of attention.

An Elder took charge of things right away, so I headed back to my office to attach a portable mike to my robe and to tell the funeral man what to do ... what *was* his name?

The church soon became packed, and ushers were busy setting up extra folding chairs. Peter Bernard, our omni-present Clerk of Session, coordinated the crowd movement, and he did a great job. He had already assured me that the fellowship hall had been set up for any overflow using our closed-circuit television. "Just like we do on Easter and Christmas," Peter said. What an ironic comparison, I thought.

Soon all were seated in the church as planned, but the arrangement looked more like a court scene than a worship service. On one end of the front row sat a uniformed policewoman in her dark blue jacket and shiny black leather straps. She sat next to little Andy, who wore his white shirt and clip-on tie. Next came Alice in widow's black, then June on her right side. A second policewoman flanked Alice and her children.

Alice was handcuffed, and her hands were also shackled to a chain around her waist. She couldn't put her arms around her confused and distraught children. They had to put their arms around her. They had to help her hold the hymnbook. They had to wipe their own tears, although the policewomen helped now and then.

As I glanced over the crowd, I realized only about half of the people in the sanctuary were members of the church. Others were probably co-workers of Alice or Stan, and some had to be curious onlookers, undoubtedly part of that constituency who had established a new sense of taste for what appeared on the front page of the newspaper.

When the organ stopped playing, I walked to the center of the chancel behind the coffin. I opened my prayer book and looked up for a moment, waiting for the crowd to settle down.

Two half-shaven young men in faded jeans entered the church through the center door. One had a large camera on his shoulder; the other toted coils of wire in one hand and a painfully bright light in the other. They moved steadily down the center aisle as their cables trailed out the front door like an umbilical cord to an unseen source.

"There will be no cameras or recorders in this worship service please," I firmly announced. The red light on the camera remained on and the blinding spotlight still shone. Alice lowered her head, unintentionally banging it on the pew rail in front of her. She started and grimaced in pain. I waited another moment, but the camera crew remained.

"Will our ushers please escort these gentlemen out of the sanctuary?" I asked. Even as I spoke two elders were already on their way to the center aisle. The cameraman backed out of the church, filming as they went.

Moments later we finally began the service. I could still see the bright light pointed toward the church from the sidewalk. Peter Bernard must have seen the same thing and closed the large front doors. I'm sure they'd show that door closing on television.

Both children were crying as I announced the opening hymn. I looked at little Andy and June. I'd seen crying faces like that before. Haunting faces of not two, but three children, crying beside their mother who hunched over a crumpled body. I had just shot their father. My buddy pulled me by the arm shouting, "Move out. We've got to get out of here. You had to, Will. Let's go. This place is crawling."

I managed to shake myself. What verse were we on? Two verses to go, thank God. I didn't think anyone had noticed me drift, but I couldn't be sure.

+++++

The drive to the cemetery in Metairie took only minutes. As the funeral procession drove through the gates, we entered a different world. All of the graves were above ground, chambers of marble built to house the caskets safely above the shallow water table. Cemeteries comprised row after row of such tombs, laid out like a little city, cities of the dead. Some of the tombs were for one person. Most were big enough for a couple; others could hold a whole family.

The tombs in this particular cemetery were well maintained, but in some parts of the French Quarter the tombs were made of brick and were crumbling. To the uninitiated, the place could be eerie. St. Louis Cemetery Number One, over two hundred years old, was crumbling badly. This cemetery held the remains of governors, pirates, plantation owners, Creoles, slaves, and Marie Laveau, the voodoo queen of New Orleans.

I remembered a trip to see this witch's tomb as a boy. Howard and Benny and I had gone on a dare, riding our bikes. When we found her marble tomb, we each picked up a shard of soft, crumbling brick and marked our "X" on the face of her stone. We were now safe from voodoo spells for as long as we lived. Would that it were so.

Looking out the limo's window as we rode silently to the designated mausoleum, I wiped a tear off my right cheek.

+++++

At the gravesite, I read familiar words of scripture about resurrection. I concluded the readings with traditional words from the Gospel of John: "I am the way and the truth and the life. No one enters unto the father except by me."

I felt myself blanch. The severity of these words hit me hard. They seemed to negate the words I had read earlier at the church: "In my father's house are many mansions."

Who knew what Stan Hendricks had believed? I watched his two children and Alice stare at the coffin. Who knew? Who knew what a nameless Vietnamese man, mourned by three children and a widow, had believed? Who dared judge? Everyone looked to his or her minister for answers at a time like this, and this minister covered his ignorance with scriptures that contradicted each other.

Alice cried softly during the final committal: "ashes to ashes, dust to dust …." As soon as I pronounced the benediction, she stepped forward to the casket and said, "I'm sorry, Stan. Forgive me." I too paused and silently asked another father of three kids to forgive me.

Funerals are for the living. The dead have no use for them. Funerals convince us there's been a death, yet suggest that there is more life beyond. Funerals give grief permission to begin its cathartic flow. Funerals bring some closure. They are a ritualized hope for an end to a pain that takes forever to end. When there has been a death, life for the survivors is put on hold until the funeral is over. Funerals are absolutely necessary for the living. And I hate them.

THOMAS GAUBERT

"Thomas, please try to be calm tonight," Ann urged me.

"I'll try not to embarrass you, honey. But what's the point of going to these Bible studies if we can't discuss things?"

"Discuss is one thing. To pull out all the weapons of mass destruction is another matter."

"Okay. Okay." Her comments teed me off. We remained silent as I parked and we went inside. The fellowship hall was already getting full, so we had to sit in the back. These Wednesday Evening Bible studies were certainly getting to be popular. Will usually began with a scripture or an issue and then talked about it for a few minutes. After that he opened the floor for questions and discussion. I liked that.

There were some folks in the group, however, that wanted Will to tell them what to believe. Others wanted to hear a Bible verse to back up everything said. I thought that most of us were there to discuss the issues openly.

Ann and I settled into chairs on the back row as Will opened the class with prayer. Now there's a silly ritual if ever there was one. The class could proceed just as well without a prayer. Besides, Will had told me on several occasions that he prayed continually throughout the day. If that's true, a special prayer to open the Bible study struck me as redundant. I guess it kept some folks happy, however, so no harm done, maybe.

"What is sin?" Will asked.

Hey, this was going to be a real doozie, I thought, smiling to myself.

"Sin is anything that is not in accord with God's laws or is contrary to God's will," he continued. I immediately wondered how in the hell you knew what God's will looked like. But I bit my tongue. I was aware of Ann's stiff demeanor beside me.

Peter spoke up. "I don't think there is anything we can do without sinning. Sin is so much a part of us that we can't get away from it."

"Don't you think with God's help we can avoid sinning?" a sweet-looking, blue-haired older lady suggested.

"Sure," Peter replied, "but without God's help we can't. That's what I mean. It's that idea of original sin Rev. McKenzie talked about in his Session devotional last Sunday night. Adam and Eve sinned by disobeying God, and we've been stuck in sin ever since."

Peter kept talking, which was usually not his style, but I tried to listen patiently. "The Bible is clear that because of our sin, things are not right in the world. Genesis talks about the man having to labor hard to grow food and about the woman having pain in childbirth -- both because of sin. Life is filled with suffering and evil because of sin. Original sin is powerful stuff."

"Wow," I whispered to Ann. "I never thought I'd hear Peter give Will's sermon for him. This is a switch."

I took a breath to say something, but Ann elbowed me, and Grits beat me to the punch. "Let me tell you what I think original sin really is all about," Grits asserted. "It's a notion that got started as a result of our infantile omnipotence."

Ann leaned over to me, whispering in my ear, "Infantile omnipotence. Here goes Dr. Freud."

"Infants and very small children think they cause everything to happen. The world almost completely revolves around them for a long time. They cry, and they get fed. They cry a different way, and they get changed. When something happens in their world, they think they caused it to happen. Therapists call that behavior "infantile omnipotence."

"I've seen that in action," Sam chimed in. "Our son spills his milk almost every night. We even keep a large sheet of plastic under his high chair to contain the mess. Well, one night recently I knocked my own glass over. Tommy immediately burst into tears and blurted, 'I'm sorry, Daddy. I didn't mean to.' I told him it wasn't his fault. I told him I did it; that it was my fault. He seemed relieved, yet he also seemed puzzled.

Tommy's reactions puzzled me, too, until I ran into a psych major at Tulane who told me about infantile omnipotence. It really is true. Little Tommy thought he caused me to spill my water." Sam smiled with satisfaction at his explanation.

"Great example, Sam," Grits continued. "Picture the early writers of the Old Testament looking around their world, realizing that life was difficult, full of pain and suffering and death. They must have wondered what caused life to be that way. Somehow they concluded that the hardships must be their fault. That's infantile omnipotence, and it's woven into the very fabric of the Biblical culture. 'It must be my fault' is written onto the sacred scrolls of scripture. That's what the doctrine of original sin is all about. In our childish arrogance we take credit for all the bad in the world, rather than just accepting it as a fact of life." In noticed that Grits paused here, hoping the class followed him. I did.

Well, Agnes Benson was livid by the time Grits finished talking. She and her husband Howard taught the Bible study that meets in the church library on Sunday night. They call themselves "The Believers" and Agnes carried that torch of orthodoxy. She countered Grit's remarks with a strong affirmation about the sinfulness of all humans, all the time, from all time. Period.

Actually, I thought Grits was on to something. Things are not perfect because they are not perfect, that's all. That's just the way life is. We didn't cause it to be that way. We're not that powerful, for goodness sake.

Grits continued. "We have to label some things 'sinful' as a matter of self-preservation, to keep society from degenerating into chaos. If we can't agree to remain civil and orderly, then the fear of God might help us do that. Trouble is, those that don't have any fear of God are usually the ones who are capable of destroying our society. We call them psychopaths, and they don't pay attention to the church or to God."

This discussion had gone on for almost an hour, and I hadn't opened my mouth. I was proud of my restraint. But Ann was still tense, and I guessed she wouldn't relax until the meeting ended and we were in the car heading home.

Will summarized the evening's discussion. I heard him say we needed to believe in Jesus Christ as our Lord and Savior. I noticed he spoke the words with a mechanical cadence, like a generic medicine being routinely prescribed by an overworked physician.

When Will pronounced the 'amen,' I watched him sigh. I felt his fatigue and sensed the weight on his shoulders. Everyone looked to him for guidance and instruction. It had to be tough being a minister to a church with so many differing views. When our eyes met he showed an awkward and barely discernable embarrassment that smacked of a soldier caught in the act of kissing up to his commanding officer. He didn't flinch, but his eyes blinked for an instant. My eyes were suddenly opened even wider to the pressures he must feel. He appeared to be a CEO constantly being badgered by fourteen hundred stockholders with a board of directors that never adjourned. I felt for him.

I felt for him even more when I watched him open the door to the hallway. Margaret, dressed all in black, was leaning up against the wall waiting for him. That woman must be crazy. She's always lurking in wait for Will. He's far more polite to her than I would be. I heard him ask her kindly to go home. I was surprised when she agreed. Poor Will; he has enough on his plate without having to deal with folks like Margaret.

CAROL McKENZIE

"Preservation Hall! Old time Dixieland jazz! I love it. Thank goodness we've got a seat." I smiled at Will and kissed him as I sat on my coat as a cushion for the wooden bench.

Preservation Hall is one of my favorite places. We often had to stand in the back, so I always wore flats, just in case. Half the room had benches and half the room had to stand. Same five dollars to get in, seat or no seat. And there was no air conditioning. There had been evenings during the summer when I thought I'd die of heat in here, but the music always made it worthwhile. Preservation Hall remained a modest place cooled by a few antique ceiling fans, surrounded by age-darkened wooden walls, serving nothing to eat or drink, and still boasting a waiting line that usually snaked out the front door onto St. Louis Street toward Pat O'Brien's patio bar.

On the stroke of eight, five old men and one old woman shuffled to their seats up front on the floor-level stage. One young man carrying a banjo followed them trailed behind. His younger presence indicated the recent death of a band member, and I sadly realized once again that these old bands were dying out. All the other musicians were old, black, and white-haired except for Sweet Emma, and it was her band. Her hair remained jet black and she wore a faded, red, pillbox hat that sat slightly askew on her head. She limped on her left side as she walked to the piano. Her left arm and leg had been paralyzed, probably by a stroke.

All the musicians wore black suits that seemed a bit too large, white shirts, and dark ties, except Sweet Emma, of course. She wore a blue flowered dress with a white sweater … and that red, pillbox hat. If there were ever any doubt who was in charge, it became crystal clear when Sweet Emma looked over her right shoulder and cackled loudly, "St. James Infirmary. Ahh, one; ah two; ah three; ah four."

The sounds of Dixieland filled the room. A trumpet, a clarinet, a bass. A trombone, drums, a banjo, and a piano. They all came alive. I noticed that Sweet Emma could use only her left hand to play an occasional chord, but she stomped a steady, time-keeping cadence with her right foot, and her right hand made up for the handicap of her left. She had energy, rhythm, and soul. Later, as she belted out the words to "Won't You Come Home, Bill Bailey," her raspy nasal voice elicited an emotion halfway between fascination and embarrassment. "She's an inspiration," I whispered to Will.

I was glad to see Will relaxing. He soon became absorbed in the music. He had entered their world, finding a happy, pleasant solace there. He even looked a bit younger. I swear he did. He leaned toward me and said, "This is truly a refreshing mini-vacation. I could stay here all night." So could I.

When the set drew to a close, a young girl stepped front and center and introduced each member of the band. Then she started hawking their CDs. Will wanted to buy one before another member of "Sweet Emma's Band" died. "I think I remember their original banjo player," Will told me.

With the music still lingering in our ears, we walked around the corner to a French pastry shop. We chose our coffee and pastry and headed toward the patio in back. Soft spotlights pleasantly lit the area. The setting was very romantic, and I felt myself turning on to Will. I reached over and touched his hand.

But I felt Will tighten up, and I became instantly irritated. I bet his thoughts had turned to the officers' retreat he would be running tomorrow morning. "Saturday wouldn't be a day off, that's for sure; but don't spoil Friday evening too," I snipped.

Will ignored my words and played with his pastry. He began rubbing the left side of his head above his ear. He does that when he gets tired or anxious. He has a small bald spot there where the skin is slick and devoid of hair and pigment. No one notices, because he wears his hair long, but that bald spot serves as a reminder to him of a very close brush with death he had in the service. A piece of shrapnel grazed, but didn't penetrate, his head. He calls it his 'miracle spot'... one of two scars from Vietnam, that one and a small scar on his chest which he never talks about. "Two miracles" he says, but not much more, even when I've asked. He clams up about Vietnam.

Nevertheless, I found myself getting very impatient with Will's anxiety tonight. His distractions were coming between us. This was the first evening we had gone out in weeks, and now he had drifted miles away. I pulled his hand away from his head, knowing that would irritate him; but he did stopped rubbing that spot.

"I'm sorry honey. I really am," he managed. "It's been a great evening, really. It's just that I got to thinking about...."

I interrupted him. "I know. I know. The Church. That other woman."

"Please don't get started on that, Carol," he pleaded, but I cut him off again.

"Look, either you go get some help like I've talked about … go to Grits, or whoever. But get some help, or …" I stopped.

"Or what?" he asked half challenged, half fearful.

"Never mind." I felt tears replace the fury in my eyes, and I looked away from him as I started quietly to cry.

WILL McKENZIE

"Dear James, I'm on my way home from work, and decided to stop, get coffee, and write. Carol and I were sitting right here in this pastry shop last night after having a great time at Preservation Hall. Then I soured-out on her, and she told me one more time that I needed to get into therapy. Her words were a bit of a threat this time, enough of a 'you'd better' to let me know she's fed up. I'm sure there are times when I must be a total pain in the neck to live with. My feelings get all confused at times and our relationship gets caught in the middle. I feel terrible about last night; I ruined a great evening." I picked at my pastry as I paused from typing.

"A lot of my dilemma has to do with basic religious beliefs. Recently I find myself responding to people's questions with answers I heard years ago in seminary, and it feels artificial. You know the drill: for questions about sin and evil, say thus and such; for issues about salvation, quote this and that; for questions about suffering, remember to quote this; and be sure to share this chapter from the Bible for concerns about forgiveness or guilt.

I dipped my croissant in my coffee, savoring the bite.

"Let me put it this way, James: how do you evaluate a religion anyway? Usually if you like the answer a religion gives to a question, you embrace that faith to be true and profound. You say that particular religion is divinely inspired. If you don't like the answer, you say it is erroneous. You may even call it heresy. Nevertheless, we are the ones who determine whether we like the answer or not. But our inner needs usually determine that process. I might feel guilty and need to be punished right now, so I hear only judgment from God. Or I might feel good about myself, so I hear acceptance and forgiveness. Religions seems to embrace a wide spectrum of

answers to our questions -- a blue one for this occasion, a red one for that, a yellow one for this situation, an orange one for another.

"A Presbyterian answer may be bluer than a Baptist answer or greener than a Roman Catholic answer. A Muslim answer might contain some blue, but it may be getting into the red areas as well. A Buddhist answer might be more orange than blue or red. It bothers me how automatically I have learned to come out with blue answers. The trouble is the correct answer may have nothing to do with any color at all.

"As you may have guessed, my head's starting to spin. So ... have another sip of French coffee. Do you want one lump of sugar or two? Maybe that's all there is to it. A question of one lump or two. Maybe it's purely a matter of taste.

"Anyway, I'm not convinced a shrink can help me with questions like these, much less what to do with those days in Nam. But would you believe I have lunch scheduled tomorrow with a shrink? We teach Sunday school together. We'll see what, if anything, comes out of that lunch. Some coincidence.

"I've got to get back to the office. Somebody at church may need an answer or two I can supply -- blue ones, of course.

"Write, for God's sake, James. E-mail goes two ways, you know."

GRITS GRAVOIS

"Margie, please call Rev. McKenzie. He's in the Rolodex. I'm picking him up for lunch. Tell him I'm on my way."

"Sure, Dr. Gravois," I heard my faithful secretary reply.

It'd been over a year since Will and I had lunch together, and I looked forward to his company. I liked Will a lot. I thought I would take him to the Southern Yacht Club. Lake Pontchartrain is pretty this time of year, and on a windy day like today there should be a bit of chop, creating whitecaps to contrast with the darkened winter water. Besides, at the Yacht Club we can get a table to ourselves where we can talk without interruptions.

I turned the corner to drive to the entrance to the church offices. Will was standing in front waiting for me, and we were soon off for the ten-minute drive to lunch

"I appreciate your picking me up," Will said. "We've got one car in the shop getting new brakes, and Carol has the other one out shopping. You know, she didn't shop as much when she worked as a nurse. However, she really has enjoyed being an at-home mother for the past ten years. Of course she rocks the babies at Charity Hospital on Wednesday afternoon and really loves that. Strictly volunteer." Will paused, and then reflected, "Wow, did I say it's been ten years since I came to New Orleans?"

"Has it been that long?" I asked with equal amazement. "Seems like just the other day when our search committee flew to Big D to scout you out. I remember we went to some place we read about for lunch, and we drove for over an hour to get there. New Orleans is a lot less spread out than Dallas and a lot more hemmed in by water."

Our idle chatter continued as we rode. I thought about an older woman I had evaluated yesterday who was in the early stages of Alzheimer's disease. Even with Alzheimer's she could keep up a surface-only conversation for a long time. What a commentary that was about the depth of most social conversations.

"Lucky us!" I exclaimed, "A parking place near the front. Let's go eat; I'm starved."

As our conversation continued, I found myself paying less attention to what Will was saying and more to how he was saying it. I could feel his depression no matter what the subject. The subject, however, was almost always about the church.

I began to wrestle with a familiar but always uncomfortable quandary. If I really cared about Will as a person, I would mention the depression and suggest some avenues of help. But I might lose him as a friend or even as a minister if I did that. On the other hand, if I cared more about Will as a friend and my minister, I'd simply ignore the depression and continue to converse as though it didn't exist. I wouldn't lose a friend or my minister that way, but Will might not lose his depression either.

A pair of sailboats, colorful spinnakers swollen with wind, angled in the lake; the glass window beside our table framed them nicely. One boat had a bright blue and yellow spinnaker, the other a sunset orange. The wind registered twelve knots according to the instrument on the wall, so the sailing was excellent.

"That sure looks peaceful," Will commented as we both admired the scene. "When I joined the Marines, I thought I might take up sailing as a sideline, but I ended up on the rivers of Vietnam instead. We didn't stay on those boats very long either. We did almost all of our fighting on land."

"Those must have been rough days," I ventured, glad to talk about something other than the church. "I never served in the military, but I've done therapy with a lot of vets."

"I bet you have. Some of those guys plumb fell apart after they got home." Will seemed surprised at what he just observed. "You know, Carol thinks I ought to be in therapy," he blurted out of nowhere.

"Well, what do you think about that idea?" I asked.

"I don't know. She raises the therapy bit from time to time and won't let it drop."

"What do you think she sees?" I asked.

"She sees me shaken by flashbacks from time to time," Will honestly responded. "But I don't think she's just referring to that. I'm really not sure I know what all she sees."

"Don't you think it might be helpful to ask her what she sees? Couldn't hurt. But how do you react to the idea of therapy?"

"I think shrinks … sorry … psychiatrists …." Will stumbled, and I broke out smiling at his correction. "I think psychiatrists," he repeated, "deal with mental illness, not religious beliefs and spiritual questions like forgiveness." Will sipped some iced tea, and then added, "I do worry about my faith at times. And that's not too cool for a minister."

"Well, we shrinks can help people sort out their feelings, regardless of the subject. Sometimes things we think are about religion are really about something else."

"I don't understand."

"Well, I had a patient who couldn't believe God could be a good father, even though she really wanted to believe in that. It turned out that her own father had abused her. So once she sorted out her feelings about him, she found she could embrace God as a good father without being suspicious or afraid. She seemed a lot happier as a result."

"That's interesting. You started off with her religious problem, discovered other stuff causing her doubts, then her faith straightened out. But what happens if you get to stuff that makes faith come out worse than before?"

"Then we would deal with those feelings too," I responded, realizing that Will was nervous about this line of conversation.

" I don't know." Will fell silent and looked out the window at the choppy lake. The sailboats had vanished from view. I let the silence happen. He resumed after a while, "Well, you're causing me to think about things, Grits. You always do. I really enjoy your classes for that reason."

"You're the co-teacher, remember?" I paused to see if Will wanted to say more, but he remained silent. "Anyway, if the idea of therapy begins to appeal to you, give me a call. I've worked with Presbyterian ministers before, and the insurance is real good. Not much out-of-pocket expense. You've got my office number if you want an appointment. Either way we should have lunch together more often."

"This has been a great lunch, Grits. Speaking of which, let me pay for today."

"No can do. I'd get kicked out of this club if you pulled your wallet out. Strictly against the rules ... Coffee?"

+++++

After I dropped Will back at church, I had time before my next patient to take a walk. What an opportunity it would be to do therapy with Will, I thought as I started walking around the block. He could become an even more effective minister if he resolved some of his inner conflicts about Vietnam and about forgiveness. They were certainly interconnected.

However, another issue haunted me. What if therapy resulted in a capable man like Will leaving the ministry? Could I live with that one?

It was the same question I faced at lunch, only with a different set of parameters. Do I care more about Will as a person, or do I care more about Will as a minister? I've got to choose the person, I told myself.

When I got back to my medical suite, Margie wanted to speak to me in private, so we went into my office.

"Your daughter Martha called while you were at lunch, Dr. Gravois. She'd gotten a call from Paul. She said he was okay and just wanted to say hello. He was in Chicago, but didn't say where. Martha indicated that she had already told Gail about the call." Margie paused to see if I wanted her to do anything. I simply thanked her, and she went back to her desk.

I stood in the middle of my office staring at the Oriental rug on the floor. That old, deep sadness rolled over me once again. Will I ever see Paul again? If only I could take back some of my words and actions during his teen years. He will be thirty-five later this month. What I wouldn't give to reconcile us.

I looked at Paul's picture on my credenza. It sat there inconspicuously with a dozen other family pictures. The portrait was his senior prom photograph. It's also the last picture we have of him.

I took a few deep breaths, pushed back my own depression, and opened the door for my next patient.

WILL McKENZIE

Mac Richards and I left just before dark for the Lower Coast to look for his son René. "René has always been on the edge of trouble, if not in the middle of it," Mac admitted sadly as we passed a familiar shopping center on the way. "This time I think he's really gotten himself in deep. As best I can piece the story together, he got caught in the middle of a drug deal. Both sides are after his hide to come up with money. A friend of René told me that he's going to a gambling house on the Lower Coast to win some money for what he owes. That same friend told me how to find the house; he was really worried about René. I just hope we're not on a wild goose chase, but I figured this would be a chance to intervene." He paused at a stop sign, and then continued talking.

"This drug stuff can get real rough. I've heard about how some coke dealers settle their unpaid debts, so I just can't stand by and do nothing. I sure appreciate your going with me Will; he respects you."

René did respect me, although I wasn't sure why. Maybe because I visited him in the hospital after he was badly beaten up by a school rival. He seemed to appreciate my coming ... and not lecturing him. If we found him, maybe he would listen to me; I didn't know. I figured at worst we would be turned away at the house, or René wouldn't be there. At least Mac and Dot would know I had tried to help.

"Mac," I said, "I've got to tell you I'm not very optimistic about this. If we're given a cold shoulder at the door, we've got to turn around without arguing. Okay?" I wanted to set some guidelines around this trip.

"Fair enough," Mac sighed. It was dark by now and he turned on his headlights.

The Lower Coast was an undeveloped, remote part of the city bordered by the Mississippi River on one side and by swamp on the other. The area had once been a large rice plantation, and it was still largely undeveloped. Only small farms, small houses, and several riding stables peppered the heavily wooded acreage on the river road that ran beside the levee.

There were no city lights, so the area was pitch black except for our headlights. The drive quickly became spooky. Mac assured me he could find the house without too much trouble. I hoped so, because not even a moon lighted our way, and we saw no other cars on the road.

As we turned right onto a gravel road, I could barely see a road sign half-covered with kudzu: "Dead End." There was darkness on either side of us and beyond our headlights. Soon, however, the lights of a house became visible. A handful of cars were parked on the edge of the road, and Mac pulled up behind the last car.

I went into an alert mode. "Mac, this was like a night mission in Nam. How about turning around so we're facing out?" He did.

Several dogs barked, but to my relief never appeared. When we stepped out of the car, I heard them lunging against their chains. They must not have been far away. We walked up to the house and onto the porch where a tough looking, middle-aged woman with a cigarette in her hand stood behind the screen door watching us approach. She wore a dirty black tank top, and had tattoos scattered on her upper chest and arms. The single bulb dangling from the porch ceiling swayed in the breeze causing eerie shadows to dart across her face.

"You're new, ain't you?" the woman snarled dryly. "You're not the law, now, are you?"

"No mam," Mac assured her. "I've just come to get my son."

"Gonna straighten him out, huh?" she cackled. "Good luck." She dragged on her cigarette and carefully picked a flake of tobacco from the tip of her tongue. She kept peering over our shoulders into the distance. "If you're looking for the games, they're in the barn 'round back." She pointed her head to the left of the house. "You can go on back now. Larry checked you out and waved me that you're all right."

I glanced behind me but saw no one. Whoever Larry was, he was elusive … and a bit frightening.

Thick underbrush and tall shrubs hid the barn from view. Only a well-worn, curved path led the way. When swamp myrtles eclipsed the light from the house, light from the barn became visible. As we approached the barn door, we could hear rowdy voices coming from inside.

"Do we knock, or just enter?" Mac asked, as though I knew the protocol.

"I'd rather knock first, and then enter if no one answers." I doubted if anyone could hear our knock over the commotion coming from inside, so I was surprised when a tall, thin man with long black sideburns opened the door.

"Come on in. I'm Larry." He spoke with a Cajun accent, showing its typical French twang. "Your money's good here, yeah. We'll be glad to take it from you." He grinned broadly and stepped aside. As we entered, a putrid stench burned my nose. Larry walked right behind us. "Your boy's on the other side of the ring, Mr. Richards. He's a new face too. Last I heard, he's winning pretty good." How did he know Mac's name? This Larry guy *was* scary.

We were standing behind a large group of men who had their backs to us. The gathering was loud and raucous, and at first I couldn't get a clear picture of what was going on. Mac started looking for a way to get across the room. This was certainly no crapshoot. A break in the human wall suddenly opened up, and I saw the action.

Cockfighting!

My God, I couldn't believe it. Right here on the Lower Coast. immediately recognized that acidic smell from a cockfight I saw in the Philippines years ago. Cockfighting was a cruel, barbaric battle to the death in which razors, called tari knives, were strapped to the claws of roosters. The cocks instinctively fought each other to a bloody, messy end.

The crowd in front of us jumped back, moving away from the vicious fracas and hoping not to get spattered with blood. The putrid odor was now front and center.

The gamecocks jumped at each other, rising several feet in the air. Feathers flew as they attacked with their razor-enhanced talons. Entangled momentarily in mid-air, the cocks fell to the dirt floor rolling for a split second before one dominated the other with slashes of its razor. Their death-struggle stirred up a cloud of dust, and I coughed to clear my throat.

This fight ended within minutes. One bird was dead. The winning owner, protected by long, thick leather gloves, stepped forward and carefully grabbed his rooster. When he picked his bird up, the carcass of the losing rooster dropped from its talons to the ground. The lifeless rooster was tossed into a nearby wash pail with other dead birds. The winner held his bird carefully so as not to be cut by the tari, then popped a hood over its head and carefully removed the razors from its claws. The game master distributed money rapidly and without rancor. The din of shouting dissolved into calmer conversations.

René, unshaven and dirty, held new winnings in his hand. He saw his father and me, and registered no surprise, like we'd been there all the time. That was René's demeanor about everything. Always emotionless.

"Buy you a beer, son?" Mac asked him after we crossed the ring.

"Sure," came René's even reply. The three of us walked to a corner where I'd seen a barrel filled with ice and beer cans, topped by a coffee-can with $2.00 marked on it. René threw some money into the can before his father could, and then added his new bills to a wad from his pocket. He popped his beer open, and took a hefty swallow, but still didn't say a word.

"Willing to come home and talk?" Mac ventured.

René shrugged. "May as well. I've won what I need. Besides, I need a way out of here since my ride already left." The kid had ice water in his veins.

Larry noticed us leaving. He invited us to come back anytime we wanted. Sure, Larry. We headed back to the car carrying with us the smell of hot, slaughtered poultry. We found the car unlocked with the glove compartment hanging open.

René quickly climbed in the back seat and fell asleep. He really did reek.

As we rode in silence, I wondered what my presence had contributed to the evening. I knew I'd been a support for Mac, and maybe that made the trip worthwhile. Nevertheless, I was greatly relieved it was over.

I was also relieved we hadn't been arrested in a raid. We would have ended up in jail for sure, which could have been the end of my career as a minister. I could see the headlines now. "Tall-steeple pastor arrested at a cockfight on the Lower Coast."

Mac looked at me apologetically as he drove down the dark road.

I shrugged my shoulders and casually wiped a tear off my cheek. Neither one of us had known we'd be walking into a cockfight, for God's sake.

+++++

When I got home, Carol was watching the end of a DVD. She sat in the corner of the sofa with her legs curled up underneath her. The television flickered light to dark as the movie ran its path. She looked at me briefly. "How'd it go?" I could tell she was into the movie and didn't want to be interrupted. I'd tell her about my evening later. I felt loneliness and sadness roll over me. The whole evening was sad.

I felt dirty and bushed, so I showered to remove the barn's dust, and after glancing briefly through a new magazine, I headed to bed. I lay down and stared at the ceiling. Eventually I rolled over onto my right side, and my pillow blotted a tear that was forming in my eye.

I leaned back against a pile of crumbling bricks and reloaded my rifle. The mud walls of the old French fort stood tall and thick, offering some security as the night settled in. I never would have dreamed Hill 471 would be such a massive slaughter … of them, not us, thank God. But we lost two men. Two good men.

Several of my men had questioned whether we should be this far north. I reassured them we were following orders. I thought the day's fighting would never end, but it was all over before nightfall. I added a memento of today's combat, an ear, to the collection dangling from my belt loop and pulled out a map to see exactly where we were. Khe Sanh in Quang Tri Province, the map indicated.

I was real glad the sergeant found us this crumbling fort south of the Hill. It actually was shown on the map, so the structure was probably historical. There was no ceiling in most places, so we were exposed to the sky, but the high, thick walls shielded us from the night wind … and perhaps from the Viet Cong as well.

It was Clipper's watch, so I decided to settle in. I knew there was a village not too far away, probably filled with Viet Cong. I figured they would wait until after dark to try anything if they were going to. I wandered outside the fort long enough to hack off some small, leafy branches of a bush to pile on the crumbling bricks to make a softer place to sleep.

"Get the hell back in here, Lieutenant," Clipper shouted when he saw me. "Sorry, sir, but we need you alive," he continued. I nodded in a foggy stupor and wondered why I had ventured out like that. I knew better.

I had just fallen asleep, or I may have been asleep for a long time, when I was awakened by a piercing scream. Female. Then something heavy landed on the ground twenty feet away from me. I startled awake, quickly looking toward the lump on the ground, my rifle pointing. Someone shined a pin light in that direction. The lump was a young girl impaled on a pole made from a tree branch. She had been thrown over the wall on that pole. She was dead, but she hadn't been dead long. The pole was bloody, and a pool formed on the ground around her bottom. A human skewer. I sickened and gagged.

The sergeant walked over with a red pin-light and barked two privates into action. Together they dragged her body to the far corner of the fort where no one was trying to sleep. Then Sergeant's calloused words sickened me even more: "This kind of crap is a good sign. It means they're out of grenades. Otherwise we'd all be full of shrapnel by now." What made his statement worse was I knew he was right. Charlie had somehow eluded Clipper's watch and had stood on the other side of this wall, so Sergeant sent a second trooper to help.

Benny, who was always nervous, readied his rifle and started moving cautiously toward the opening of the fort. "Hold on, Benny," I said, "they're long gone, and we've got to get some sleep if we can." It was now twenty-three thirty. I looked again in the direction of the dead Vietnamese girl. I also tried again to put the death of Jackson and Hebert out of my mind. It wasn't possible. They were my men. They were eighteen and twenty. The dead girl may have been twelve.

At almost exactly zero two hundred, a second tortured scream cut the night's silence. Seconds later we heard another thud followed by two whacks of a pole on the ground. Then silence. Everyone froze, rifles in hand. Nothing. Not a sound. Nothing. Not even night sounds. Particularly not night sounds.

Benny screamed, charging out of the fort like he was leading the entire platoon on an assault. There was no stopping him. But nothing happened. No one fired at him, and he found no one to shoot at. By the time he returned, this girl's body had been laid in that far corner next to the first. The poles hadn't been removed, and I asked Sergeant about that. "No telling how much of their insides will come with those sticks, Lieutenant. It's messy enough now," came his blunt reply. I wish I hadn't asked. "They'll cut this crap out soon," he stated with conviction.

At zero four twenty-six a third scream awakened us. This time the body landed two feet from me, and she was still screaming. The pole clobbered my leg with a force I thought might have broken it. Not so. The moon shone brightly now, and I could see her face clearly. Her eyes met mine, eyes of absolute terror and unspeakable pain. They were pleading eyes. They were eyes of a very young girl. I turned my rifle toward her head, but she coughed up blood and slumped. Dead. I turned away and vomited uncontrollably.

Carol was shaking me. "You're screaming, Will. You must be having another nightmare. Come on; wake up. You're home. You're here. It's all right, honey. It's all right."

"It's not all right," I managed to say as I sat on the side of the bed, wiping my face with the sheet. I was a sweaty mess, and I felt like I reeked of death. I found myself praying for forgiveness, for them and for me.

"Talk about it," Carol insisted. "You've got to talk about it."

"No. I'm not going to talk about it. I don't want to talk about it. You don't need to know what happened over there, and I don't want to hear myself tell about it either."

"I'm sorry, Will. Get up and put on some dry pajamas. I'll change the sheets. Then we can get back to sleep."

I did change my pajamas, but then I headed for the family room. "I'm going to surf the net for a while and maybe write James. I'll try to sleep later." I felt like a little boy who was too frightened to go to sleep.

+++++

"*I wish you were here now, James. I could use a long talk. After reliving that night in the fort near Hill 471, I got to thinking 'why on earth am I a minister?' The marines taught me to kill, and I had plenty of practice at that for two damn years, as you well know. Then I went to seminary where I was taught that life is sacred, that we should love one another, turn the other cheek, and forgive seventy times seven times. I'm sure you had the same kind of turn-about experiences when you went to med school. Will God ever forgive us? … and them?*

"*One trouble is, the enemy had faces. Charlie had faces. Friendly Vietnamese had faces. Our buddies who were slaughtered had faces … and names … want to hear them again? There was Roger Jackson and Allen Hebert at Hill 471; and there was Henry Burgess and Matthew Cummings and Roger Boudreaux and John McMillian and Henry Ivers and Joshua Stone and Washington Johnson and Randolph Milling and Leonard Blueberry and John Talmadge and Dick Everett. Thirteen men whose lives, names, and faces I remember every day. Every damn day. Dead; and I'm still alive. Why?*

"*Remember old Professor Steinberg at Tulane? The holocaust survivor who taught history. I can still see him looking out the classroom window with glazed eyes and saying, 'One thing we Jews learned from the holocaust is that God won't look after you.' I've never forgotten his words. Vietnam played out his words. Now we've got war in the Middle East and disease in Africa and all over the place. Even my rich church is filled with death and dying that doesn't respect person, rank, or creed.*

"*Seminary taught us, the church has always taught us, and for a long time I have taught others, that unless you believe in Jesus Christ, you aren't forgiven or saved. Well, if that's true, what on earth is God saving His salvation for?*

"*It's late. I'm going to log off. Ciao.*"

+++++

I showed the guard my driver's license as I signed the prison registry to visit Alice. The heavy, shiny steel gate in the city jail shut tight with a loud, echoing ring like an industrial cymbal. I was now locked in a holding room. The prison guard, chatting about how we've been spared a hard freeze, patted me down with disinterested professionalism, and required me to surrender my penknife and my belt. Then he gave the word, and a gate at the other end of the room unlocked and noisily slid open. "One door won't open unless the other one is locked," the guard explained. It was an escape-proof entrance and exit.

The stark nakedness of the walls, the high, white ceiling, and the immaculately shiny marble floors all served as a constant reminder of invincible confinement. The building created an unforgiving, judging aura. This whole place intimidated me, and I wasn't a prisoner. If it worked on my head, what must it do to those who are incarcerated?

The room where I visited Alice looked like the ones you see on television, complete with booths, wire-meshed glass, and closed circuit telephones. The guards told me the phones were connected only to each other and that no one else could listen. I wondered. There was about as much privacy in this room as there was at a crowded row of urinals during halftime at a football game.

Alice looked sad. "I'm not angry anymore, Rev. McKenzie. I'm numb … and filled with guilt and regret. Maybe we could have worked it out. If only I hadn't lost it." She looked at the table top in front of her. "If I'm sent away, my children will be put in a foster home. My folks will have to file petitions to get custody." She started to sob -- a sob less hysterical than she sobbed in the church, a sob slower and more paced than she sobbed at the funeral, but a sob as though her entire life were summarized in the spasms. "Can I ever be forgiven?" she asked desperately.

I offered supportive words, words of comfort and reassurance, words that showed her I cared. My mind jumped in a dozen different directions at once, and the cadence of her sobbing pounded against my confidence and battered my heart.

"Can I ever be forgiven?" she asked again.

"God forgives you, Alice. Jesus forgives you. I forgive you too." The words rolled out of my mouth almost automatically. But they were heartfelt; they expressed my highest hopes.

But, Alice, I thought, why is it so easy for me to say you are forgiven when I don't feel forgiven myself? Maybe it's because you killed out of anger toward Stan. When anger prevails, killing seems to be more justified, more forgivable. When they killed my buddies, I could kill them with righteous anger. What if you killed without any emotion toward your victim -- no jealousy, no revenge, no personal insult to settle, no humiliation to blame it on, no fury? What if you killed because you were a killing machine doing a job for a cause in which you didn't fully believe? What if you killed because you were simply scared? What if it boiled down to kill or be killed?

Ultimately, Alice, your killing and my killing were about the same. They both produced a dead human. But then look at what happened afterwards. They gave you a warrant, and they gave me a medal. You'll go broke paying attorney fees, and I got a raise in rank and pay. Your friends and family feel ashamed and sorry for you, and my family welcomed me home. They clipped handcuffs on you and they pinned a Silver Star on me. That's right, a Silver Star. And believe me, I'm proud of that Silver Star.

But no one is less dead either way. With any luck, Alice, you'll soon develop two lives. You'll develop a life for killing and a life for living, and you'll close one door before the other door opens. Your innocent life will be separated from your guilty life by glass impregnated with chicken wire … chicken … wire ……..

Our time was up and the guard tapped Alice on the shoulder. I smiled a "you're welcome" to Alice in response to the lavish appreciation she expressed to me for visiting her. I promised to come back soon. Maybe next time would be better … better for Alice … and maybe for me. But what did 'better' mean?

The second exit door slid open and I left. Exit, entrance. It was just a matter of which way you were facing.

CAROL McKENZIE

"Miriam baked a King Cake for the staff to enjoy," I said as I stuck my head into Will's office and handed him a napkin-full of the cake. Will was working on his sermon and mumbled a thank you, not really looking up from his laptop.

"Besides," I continued, "this is your opportunity to say hello again to Janie."

Will looked up then and stood to shake hands with my nursing school roommate from Dallas. "Good to see you, Janie. It's been a long time; I'm glad you finally got to New Orleans. This is a delightful surprise. Are you in town for long?"

"Just today and tomorrow for a cardiology conference at Charity. I just have time for lunch with Carol before the grind begins."

After a few minutes of talk, Janie and I excused ourselves. As we walked down the hall, Janie asked what the King Cake was all about.

"Last night was Twelfth Night, the night the three kings arrived to visit the Christ child. So today is Epiphany, celebrating their discovery. Today also marks the beginning of the Carnival season, and the Carnival season is a very serious matter in New Orleans."

"I never thought of it as serious," Janie showed surprised at my comment.

"Well, the debutante season also starts today, and the different Carnival Krewes now begin holding their annual balls featuring this year's debs."

"Krewes?" Janie asked?

"Yeah; the Carnival clubs are called Krewes. At last count there were over seventy Krewes participating in the Carnival season. King Cake, by the way, is this oval shaped, doughy cake topped with purple, green, and gold icing, the three traditional colors of Mardi Gras. Years ago, the King Cake determined who became the King of Mardi Gras. A small china baby was cooked into the cake. The King's Guard all cut pieces of the cake, and whoever got the baby became the King of Carnival.

"Today the King is secretly chosen within the old-line Krewes. As for the King Cake, now a plastic baby is still cooked into the cake, and whoever gets the baby must bring a cake to the next party.

"Will's one of the few people I know who doesn't really like King Cake. Too sweet and too messy, he says." I laughed. "Sure it is, but it's also delicious and festive, and fun. I've saved us a generous piece to go with our coffee later this morning."

By this time we were in the parking lot, walking toward my car. "Will doesn't like to admit how much control the members of the old-line Krewes have in this city. Business and social interests are intricately intertwined in New Orleans, and the Carnival Krewes embody this dual identity. Krewe members scratch each other's back. That's the way things are here.

"Will likes to think the church plays a major role in the life of the city. He says that many of the 'right' people are in our church, and that's probably true. What Will continues to miss is that what makes these people influential is not that they belong to the church, but that they are members of an old-line Carnival Krewe. Sure, faith has its place here in the Big Easy, but that's exactly what it is -- just a place, rarely the cornerstone.

Janie and I parked at Whole Foods grocery. We planned to grab a sandwich and find a scenic spot in City Park to eat it. I knew of a bench we could use overlooking a beautiful lagoon, and it was warm enough to sit outside.

"So who has the power in this town and what does that have to do with religion?" Janie asked. I was surprised she still wanted to pursue this line of conversation.

"In some cities," I said, "power is in the hands of old wealth. In some cities it's in the hands of a political machine. In some cities power may be in the hands of a few dedicated Christians. In some cities power may even be in the hands of the Mafia. However, if Christ were to come to the Crescent City, he would first have come as Rex -- the King of Carnival."

WILL McKENZIE

I felt out of my element. School affairs, with all of their ins and outs, were Carol's strength, not mine, but she had to take David to the doctor. He woke up in the middle of the night with stomach cramps that had gotten worse.

"All you have to do is check the acceptance list," Carol said. "It should be posted on the library bulletin board by the main checkout desk. If David's name is on the list, you write them a check for $75. That's it. If his name isn't on the acceptance list, see how far down the waiting list he is. Everyone who's accepted has until seven o'clock tonight to pay. From seven to nine tonight the waiting list opens up. It can get complicated, but you either pay for him while you're there or find out where he is on the waiting list. I'll take it from there when we get back from the doctor."

"Ok," I agreed. David was dressed but lying on the sofa. "David, I hope you're going to be all right. I'm worried about appendicitis. Carol, give me a call when you find out what the doctor says, will you?"

I had forgotten that David would hear about the Summer Scholars program today. He had applied long before Christmas. Only 28 are accepted in the entire city, so it's very competitive. Being accepted into the program was a sure ticket for entrance to the gifted and talented high school in the fall, and that's what this was really all about. Carol had indicated people would go to any length to get into that particular high school.

+++++

80

The Latter Library is a beautiful mansion occupying a city block of prime uptown real estate. This elegant home, evoking feelings of grandeur, is also an excellent public library.

I climbed the marble steps up to the front door. When I was a kid there seemed to be a lot more steps than there are now. I am always fascinated at how our perception of reality changes -- because of the passage of time, because of our age, because of our circumstances, or maybe because of our experiences. Same steps, but viewed quite differently. Combat did a lot to change my perceptions and my perspective on things.

Halfway up the steep steps, I suddenly saw one of my men, John Talmadge, slump forward and slide several feet back down the hill. I reached back toward him, but a large circle of red grew on his back where the bullet exited. He had died instantly. I felt the sadness overcome me. Then my flashback faded as a man came down the library steps toward me. We both adjusted our position and stride to allow the other to pass, and we both nodded cordially. I shook my head and looked up at the library doors.

Inside, this mansion looked just like a library, complete with a librarian who wore her gray hair up in a bun. Three women were gathered around a small bulletin board on an easel over to one side. That had to be the acceptance list, so I moved in for a closer look. I couldn't see over the women, so I asked in a polite tone, "Is McKenzie on the list?" None of them answered. One woman turned and walked toward the librarian's desk with a smile, while two looked disappointed and left.

As I stepped forward to look at the list, one woman who lingered by the board suddenly jumped to the side and let out a yelp. She startled me and everyone in the lobby. Then she made a beeline for the door and walked out. Puzzled, I watched her leave. When the front door closed behind her, I turned back to the bulletin board. David had made the list, and I was excited and pleased.

I, too, wore a smile as I pulled out my checkbook and paid for David's registration. I was proud of David, and I was also relieved. Both Carol and I were eager for him to get into that gifted and talented school. We could never afford one of the private schools, and the other public high schools were pretty bad.

The librarian located an index card with David's name on it, checked a box marked "paid," and handed me a receipt. "A letter with full details will follow shortly, Mr. McKenzie." I smiled and thanked her before I left.

The woman who had yelled in the library was waiting on the columned veranda. She looked at me gruffly. "You're Reverend McKenzie, right?" She paused for emphasis. "I see your son got in. Mine is first on the waiting list. Well, Reverend, you've got until nine tonight to withdraw your son from that program or I'll file charges that you groped me. I have at least three witnesses who heard me scream. Withdraw, got it? I'll be checking the board this evening."

She turned heel and clamored down the steps. I wanted to say something, but I didn't know quite what. "Wait!" was all I could muster. She turned her head to the side and without missing a step shouted, "Before nine. I'll be here waiting." I stood frozen on the top step, watching helplessly as she got into a blue Mercedes convertible and burned rubber onto the Avenue.

After what felt like an eternity, I went back into the library. I debated whether to tell the librarian what had happened, perhaps as a way of buying some insurance. However, telling her might also backfire, so I simply asked her who the woman was that screamed. She had no clue and couldn't care less. I finally thought of the waiting list. "Alternate number one: William G. Erwin." I grabbed a pad and pencil from the card catalogue shelf and wrote down his name.

Pale and slightly dizzy, I walked out, smiling feebly at the librarian, whose expression hadn't changed. She pushed at her hair bun and silently went about her tasks, just as librarians are supposed to do.

+++++

At home, I waited and waited for Carol and David to return from the doctor. I was alternately concerned about David's illness and what could happen to me. I was alternately scared and furious as I thought about that woman's threat. I knew, and that woman obviously knew, that such an accusation would ruin my career. All it would take would be her accusation … a mere accusation. I knew this could happen to any man, and I knew two men it had happened to. I had trouble believing I was being blackmailed like this.

I've always been so damn careful. I never accepted evening appointments for counseling with women. Even in the daytime I scheduled women only when Marie was working just outside my office door. I always took someone with me whenever I visited a woman in her home, and when visiting with women in the hospitals, I always left the room door ajar. I've always been discrete. Now I felt furious, scared, and felt totally at this woman's mercy.

My first priority was to tell Carol all about it, detail by detail. We've got to be together on this. I also needed to be at the office, but I knew I'd be totally useless there right now. I called Marie to reschedule my appointments for another day. 'I'll be in when I can," was all I told her. She never asked where I was, or why. Marie's good about that.

Yet how long were David and Carol going to be at the doctor's? I poured another cup of coffee and paced, fully realizing that neither helped.

About an hour later Carol came home, but without David. I thought 'hospital.' "Is everything all right?" I asked with yet more panic.

"I was about to ask you that?" Carol answered. "What are you doing home at this hour? Anyway, Dr. Long says David has the flu that's going around. He's dehydrated and is now sleeping on an examining table with an IV drip in his arm. The nurse will call when the IV's finished. What's up with you? You look like a ghost. You're not coming down with the same stuff are you?"

I explained the whole thing to Carol, needing to pace as I talked. She listened carefully. When I finished she didn't say anything. She simply stopped my pacing with a big hug. I sloshed my coffee on the kitchen floor, but her reassuring hug meant the world to me.

"William Erwin," she paused in thought. "Then I'm sure she must be Mildred Erwin. William used to be in David's class until they went to different middle schools. Mildred owns her own construction company. She's quite capable of out cursing a dump truck driver. She's a tough cookie. Yea, I think she's quite capable of doing something like this." Carol fell silent.

"I'll go back to the library about eight-thirty," Carol concluded. "She may not remember me, but I remember her. She will have had some time to think about her threat. My going will be much better than your going; she will know you and I are together on this if I go."

"Your plan makes me feel like I'm hiding behind your skirt. What about calling Bill Hamilton? He's known all over town as a good trial lawyer."

"Oh for God's sake, Will. There's nothing he can do right now. Although I'll keep his name in mind in case I need to drop it on this Erwin woman."

+++++

The rest of the day was rotten. I rode with Carol to pick up David from the doctor's office. He crawled back into bed as soon as we got home. Then I managed to meet Peter for a late lunch, and on to the office afterwards. But my heart wasn't in church work today.

Marie took one look at me and expressed concern that I might be "coming down with the crud that's going around." Flu symptoms can cover a variety of ills, I thought. I was getting very little done at my desk, so I decided to visit the hospitals, even though I had just done that yesterday. I needed to keep moving.

+++++

Carol left in time to be at the library by eight-thirty. I cleaned the kitchen more thoroughly than it has been cleaned in months. Soon Carol came back home. "Three names on the acceptance list had been stricken with a red pen. Three names on the waiting list had check marks added in front of them with 'accepted' written behind their names. William Erwin was checked as accepted. Someone else must have dropped out."

I let out a huge sigh.

Carol burst into tears, then smiled and kissed me. She'd obviously been more nervous than she'd let on.

It was late, but we went to the levee for a walk. A strong moon lit up the River and the evening was very pleasant. The walk helped us both unwind. But knowing, just knowing, there was a woman out there capable of such ruthless blackmail caused a knot to linger in my stomach.

CAROL McKENZIE

I enjoy going to the parades with our friends. Will and David run hot and cold on the subject, but you can count me in every time. Tonight's parade was one of the first of the Carnival season, and it rolls up Prytania Street just a block from Lil and Douglas Mann's house. After a quick supper we all headed over there. David wasn't very eager to go until he heard that Mike Charbonnet would be there; then he was all for it. We asked Will's dad to go, but he declined. Pops needs his wheelchair almost all the time now, and it was difficult to use on the sidewalks and streets at night. As the resident nurse, I was glad he turned us down, as much as I love the dear man.

"Did you finish your homework?" I asked David. After all it was aThursday night, and there was still school tomorrow. I tolerated his elongated, disgusted, "yeeees, Mom." Will, who likes to be prompt for everything, was already in the car, honking for us.

"Wouldn't it be neat if our church had a float in a parade?" Will suggested as we drove. "We could make it a witness. Perhaps throw those little aluminum crosses some people carry in their pockets."

"Yeah. Sure, Dad. Right." David chimed in sarcastically.

I looked at David and laughed. Then I turned to Will, "Over Peter's dead body."

"Well, half the church is in at least one Krewe. Some are in two or three," Will added, making one more stab at the idea.

"Give it up, will you, Dad?" David barked. Will fell silent, and I smiled to myself.

"Personally, I think Mardi Gras parades are spectacular as they are," I said. "The maids and ladies-in-waiting are always on the early floats, and I love their exquisite gowns. Then the king of the Krewe arrives on his own float, and he's always majestic. I love all this pageantry. Then twenty to thirty more floats follow, filled with masked riders throwing beads and trinkets. And high school bands march between floats, providing constant music throughout the parades. And it's all free." I beamed and my two men tolerated my enthusiasm. We parked and headed to the parade route.

A truck from the Power Company drove past where we standing. The truck had a pole sticking up from its hood the height of the tallest float, checking for clearance. I always wondered what would happen if that pole slapped into an electrical wire. Surely they figured all that stuff out before they built the floats. It was certainly too late now. The crowd waited three deep now, and everyone craned their necks, standing on tiptoes looking for the parade.

The first band appeared -- a colorful, drum-tapping group who started playing "When the Saints Go Marching In." The bands always sounded better as they approached and after they passed. While they were marching beside you, you heard the song played only by one group of instruments at a time -- now only trumpets, and now only clarinets, now only trombones, then drums, then basses with their two or three deep notes puffing in a rhythmic sequence.

The flambeaux followed this band. I particularly liked the flambeaux; they elicit a more primitive and native time. The flambeaux were white-robed black men who carried multiple torches mounted on poles they twirled as they strutted to the beat of Zydeco music. The dramatic yellow flames flickered in the evening darkness, creating a romantic atmosphere for the floats. Pops once told us that when he was a boy, the flambeaux walked beside the floats to illuminate them. That had to be quite a fire hazard. Now the dozen or so flambeaux marched together in a group at the front of the parade. In Pop's day mules also pulled the floats. Today tractors did the job, and their generators provided ample power for extensive lighting effects without the flambeaux' torches.

At last a real float rolled in front of us. We were peppered with beads, doubloons, cups, and medallions. The noise generated by constant cries of "Throw me something, mister" got louder and louder until the roar became the familiar Carnival din that all but deafens. The riders on the floats throw lots of stuff. Mostly beads. Mostly trash, actually. But after the first five minutes of a Carnival parade, even an uninitiated visitor is ready to fight for a string of plastic beads, or a plastic cup, or an aluminum doubloon. It's not uncommon to bring home a grocery bag filled with beads and trinkets. Of course, when you get home, you have to figure out what to do with all that stuff you caught. This year we decided to make another Mardi Gras lamp by filling a five-gallon water bottle with beads, then wiring it for a light bulb and shade. We had already made two in past years.

A well-built, tightly-sweatered woman stood nearby on a ladder for a better view – a better view of her, that is. The riders seemed to enjoy what they saw and bombarded her with beads. Between floats, the younger kids scavenged the ground for fallen beads or compared the treasures they had caught. I fondly remembered when David would do that. Now he's into being with his friends more than catching stuff. Still, I saw Mike and David over to the side comparing what they had just caught.

I noticed that Will and Brad Dunes had stepped back from the crowd and were engrossed in conversation. Brad was a very wealthy contractor. He was also opposed to our proposed building program at church. I'd bet my bottom dollar Will was trying to get him to change his mind. By the looks of things, Brad was getting irritated. He started punctuating his remarks with jabs of his finger into Will's chest, and Will had assumed his marine-firm, not-to-be-intimidated stance. When Brad finished his point, he turned sharply and rejoined our crowd. He was clearly teed off. Will remained stoical and casually rejoined us too. Everyone's attention quickly focused on the approaching float, and the action continued into the evening.

Back home when Will and I were alone in our bedroom, I said to him, "Brad looked plenty angry after talking with you, and you had on that military poker face I hadn't seen in a while. What were you two talking about that got him so hot?"

"The building program," Will answered. "He never did agree to give any money, but he finally agreed to stop actively opposing it."

"How did you pull that off?"

"I told him this was the first time I had ever asked him to do anything for me and reminded him I had helped Lil and him on several occasions. That's when he got pissed."

"I'm aware you spent a lot of time with him when he and Lil were having their difficulties. Is that what you were referring to?" I paused and could tell from Will's silent demeanor that I was on target. "I don't believe what I'm hearing. That's emotional blackmail, Will!"

"Look, I just mentioned that I'd helped him out on occasion, so now would he help me out. I didn't get specific."

"Just like that. Nothing specific. Just reminding him of the time he was down and you helped him, so now pay up. That's terrible, Will. You're just as bad as Mildred Erwin."

"It's not anything like Mildred Erwin. It was just give and take, that's all." Will gritted his teeth in anger.

"Will, you can try to fool me if you like, but you sure didn't fool Brad. He knew exactly what you were saying. For God's sake, Will, don't kid yourself! Jes'um."

Will fell silent as we lay there in the bed next to each other. After a minute or two of silence, I turned out the light and rolled over. Will was staring at the ceiling when the light went out.

Sometime in the middle of the night, I got up to go to the bathroom. I could see that Will remained awake. "Good," I thought, never acknowledging that I noticed.

WILL McKENZIE

I hit my stride jogging on the neutral ground of St. Charles Avenue, where I shared the space with streetcars running in both directions. The Avenue offered a wonderful place to jog, passing beautiful antebellum mansions and beautiful people as well.

I usually ran for a few miles heading uptown. Then I reversed and headed downtown. It took Carol a while to learn directions in New Orleans. Uptown and downtown. The other two points on the compass are the River and the Lake. "Go toward the Lake six blocks, then turn uptown for two blocks." No one says North, South, East, or West.

I jogged to Audubon Park to run the loop around the oak-lined golf course laced with lagoons. I had to weave in and out of baby-strollers and couples holding hands, but the park was still a jogger's paradise.

My mind churned busily as I ran. Carol and David were at each other's throat these days, and Carol expected me to resolve things between them. I can't resolve their problems; they've got to. To begin with, fifteen-year-old boys are like that with their mothers. The subject of the squabbles varies, but the message is usually the same: "This place isn't big enough for the two of us." Their arguments would often start in the kitchen, which soon became the scene of a "Dodge City shoot-out." I teased them about that, but my teasing just evoked more irritation. The fact that I cannot -- in Carol's mind "won't" -- resolve their differences had become a big issue. Carol wants me to take her side and "stand up for your wife." Today they were at each other hot and heavy after breakfast, arguing about how David was going to spend his Saturday morning. You'd think the issue was a federal case.

"Yeah, just run away as usual," were Carol's words to me as I headed out the door. But hanging around to become a part of their arguments didn't help. I would get involved if it did any good; but when I did, there ended up being three frustrated people in the house, not two.

My father also complicated our domestic situation. Pops was steadily slipping into Alzheimer's, and it was getting unsafe for him to live alone. Last week he smoked up his house when he put a frozen turkey potpie into the oven, cardboard packaging and all. One incident among many. So now he spends the entire day with us, and we drive him back to his house for the night. Carol and I both know this arrangement isn't a lasting solution; it's already getting old. The whole thing remains a dilemma.

We'd been looking for a good assisted living facility. Then my Aunt Ruth heard about our search and jumped all over us for wanting to "put Pops away." My talks with Ruth got nowhere. Her interference didn't help, and it contributed to our stress.

Pops care took more and more of Carol's time, while my church responsibilities prevented me from being home as much as I wanted to. Day or night, when someone died or was rushed to the hospital, I had to go. Carol knew that, but still resented it. "That's why I didn't marry one of those doctors at the hospital," came her standard retort. In addition to abandoning her, I'm also saddling her with taking care of my father. Carol is an angel with Pops, and I think she really does know how much I appreciate her. At least I hope so. Nevertheless, Pop's a real burden, mostly on Carol. David also loves for Carol to spend time with Pops, not because David's concerned about grandpa's well being, but because Carol's not on his back when her attention is focused on Pops.

I jogged in place waiting for a red light to turn green.

"Hello, Charlie. Only two more miles and you're home!" I smiled as I crossed paths with a friend. We jogged on in opposite directions.

David seems to be on a positive plateau in school right now. I am relieved about that. He's also very introverted, and that bothers Carol. She wants him to be more "social." I told her David was born an introvert, hardwired from the moment my sperm met her egg, but she's not convinced. So far David doesn't seem to be bothered by peer pressure to be more outgoing. I'd seen that pressure upset introverted teenagers. Our society is geared to extroverts, no doubt about that.

The harsh clang of the streetcar's bell startled me. I had wandered too close to the track, causing the driver to slow down. I jumped to the side on my next stride, and the rattling, clanging vehicle swayed past me as he stomped on his bell angrily. Streetcar drivers are very impatient with joggers.

Memories filled my mind. Memories of when my friend Roger and I rode the streetcar as kids. We rode often, sometimes simply to pass the time on a slow summer afternoon. Streetcar drivers always sat or stood in the front where passengers got on and paid their fare. The fare was seven cents when I was young. Now it's a dollar. Before the driver pulled away from a stop, he clanged that bell by stomping on a metal button with his foot. Then he rattled off to the next stop two blocks down the track. Stop, clang, and start, every two blocks. It wasn't a smooth ride, but it got you there.

The seats inside were oak. There were bench seats near the conductor, followed by seats for two on each side of a center aisle, followed by more bench seats at the other end. The streetcar never turned around. When it reached the end of the line, the seats were flipped to face the other way. Then off the trolley went in the opposite direction. Going Uptown.Going Downtown. The streetcar represented a romantic remnant from the past still enjoyed in the present. It was also an efficient piece of transportation.

My thoughts focused on the top edge of a streetcar's seat. Each seat had two holes drilled into the top edge, and those holes were embellished with a brass grommet. They were the "sign holes," as we used to call them. Those two holes, which could still be seen today on seats that hadn't been replaced, were reminders of a very troubled time in New Orleans.

A wooden sign mounted those holes. One side read, "Colored only behind this sign." The other side read, "Whites only in front of this sign." When a white person boarded the car, he or she would choose a seat and place the sign on the seat back. No colored people could sit in front of that sign, and no whites would sit behind that sign. Colored people rarely regulated the placement of that sign; the whites did that.

"Colored" people included African-Americans, Cajuns of mixed heritage, native Indians who had mixed with African-Americans, and anyone else who didn't pass the "grocery bag" test. If your skin was darker than a grocery bag, you were considered colored. If your skin was lighter than a grocery bag, you "passed for white." It had been as simple as that, cut and dried, and ruthless.

A young mother went jogging past me pushing her baby-stroller. The child, perhaps a year old, was asleep, and the mother smiled from ear to ear as we passed each other. I wondered what was being taught to the child. The mother jogged; the child slept. Does Pavlov make any connection for the kid? Well, at least *she's* jogging.

My mind returned to those racially troubled days in this city. I remembered getting on an empty streetcar with my father and sitting on the very first bench, putting that sign at our backs. My father was a liberal. Ninety percent of the car was then open to coloreds. Yet every colored person who boarded that streetcar walked to the very back and sat down. Every white that entered would find an empty seat behind us, moving the sign farther back. Not infrequently "colored folks" would have to stand, even when seats remained empty in the white section. They would hold tightly to the overhead bar to keep from falling as the clumsy streetcar swayed back and forth down the tracks.

One time as teenagers, my friend Roger and I got on the streetcar and pulled the sign out of the half-way-back position where the conductor always started it. We walked all the way back to the rear to where there was a colored person sitting. We sat immediately in front of that colored person, placing the sign on our seat back. No colored person could sit in front of us in an almost empty streetcar. We acted naïve and innocent when a colored person asked us to move forward to free up more seats. We pretended we didn't understand the request.

What was worse, we thought the whole scene was funny. I still get a bit sick thinking about what we did. I pray now that dozens of unnamed people of color will forgive this white kid who remained unnamed to them. What I did was totally shameful.

Soon full racial integration confronted the city, and the streetcar was no exception. Blacks, as they then wanted to be called, soon became aggressive and belligerent. A miniature civil war played itself out inside every streetcar. Blacks would jockey for position in the queue at the streetcar stop in order to be the first to get on. They would sit as far forward as possible, putting the sign on the seat-top in front. Whites then had only the sideways bench to sit on or to stand beside. Tempers flared. Shoving and pushing followed. Whites and blacks maneuvered to place that sign to the advantage of their race. The controversy all revolved around that stupid sign, as though the piece of wood had some power or authority.

Conductors, both white and black, clanged and clanged the bell and yelled for order and quiet and demanded everybody sit down in ANY available seat. I remembered a policeman boarding the streetcar with his "Billy stick" in hand. He forced one black man off the streetcar amidst loud protests from the other blacks. The streetcar started up again and everybody became very silent – an angry silence.

Now another streetcar glided past me on the Avenue. The conductor did not ring the bell at me. That was a nice change. I watched the streetcar vanish into the distance as I continued to jog.

Going Uptown. Going Downtown. A romantic piece of transportation became a stage for acting out our country's struggle to obtain civil rights for all people. Precious little forgiveness was given or requested on streetcars during those tumultuous days.

Years later the signs were removed, but the brass-trimmed holes in the top of many bench-backs remained for years as a scar, reminding me of my blatant prejudice and irrational behavior.

Shame filled me as I jogged, and I stumbled on the track. I scrambled to regain my balance. How could I have done those things? How could I have laughed? How could I have been so blind? How could I have been so cruel?

A great sadness filled me. Was it just the streetcar? Or was it Carol and David as well? Or was my sadness aggravated by the plight of a church member who murdered her husband? Or was it millions of people who live and die without ever knowing love and forgiveness?

I stopped running and panted deeply. I stared at the steel tracks with my hands on my knees. They were the same steel tracks that had carried me from childhood into adulthood.

I had no energy to run any further.

+++++

Because I was asleep, it took me a minute to realize the phone was ringing, not the alarm clock. Fumbling for the phone on the bedside table, I knocked my glasses to the floor. The clock glared rudely at me: two forty-six. I fumbled to pick up the phone.

The husky voice on the other end sounded hysterical, but it was clearly the rasp of Ralph Founier. Something must have happened to Ruby, I thought.

"Hold on, Ralph," I urged. "Take your time. What's happening?" He wasn't making a lot of sense. He was also trying to talk to someone else while he talked to me. I had never heard Ralph this upset. He was usually as calm and placid as his fishing pond in the country. But not tonight. He blurted out what he wanted to say, almost like a recording. I simply responded, "I'll be right there, Ralph. I'll be right there."

"What's the matter?" Carol asked as she rolled onto her elbow and opened her eyes too wide, trying hard to awake up. "Who was that?"

"Ralph Founier. There's been a fire at their house, and Mitch is dead. The fire started in Mitch's room. That's all Ralph said. I'll know more when I get there." Carol offered to go with me, but I told her no. I didn't know what I was going to be walking into or for how long. I threw on some jeans and a knit shirt and headed for the garage.

I sat for a moment in the still, dark car. The night seemed timeless as I found the correct key and turned it in the ignition switch. The clock on the dashboard came to life, renewing my sense of urgency.

The street was hauntingly empty, and I knew the way well. I turned onto Octavia Street, drove away from the River, and flicked the tear from my right eye.

I started thinking about Mitch. What a tragic end to a sad life. I slowed and rolled through a stop sign. Mitch was retarded. He had the mind of a five-year-old with the body of a sixty-five-year-old. We had celebrated his birthday two weeks ago. Ruby, Mitch's sister, must be in her early seventies. Her husband Ralph must be in his mid-seventies.

Ralph and Ruby had been married only a year when Mitch came to live with them in a trailer they attached to their kitchen. Mitch had lived with his mother in prior years, but she had died, and Ralph and Ruby took him in. That was over forty years ago. He had been an enormous burden to Ralph and Ruby ever since, yet they rarely complained. They seemed to take Mitch as part of the given of their married life … for better or for worse … and it was usually for worse when Mitch was involved.

I pulled my car between a fire truck and a black Mercedes. I had barely stepped out of the car when I found myself holding Ralph in my arms, crying like a baby. I felt strangely proud that he trusted me so completely.

"He's gone, Will, he's gone," Ralph repeated over and over. Suddenly Ralph straightened up and instantly stopped crying. "Come on into the house, Will. Ruby needs you."

We stepped over limp fire hoses and dodged tired firemen who were busy collecting their equipment. Only one truck still pumped water onto the smoldering trailer and kitchen at the back of the house. Powerful lights from the hook and ladder truck lit the scene. I stepped over one mud-puddle only to step into another one. I felt my sock go cold as my shoe filled with water; it now made a ridiculous squishing sound when I walked. The fire hoses had created all this mud. It hadn't rained in over a week.

A figure approaching from the right caught my attention. Susan White came flailing forward. Susan was last-year's runner-up in the Miss Louisiana pageant. I'll never know why she lost.

"Mitch is dead. Mitch is dead," she blurted with panting breath. "He didn't have a chance. He was burned alive in there," she hysterically proclaimed. Her flimsy nightgown pressed against her breasts revealing their slight, natural uplift as her arms gestured wildly toward the smoldering trailer. Her shapely body was clearly silhouetted by the fire truck's powerful lights as her sheer pink nightgown became transparent in their glare. She made sure she had my full attention, which she most certainly did, then she ran off in another direction, relaying the redundant news to a couple who were standing beside their car watching the house.

I shook my head in disbelief and turned again toward the house. Shamefully, I found myself hoping she would stand with those lights behind her again before the night was over.

Ralph waited, holding the screen door open for me. If Ralph had even noticed Susan he gave no indication of it. Stepping over another hose, I rubbed my hand over my hair and was pleased to think my middle-of-the-night cowlick was finally lying flat. I caught myself and realized I liked to be recognized for my looks too, just in a different way than Susan, that's all.

As I entered the living room, I saw Ruby sitting in a daze on the sofa. I sat down beside her even though I didn't really want to, because the acidic stench in the house was overwhelming, and the sofa seemed to reek with a power of its own. The front rooms of the house didn't seem to be burned, but they were filled with soot and ash, the floor was soaked with water, and the noisome smell burned my nose. All the furniture appeared to be covered with a greasy smoke film.

When I sat down, vivid memories from Nam filled my mind. A burned out village. The stench of burning flesh. The smell of huts turned into smoldering charcoal. A screaming man lying under a burning beam too big and too hot to move. He screamed until he died. I had given the order to the flamethrower.

I looked around the room nervously checking for danger. My eyes met Ruby's, and I shook off the haunting memories. Ruby was alive, unburned, and sitting beside me. I reached out and held her thin, wrinkled hand. She immediately started telling me what had happened, as though she had been waiting for someone to tell. She spoke in a measured monotone, almost without feeling, like a recording that had been turned on and had to play itself out. Ralph listened intently while he sat in a rocker across from us. He seemed greatly pleased and relieved that I had taken charge of Ruby for a while.

As I listened to her, I thought of my own encounters with Mitch and the many stories about him that had circulated around town through the years. I remembered coming home years ago to find Mitch rolling and laughing with David on the living room rug. David was in kindergarten at the time. Mitch held him with one arm and tickled him with the other hand, but in places that were inappropriate. David was laughing loudly, but I was plenty upset.

Mitch looked up at me like a caught child. Before I could say a word, he jumped up, ran out the front door, and peddled away on his bicycle. Had he molested David? No damage seemed to have been done and David seemed to be fine. The incident was confusing and very disturbing.

When Carol came in from the backyard where she had been gathering flowers, I told her what I had found. She immediately insisted I tell Mitch never to come inside our house again. Never. I certainly agreed. Later that day I found Mitch and told him. Although he was disappointed and hurt, he obeyed like the child he was.

Other families had resolved situations with Mitch differently. Ralph was forever getting a phone call to pull Mitch out of a roadside ditch where he lay beaten beside his bicycle. On at least two occasions, Mitch was admitted to the hospital. Once he had been beaten to within an inch of his life. I wondered why no one had ever called the police, or why no one ever killed him. I heard of a wife who came on to Mitch, inviting him into her house. The beating then came from a jealous husband, not a fearful parent. Ralph would always find Mitch, bring him home, bathe his wounds, fix his bike, and hold his breath until the next incident. He'd long ago given up on changing Mitch, and I always had the feeling Ralph shielded Ruby from the things her brother had done.

Now Mitch was dead, and Ruby's love for him led her to speak only of his simple innocence, and how their mother had given special care to her "special angel." While she was talking, two men emerged from the back room carrying a black body bag by both ends. It drooped in the middle. They brought Mitch's body right past Ruby and Ralph.

Ruby seemed totally undisturbed by the callously morbid routine. Ralph maintained his stoical countenance. They both simply watched passively as the men trudged through the room, bumped a table with Mitch's bagged body, and vanished out the front door into the darkness.

In the silence that followed, I wondered about Mitch. Mitch didn't have a malicious bone in his body, but he certainly was retarded. He couldn't read, but he could proudly play one hymn with one finger on the piano. He would often find a piano at church and play that hymn over and over and over until someone came and distracted him from it. Surely God has a special place for "special angels."

When Mitch joined the church, just a few years ago, Ruby tutored him for weeks on how to answer the questions. "Are you a sinner? Do you accept Jesus Christ as your savior? Do you promise to follow Jesus?"

When the Sunday arrived, Mitch and I stood before the congregation. I began with the first question: "Are you a sinner?" Mitch got the most horrified look on his face, took a step back, and belted out, "NO!!" When I regained my composure, and when the congregation stopped giggling uncomfortably, I tried breaking the question down into even more simple questions. "Do you sometimes do what you shouldn't do, Mitch?" He answered those questions to everyone's satisfaction.

Surely God has a place in his kingdom for the likes of Mitch, even if he wasn't sure he was a sinner. Even if he had no clue as to what he believed. God had to love and forgive Mitch, or no one could be loved and forgiven; not Alice, not the Viet Cong, not me.

+++++

The moon shone brightly as I left Ruby and Ralph. I walked back to my car, nodding to a handful of people who remained on the sidewalk. The firemen and the police had gone, and the coroner was closing the back door to his hearse. The black Mercedes was still parked next to my car, and I reminded myself not to ding it opening my door. As I started to get in, I was startled by a female voice calling my name thorough the open passenger window of the Mercedes. I hadn't noticed anyone in the car.

"When will the funeral be, Reverend McKenzie?" the soft voice asked.

It was Susan White again, leaning toward the passenger window from behind the wheel. Someone had loaned her a leather jacket that swallowed her shoulders and arms, but the moonlight revealed her slim, shapely thighs, which seemed unaffected by the night's chill and unembarrassed by their bare beauty as she leaned and squirmed to talk to me through the car window. She leaned toward the window some more in order to see me better ... or was it to be seen better?

"We haven't talked about the funeral yet, Susan. We'll get into all those arrangements tomorrow."

She stretched toward the window even more to hear better. Her gown slid higher up her thighs. The faint, pleasant smell of her gardenia perfume offered a wonderful contrast to the nauseous stench in the house. I wondered how long to pause here. I wanted to linger at her window, to savor the moment. I felt an excited tingling between my legs as I relished hers.

I realized how easily I could talk with her for a while about Mitch, about the fire, about Ruby, and about the house, squeezing as much pleasure from the moment as possible. I also knew she would enticingly oblige and would enjoy each moment as much as I. No one could possibly accuse me of improprieties as long as I just stood at her car window and talked. No one else could see what I enjoyed seeing.

But she would know why I had lingered, and a chip of my soul would belong to her, and my interest would provide fuel for the next unexpected, but surely heightened, encounter. Reluctantly I decided to bring our tête-à-tête to an end.

"I'm going to call it an evening for now, Susan. You drive home carefully."

As my car bumped out of the driveway onto the road, an old country song came into my mind, and I quietly hummed "Trashy Women" as I headed home.

+++++

"You stink." Carol curled her nose as I tiptoed into the bedroom. "Go back to the laundry room and strip off those clothes. I'll wash everything in the morning."

She was half-asleep, but still functioning on "efficient." As I grabbed my pajamas and crawled into bed, she curled her nose anew. "Pew, even your hair stinks." She got up, rolled into the bathroom, turned on the shower, and then crawled back into bed. "For you," she stated as she curled up and closed her eyes.

It was a cold shower....

+++++

I left for the office at nine thirty, still yawning and feeling a bit dragged out. My Palm Pilot reassured me I had made no appointments before lunch today, thank goodness. Then I realized Joe Miller was driving slowly beside me in the parking lot as I walked from my car to my office.

"Quarter to ten." He pointed at his watch. "Must be nice, Will." Joe sank his barb, rolled up his window, and drove off before I could say a word. I fumed into my office.

"Burns me up," I vented to Marie who was busy finishing Sunday's bulletin. "I was at the Founiers' until almost four this morning, and Joe Miller chews me out for coming in late. He drove off before I could say anything. Hit and run."

"He'll hear all about it later. Then he'll feel bad about his comment," she replied without looking up from her computer.

How nice to have a supportive secretary, I thought. I wished everyone were as understanding and accepting. Just like Momma used to be.

"I'm going to meet with Ralph and Ruby this morning after they return from the funeral home. They're talking about having the funeral on Monday, of all days. I wish they would wait until Tuesday, but they were pretty set on Monday."

I let out a deep sigh. "This will be the third week in a row something has prevented me from taking my day off. I can use a day off so bad I can taste it."

"Pretty hard on Mitch too, wasn't it?" Marie retorted without missing a stroke on her keyboard.

Ouch! Touché.

So much for momma's unconditional love.

+++++

I entered the prison to visit Alice again. I tried to visit once a week. I was now allowed to visit her in her cell, as was her lawyer, so I didn't have to be frustrated by the glass visiting booth. After they locked the door behind me in Alice's cell, the guards moved to the far end of the hall as a gesture of privacy. I still felt like they could hear every word we uttered. Alice whispered, and I did too.

Alice was now devastated by what she had done. The full import of her actions had hit her. This time she talked of suicide, then negated the idea because of the children. I was aware I had no belt, no necktie, and certainly not my customary penknife. I was also aware that prisoners who were determined to kill themselves would find a way in spite of the best precautions. I banked on Alice's love for her children to keep her from doing anything self-destructive. I think the guards were counting on that too.

She was now looking to Jesus. She expressed her regret and asked for forgiveness over and over again. I felt like I was sitting in a confessional booth at Ellis's church, a priest hearing the confession of a murderer. But Ellis heard confessions through a darkened grate. That grate protected the anonymity of the sinner. I think it also protected the priest, offering him an emotional buffer, just as I listened to Alice filtered through a defensive grate of my own making.

Her whispered confessions were mixed with anxieties about what might happen to her. Her plea for forgiveness flowed into a plea for the removal of consequences. Naturally enough, she wanted an acquittal. "Innocent by reason of temporary insanity" remained her plea. True, no one in her right mind would drive a butcher knife through her husband's heart, leaving two children without a father and putting their mother in jail.

I wondered again if we were temporarily insane to do what we did in Vietnam. The public sanctioned wartime killing when they felt the cause was just. However, the public turned against our being in Vietnam. The war there was soon seen as an unjustified conflict with unjustified killing. Was the killing I did all right as long as the country supported the war and not all right when the country turned against that war? Who decides the guilt, and who grants the forgiveness?

My mind pictured a Vietnamese sniper taking a shot at me from a rooftop, followed by his fall to the ground when I shot him through the neck. The image disappeared as quickly as it appeared. I dismissed the thought. Crazy stuff. Insane. Temporarily insane.

Alice's whisper trailed off. She was silent … and waiting. She was waiting for me to absolve her. For better or for worse, I was her priest, and this cell was her confessional.

"Alice, God forgives you," I told her with genuine confidence and therefore with convincing authority. She burst into sobs. I had given her assurance of what I believed to be true, and I hoped Alice could embrace that forgiveness as her own.

Giving that same gift to myself was more difficult. I wish I could put my guilt to rest once and for all. Put me in front of a jury and get on with it. But how would I plead? And would I believe the jury if they pronounced me not guilty? I didn't know.

+++++

I left the jail in time to meet Doug Neal at my office. We were having lunch together. I suspected our discussion was going to involve a heavy conversation about his marriage. After a while you developed a sixth sense about these things. When a man calls and asks to get together without saying why, you can lay good odds it's about a family problem. Women, on the other hand, usually come on out and say they want to talk about problems in their marriage. Mars; Venus? Who knows?

When I walked into the office, I was greeted by a pleasant surprise. Evelyn Morrow was talking to Marie about materials she needed for her Sunday school class. Evelyn was one beautiful person, as beautiful on the inside as she was on the outside. She and her husband Ed were exceptional people. It was always a joy to see them.

Evelyn was in her late-forties, slim and shapely, and blessed with an exceptionally beautiful face. Her hazel eyes always seemed to sparkle. Her lightly frosted hair bounced gracefully as she talked. She was also Phi Beta Kappa at Stanford. Ed owned his own printing company and did exceptionally well with it. Their children, both boys, were smart and well rounded. But mamma won first prize. Some people seem to be the repository of so many blessings and so much grace that it almost seems unfair to the rest of us mortals. Evelyn was one of Carol's favorite people. The four of us had enjoyed dinner together on several occasions. As I enjoyed talking with her, I thought how much better this was than talking with Susan White through a car window in the middle of the night.

Doug Neal came into the office. He was obviously struck by Evelyn's beauty since he stumbled slightly of a floor-board as he introduced himself to her. We soon said our goodbyes and headed to the parking lot.

Once outside, I saw Margaret sitting in the passenger seat of my car. Margaret was mentally ill and had become a real nuisance, always following me. This time, however, she missed her target because we headed directly to Doug's car instead of mine. I tried not to look in Margaret's direction and Doug didn't notice her. What was I going to do with Margaret, I wondered.

"Boy, that woman in your office was stunning," Doug ventured as soon as we got in his car. "I've never seen her before."

I couldn't resist the opening and laughed, "If you came to church more often you would have. She's usually there." I rubbed the gathering tear from my right eye. We both smiled broadly.

"How's Chinese?" Doug asked. "The Five Happiness on Bienville Street is always good."

I clutched. I just couldn't do it. I had tried again with Carol and David about a year ago and made it to the front door of the "Golden Chopsticks." I couldn't go in. I remembered David's remark about 'Mr. Brave Marine' as we turned away and went somewhere else.

I felt nervous sweat on my upper lip and ran my hand over it. "I can't tolerate anything with MSG in it, Doug. I know they say some of the dishes are free of that stuff, but there's still enough in it to give me big-time cramps."

"That's fine. How about oysters? Are they okay? Acme Oyster Bar?"

"You bet. Now you're talking about one of my favorites. I love their oyster po-boys."

I wondered why I couldn't simply tell Doug that oriental restaurants stir up bad memories about Vietnam. Will that war ever cease being destructive in my life? Will I ever stop having to deal with it? I paused, mustered my courage, and decided to admit what was going on.

"Actually, Doug, the MSG was a smoke screen," I began. But he wasn't listening, so I didn't go on. After all, we were here to talk about his troubles, not mine.

So it goes.

Sure enough, my instincts had been right and Doug started telling me about his marriage. However, not only was Acme known for its oysters, it was also known for its noise. We had to shout to hear each other, and that struck me as funny. Here sat Doug, shouting loudly that his marriage was on the rocks, while we opened our mouths wide to eat the succulent bi-valves. He painted vignettes with a very broad brush. Both he and his wife sounded miserable, to hear him tell it. His story boiled down to a simple conclusion: "I'm leaving." He talked about how hard it was to do that.

Done. Finished. End of discussion, and still half a Dixie beer left. Doug had chosen to take me out to lunch to ask for my permission to leave his wife after 26 years of marriage. I wondered if seeking permission and seeking forgiveness were related.

When he had wrapped up his story, I simply commented, "I really am sorry to hear all this, Doug. Keep me in touch with what you do, will you? My guess is that until you can grant yourself permission to leave, you won't." That's about as close as he was going to get to receiving permission from me over po-boys in a crowded, noisy oyster bar on Iberville Street in the city that care forgot.

When I got back to church, my mind massaged our conversation. How do you grant yourself permission on some things? As that thought started to swirl around in my head, the phone rang. Once again I started tending to someone else's needs. Maybe that was easier.

+++++

A day off finally arrived. No alarm clock today. I awakened to a leisurely morning with a second cup of coffee, the morning paper, and my favorite online sites. I had a tennis game at ten with Bob, a minister colleague. That was my only plan for the day, no other engagements. We played on the Tulane courts. My alumnus status brought very few local privileges, but the use of the tennis courts was a good one. Parking, however, remained a problem.

Promptly at ten Bob drove up, honked, and we went searching for that evasive parking spot somewhere near the courts. We slowed down for the flashing lights ahead and crawled past a rescue squad van that almost completely blocked traffic on the Avenue. I noticed two wrecked cars, one with a crumpled rear, and the other with a crumpled front-end. A medic squatted beside a young man sitting on the curb. He didn't seem to be hurt badly. When we were parallel to them, I saw his arm, spattered with blood, dangling limp in his lap. Feelings of guilt flooded over me. I couldn't figure out what triggered those feelings. Probably Nam again, but what and where? It didn't connect.

Bob commented about how good the emergency medical service was, and we continued on to the tennis courts.

+++++

I played well. My backhand remained strong for a change, and I managed to get my serve in most of the time. Bob still beat me, but not by much. I always comforted myself by remembering he played on our college team and went on to play in the Davis Cup, a career which quickly ended when he tore a ligament in his ankle. The fact he was willing to play with me made me feel like I must be half-decent. But then, neither one of us was a college kid anymore.

As we gathered up our equipment, George Nelson walked onto the court. "Hello, Will," he greeted me, "I was walking to my class, but you're just the man I need to see."

Ignoring Bob, George started laying out his agenda. George was chairman of the Men's Fellowship. He had an idea for the group, the name of a man to implement it, and a timetable to make it work.

My resentment smoldered. I was on a tennis court with a friend on my day off, and, by damn, I didn't want people coming at me with church work while I tried to enjoy some freedom from parish work. Was there no time when I was "off duty"? On the other hand, what was I supposed to do, curse George out for his enthusiasm and dedication? Instead I politely pushed him off.

"Good idea, George. Let me mull it over. Give me a call at the office in the morning and we'll talk some more. I have to go now. Carol's expecting me back at the house in about fifteen minutes. Good to see you. Say hello to Sally."

Bob and I walked back to his car in silence. Then Bob asked, "No time for that beer at my place?" I was embarrassed to be caught in a lie. I apologized for my clumsy way of getting rid of George. Bob smiled and simply asked, "Ok. Coke or beer? I've got both." We headed to his house.

+++++

Friday morning, Carol woke me up. "Look, snow! Real snow!"

It was barely light outside, but as I looked out the bedroom window I could see it coming down ... thick and heavy and wet ... and it was definitely snow.

"How 'bout this," I exclaimed. "I wonder how long the snow will last. Wasn't it about the second year we moved here that it snowed before?"

"I think that's about right," Carol replied. "Wow, that's nine years ago. They predicted freezing rain on the news last night, but certainly not snow.

"Look at it come down. I don't think I ever saw snow this wet in Dallas."

"I bet everything will be shut down as a result," Carol said. "I'm supposed to rock the babies at the hospital this afternoon, but that probably won't happen today. Let's build a fire and see what they're saying on television." Carol headed for the family room. The local station was filled with announcement of closings. Government offices were closed; most of the schools were closed; the bridges across the Mississippi River were closed -- a major happening. As the list lengthened, the station converted to ticker-tape announcements across the bottom of the screen while the anchorwoman called upon various reporters scattered throughout the city to highlight the event.

I glanced at our back yard. The snow stuck here and there, and it seemed to be a bit drier than when it first started. The television reporter warned everybody to stay indoors and not get out on the streets. The wet snow will turn to ice shortly, he predicted.

New Orleans, the Big Easy, was being immobilized by less than an inch of snow. The city didn't own a single snowplow, nor did the city have supplies of ash or salt. Almost no one owned a pair of chains, and snow tires were not an item you could find in the auto stores. An inch of snow was bringing the entire city to a halt, yet another inch was predicted to follow. At least this wonderful phenomenon was happening early in the morning before the beginning of a business day, so there wouldn't be traffic jams caused by people trying to get home.

The phone rang. It was Peter, our Clerk of the Session, who felt a responsibility for the church. He suggested we call the television stations, asking them to add our church to the list of public building closings. I asked him if he would do that for me, and he quickly agreed. I thought that was probably why he had called in the first place. Permissions, permissions, permissions. Everybody wants permissions. Well, if you couldn't get permission, then how about forgiveness?

The snow still fell, and our outdoor thermometer registered thirty-two degrees on the nose. Carol looked in the refrigerator. "How 'bout an omelet?" she suggested. She looked at me and continued, "You've got the day off, Will! Enjoy."

When she actually put that fact into words, I felt both guilty, and stupid for feeling guilty. It wasn't my day off. I'm not supposed to have a free day today. In spite of all the media warnings, I had actually thought about going to the office. I had trouble giving myself permission simply to do nothing but watch the flakes fall. I had privately resolved to work on my sermon and was privately embarrassed that the thought of working made me feel better. That's sick, came my second thought.

I pushed aside the thought of doing work, and then finally replied to Carol, "Yeah, an omelet sounds great. I'll set the table. Should we wake David?"

The lights blinked, turned brown, and then faded entirely. We heard the unique sound of a transformer blowing out. Now we were without electricity. Not even the computer would work. Carol tried the telephone, but it was dead. In spite of it all, I still pushed off feelings of guilt, and looked for ways to … to … well … work. Carol kept cooking the omelets; thank goodness for a gas stove.

I couldn't seem to relax. I looked for the portable radio we kept for such emergencies. I found it in the hall closet, but the batteries were dead. Carol put her spatula down and looked at me as I wandered around the kitchen.

"Will," she emphasized, "There's nothing you can do about the snow. There's nothing you can do about the electricity. For goodness sake grab that mystery you didn't finish at the beach last summer and do yourself a favor, will you?"

I was embarrassed that I couldn't seem to let go. I thought back to yesterday's incident on the tennis court, realizing that George personified my own over-active, guilt-generated work ethic. Keep pushing. Keep improving. I had turned my profession into a twenty-four/seven endeavor. Come to think of it, I had done the same thing in the Marines, but I did make Lieutenant quickly as a result.

I nodded to Carol and smiled, knowing she was right. I found my book and sat by the window near the light. After a few pages I announced, "I'm going to shave. At least we have a gas water heater."

"Hey, Dad, look at the snow!" David exclaimed as he staggered sleepily into the family room. "No school today I bet!"

"Nope," Carol nodded as she smiled … at me.

"Good deal! I'm going to call Janie." David grabbed the phone and discovered it was dead. "Well I'm going to go outside and taste it as it falls. I wonder if we can build a snowman. Maybe a midget, huh?"

He tightened his robe around himself, opened the back door, and ran leaping barefooted into the whitened back yard.

Unshaven, I followed him out, packed a handful of wet snow into a soggy ball, and threw it at him. Before long we were both joyfully scraping the grass for ammunition.

+++++

The next day was sunny and much warmer. The snow had entirely gone, and Carol and I were glad because we had been invited to a very prestigious Mardi Gras ball. This was one of the oldest Mardi Gras Krewes. Carol received a "call out" card, and I received a "committeeman" card. This meant we wouldn't sit in the balcony to observe the ball passively as most guests did. Rather, Carol would be invited to dance, and I would join the mystery Krewe member who was in the Krewe's Den.

No one was supposed to know who invited them to a ball. That preserved a veil of mystery, at least in theory. The truth was everybody always knew. In our case, we were the guests of Grits and Gail. When he called a month ago to ask if we'd be free this evening, that not only gave away who would invite us, it was also Grits' way of not wasting his limited number of invitations.

I pulled out my white tie and tails from the back of the closet, examining all the pieces to make sure nothing was missing. Carol decked herself out in a floor-length evening dress I'm not sure we could afford, but which we had purchased anyway. Her dress was pastel pink and blue with white lace running down the side. She put her hair up into a fashionable bun. She looked ten years younger and absolutely sexy. David even whistled as he passed by our bedroom door. Now that really was something.

I gathered our invitations, carefully putting them in my coat pocket. We had heard stories of guests being turned away at the door because they couldn't produce their invitations. If you asked for the Krewe member to come verify that you were invited, the gentlemen at the door would deny that such a person was in the Krewe. Membership remained secret, and there would be no crashing the ball, even if you were wearing tails or an evening gown.

Dressed in our finery, we attracted some stares at red lights as we drove to the Municipal Auditorium. The Auditorium was located in a terrible neighborhood with a very high crime rate. There was extremely limited parking in its lot, and the neighboring streets were poorly lit. Everyone ignored these realities when they went to a ball. The ball became the supreme focus and overcame all obstacles. It all sounded a bit like the king's new clothes to me.

We found a parking place on the street about two blocks away. I had barely helped Carol out of the car when three teenage boys stepped in front of us. They appeared from nowhere out of the dark tenements that lined the block. No one else was in sight, just them and us, and the Auditorium seemed to be a mile away. My heart raced and my muscles tensed, ready for one-on-one combat, which I knew I could do well, tails or no tails. I stepped between Carol and the boys, preparing to respond. I really didn't like this. A confrontation would not be a price worth paying to go to a ball, even this one. Simply not worth it, high, elite society or not.

The boys were smiling at us. The biggest one, about David's size, stepped toward me boldly and asked, "Watch ya car, missa? One dolla." Like two echoes, the other boys repeated the phrase, "Watch ya car?" "Watch ya car? One dolla."

I paused as their message sank in. "One dollar total? And my car will be safe?" I asked, as I moved my hand slowly to my pocket while keeping a hawk's eye on them.

"Yessa," the biggest boy affirmed, "It'll be safe. One dolla to watch ya car."

Aware they might try to grab my wallet, I managed to remove it from my coat, secure a dollar bill, and return it to my pocket -- all in one smooth movement. The boys only stood, watched, waited, and smiled. I held out the bill to the bigger boy who nodded his head in a bit of a bow, saying, "Thankya, sir. We'll watch ya car good." They instantly vanished into an alley beside the nearby duplex.

"I'll be damned. Protection money. I hope the car will be in one piece when we return." I grabbed Carol's arm and hastened her down the block into the lights of the Municipal Auditorium. Neither of us referred to the incident again. Tonight the ball was the thing.

Once inside the Auditorium, I escorted Carol to the elevator that would take her to the "Queen's Room." There she would join Gail and other women for champagne before the ball began. Later, when the magic hour of nine drew near, the elite ladies of New Orleans society would descend the marble staircase to the floor of the Auditorium and find seats in the section to which they had been assigned.

"See you later, honey. Have fun." I watched the elevator door close. We would later laugh at how the socially elite ladies gathered in a stark room bare of any décor. The "Queen's Room" had concrete floors, and two, long, Formica-topped tables filled with plastic glasses of champagne and swirls of little paper napkins. Not a servant around. Not a picture on the wall. Not a flower on a table. No tablecloth. No carpet on the floor. Not a window in the room, which was harshly lit by bare-bulb fixtures, suspended from the ceiling at random intervals. Such comprised the majestic "Queen's Room."

But everyone completely ignored such trivia. The crème de la crème, in their finest attire, spoke in animated conversations about the last ball they had attended or what debutante presentation they had helped to organize. Such pleasantries were carried on amid deafening echoes created by the bare walls and accented by heels clicking against the off-white concrete floor.

Last year's queen held a bouquet of roses in addition to her plastic glass of champagne. The roses were real. This year's queen had been carefully hidden away in an undisclosed location. For an hour the ladies drank, smiled, and wore their polish thin. They were all proud to be there, every single one of them.

Meanwhile, I joined Grits in the Krewe Den among some two hundred other Krewe members and their committeemen. I recognized the president of my bank, the leading surgeon at Memorial Hospital, the owner of most of downtown New Orleans, the owner of the most famous restaurant in town, the city's most prominent judge who was already slurring his words, and several other members of my congregation. They smiled and nodded when they saw me, extending to me the casual assumption: "of course you're supposed to be here, or you wouldn't be." They extended the same attitude to each other and expected it for themselves. Everyone talked as though the rest of the world didn't exist.

I overheard one Krewe member tell another, "We've got this smart ass VP in Los Angeles that couldn't get it through his thick head that tonight is our Ball and the report he wanted would not be ready by noon tomorrow. He just doesn't have a clue." They both laughed.

We too gathered on concrete floors under harsh, bare-bulb lighting in a room without windows. A bathroom with open double doors at one end of the huge hall exposed rows of urinals-in-waiting. The deafening noise was tempered only by rows and rows of costumes hanging on racks made of steel piping. Long tables filled with ice, set-ups, and plastic cups paralleled the rows of costumes. The tables were lined with wooden folding chairs. Every Krewe member put his own bottle on the table, freely offering friends a drink as they wandered by.

The costumes were colorful satin, each tagged with a number. Grits was number 124. His costume consisted of a pair of bright pink, baggy pants with a tie-sash adjusting the waist, and a blue polka-dotted top that slipped over his head and tied behind his neck. They resembled extremely colorful hospital scrubs. A separate plastic bag contained a pair of cotton gloves, a satin hat complete with chinstraps, and a satin bag to hold the favors he would give his call-outs after he danced with each of them.

All Krewe members, while outfitted in deliberately different colors, would wear the standard, uniform carnival mask – a skin-toned face of plastic with holes cut for the eyes, mouth, and nose.

"Porters" helped all the Krewe members with their costumes. These elderly black men shuffled between members and talked repeatedly about how many years they had been doing this. "Why, I helped your father put on that same costume. Wonderful man, he was." Their main, if not only, function was to use scissors to enlarge the eyeholes and mouth-holes of the mask so you could see and breathe more freely. Even so, the mask would become terribly hot and quickly became your own private facial sauna. But once masked, everyone was uniformly disguised, and the masks were very effective. No Krewe member was allowed on the ballroom floor without one.

As the Krewe members waited for the time of the ball to arrive, most of them had very little on at all. Most had taken off their tails, carefully hanging them next to their costumes so they could wear them to breakfast after the ball, but most members were reluctant to deck out in those uncomfortable costumes any earlier than they had to. So the distinguished gentlemen of this elegant city stood around in their underwear, getting progressively drunker as the hour of the ball approached. I began to believe there was a direct correlation between how many years a person had been a member of the Krewe and how drunk he became by the time the ball actually started. A few old timers never made it up from their chair around their table. Some stayed seated in front of their costumes, dressed only in their white shorts and undershirts, slumped, drunk, and asleep. No one cared. They were just left alone. It struck me as a strange way to show acceptance.

Grits seemed to take the evening in stride, and he drank modestly in a measured manner. He offered me some of his bourbon, which I accepted. No eyebrows were raised; nobody cared. Over to one side of the room, hot turtle soup could be dipped from an igloo into Styrofoam cups. Ham and cheese and roast beef po-boys were spread out on a table next to the soup. Most of the Krewe members didn't bother with the food. I took some of the turtle soup, which was superb, even if it was in a Styrofoam cup … dipped from an igloo.

With ten minutes to go, the Captain stepped up to a microphone and blew a deafening whistle. "Time to get dressed and line up!" the Captain ordered … three times. Before long almost all the Krewe members had donned their costumes and masks.

Two lines formed at the door leading to the ballroom floor. Every Krewe member had a noisemaker, and the racket was unbelievable. Another whistle blew, this time from on stage. The pair of lines, masked and colorful and noisy and drunk, began moving forward onto the stage floor of the auditorium.

The ball had begun.

CAROL McKENZIE

I sat next to Gail in call-out section J. We were on the first row. You couldn't ask for a better seat. The air was filled with excitement, and at the strike of nine the Captain of the Krewe marched on stage in front of drawn curtains and blew his whistle. Dressed in white, he had a short cape of white ermine flying behind his brisk, military walk.

The band in the balcony, featuring an overload of saxophones, started to play a lively tune. From the left corner of the stage, brightly costumed Krewe members ambled onto the stage. They shuffled with abandon around the floor, rattling noisemakers as they circled. The festive scene continued to be alive, exciting, and colorful. I loved it! Two men, dressed in fancy knee boots and capes directed traffic. One or two members of the Krewe stumbled, but no one fell, thank goodness. I wanted to think their unsure footing was because of their masks, but I knew better. Alcohol was flowing like water tonight. I sure hoped Will would behave himself. I looked around the Krewe members for Grits, but because of the masks, everyone looked alike. Even Gail couldn't find him among the mass of revelers.

After a few minutes of festive confusion, the members of the Krewe sat down on the floor in front of us facing the stage. They remained noisy. One Krewe member turned around and flirted with Gail. I got amused, but hoped he didn't turn my way. Gail laughed and tried to ignore him. Then he did try to flirt with me, and I started giggling. He finally turned back around facing the stage again. I figured that an anonymous mask and too many drinks created all kinds of license – kind of fun actually, and I felt myself blush at the thought.

Without announcement the band shifted the mood by playing a smooth, romantic melody. The huge curtain rose, and we found ourselves sitting in front of a gilded royal room featuring a large gold throne in the center. Two massive, gold chandeliers hung from the ceiling. The staged scene was dramatic, beautiful, and regally convincing. Its grandeur was quite a contrast to the earlier scene backstage. I felt very special to be a part of this pageantry.

A trumpet sounded a fanfare, and the King entered. He pulled an elaborate ermine train behind him, while two pages scrambled to keep his train open and straight. The King graciously waved his diamond-studded scepter to everyone as he processed around the room. Then he walked majestically to his throne and stood there masked and regal. I waited excitedly for what was next. Gail looked at me and smiled. How many times had she seen this splendid presentation, I wondered.

One by one, gentlemen in white ties and tails presented the ladies-in-waiting. Six of them formed an aisle through which seven maids walked to the throne, also escorted by men in full evening dress. One by one the maids were presented and positioned to stand to the left and to the right of the King. I loved every minute of this gala pageantry.

Then the music changed yet again. The Queen appeared, escorted by the Captain of the Krewe, and we all stood. The Queen processed around the room with a long train flowing behind her and holding a diamond-studded scepter with which she greeted everyone. The ladies around me were atwitter, passing comments back and forth. Everyone knew the queen, of course, or if they didn't, they pretended to.

"I just knew Claire would be the queen," a lady behind me bragged to her friend. "Her sister was Queen four years ago, you remember. Claire is even more beautiful."

"Always has been," the other lady added. "Did you know she has been accepted into Tulane Med next fall? Following in her daddy's footsteps."

I heard another woman ask, "Did her younger brother ever straighten out that trouble he was in?" I listened for the answer, but the two women whispered in each other's ears.

Queen Claire met her King on the gilded throne, and then everyone on stage joined in the Grand March around the room, eventually ending up where they started. The King and Queen finally sat down, and so did we. The scene was spectacular, and I could hardly believe how grand the occasion was. Then the dancing began.

Committeemen called out names up and down the aisles. "Gail Gravois" came the call, and that committeeman soon found Gail and escorted her to the dance floor to join her "mysterious" partner. Once they were together, I could easily recognize Grits even with his mask. I would never be able to identify Grits without Gail beside him, however. They danced, and then he gave her a "favor"– a nice, silver, miniature picture-frame. Another committeeman returned her to her seat. That committeeman was Will, who turned around and called my name, smiling at me.

"This is unreal," I whispered in Will's ear as I took his arm and walked toward Grits on the dance floor.

Just before I met Grits, Will kissed me on the cheek and whispered, "You're the most beautiful lady present." I blushed as Grits and I started dancing.

+++++

The Queen's Breakfast at the City Club followed the ball. Grits had changed back into his white tie and tails, and we all met at table number twenty-nine. Two other couples from church were at our table as well. We had barely been seated when a waiter asked us what we wanted to drink. I looked at my watch … eleven forty-five. Everyone chose the hard stuff except me. Even Will ordered a bourbon. No one seemed to care about my choice, or his. I wondered how many he'd had tonight, but he seemed completely sober. Marine training? The prattle of social conversation continued, mostly centering on the maids and the Queen. My adrenaline was still pumping and I was not the least bit sleepy, which surprised me. I was having a ball.

A jazz band played in the adjoining room, and I thought the music was too loud in our room. I could see a dozen or so couples dancing in front of the band. How did they stand the volume? The royal court had its own table where the Queen and her Maids and all their escorts were seated facing the dance floor. Most of them looked bleary-eyed, but smiled anyway. One maid had to be helped to the powder room. I felt embarrassed for her, but nobody paid much attention.

A trumpet fanfare sounded, and the court began a procession through the rooms of the club. We all clapped as they passed our table. I realized that the King was not a part of the processional. He had removed his mask, changed back into his tails, and was once again an anonymous member of the Krewe in our midst. All I knew for sure was that the King wasn't Grits, because I danced with him.

Without announcement, people started getting up and heading toward a buffet table. Everyone at our table grabbed their drinks and went to the end of the line. We continued to visit as we stood and waited for "breakfast." It was two in the morning.

The grillades and grits were a welcome dish when we finally reached the serving table. I passed on the coffee, but most people at our table drank one or more cups of the strong, black syrup. Coffee replaced mixed drinks for the balance of the evening. That comforted me, because I knew this club-full of people had to drive home sometime this morning. Will remained sober, so I felt okay about him.

He wiped a tear from the corner of his eye as we got up to leave; it was two-forty in the morning.

WILL McKENZIE

"Well, do you believe this evening or what?" I asked Carol as we drove home. "The regal splendor of the evening was surreal. I marveled to think there would be several more balls later this week and in the weeks to come, and many of the same people would be participating in them. Everyone seemed to take the ongoing Carnival festivities quite seriously, while having fun at the same time." I shifted lanes to make a left turn.

"The whole thing makes you wonder what's real and what's not," Carol mused. She reminded me about the Stoddards who left New Orleans because they didn't want their children to grow up thinking this was the way life really was. I'd forgotten about their startling move to Memphis. However, for hundreds of Krewe members and their families, Carnival *was* their life. I've been in their homes at other times of the year, and Carnival would still be present in pictures on tables, in talk about next year, and in references to last year. I've seen prominent families forego vacations and wear a threadbare suit in order to buy their daughter a dress or to purchase throws for the Krewe's parade.

My mother once told me with great pride how several friends of a prominent family paid the expenses for the daughter's presentation at the ball because her family couldn't afford it. She had to be presented, of course. It also went without saying that my mother was one of those friends. "Quality people," my mother called them. "Quality people." I cringed remembering her words.

My queen and I cuddled together while sleep rapidly overcame us. Our grandfather clock in the hall chimed the Trinity.

CAROL McKENZIE

A phone call from the police department came as I put poached eggs on the breakfast room table. My heart raced as the officer asked me if I were the parent of David McKenzie. David had left for school an hour ago. I pictured David in an accident or in the hospital.

My panic quickly turned to shock when I heard the policeman say David was being held at central lock-up; he had been caught buying a joint on the way to school. The policeman asked if I could come get him and talk with them. I took down instructions and hung up, starting to cry.

Will looked intensely at me as I shared the story with him. He went pale and silent too. He got up from the breakfast room table, grabbing his jacket. He nodded his head toward the door, and I grabbed a jacket too. We got in the car and were on our way … to the jail.

"I just know it's because I'm a minister," Will mumbled with watery eyes. "It's hard to be a minister's son, and I worry a lot about him. Then out of the blue my worries come true. I feel terrible." He paused and shook his head. I cried quietly and had no immediate reply. I felt like it was all my fault. Will then asked me, "I didn't see any warning signs, did you?"

"Warning signs? Not really," I paused in thought. "David's test scores had dropped off a little in two classes, but I didn't make too much of it. He doesn't like that teacher, so I chalked it off to that. That could have been a warning sign I didn't recognize. Where was my nurses' training when I needed it? You never know what goes on in a kid's mind nowadays." I fished in my pocketbook for a Kleenex. "I just hope this doesn't go on his record. It could keep him from getting into a good college later on. I wonder who else was involved." I knew there had to be much more the officer didn't tell me over the phone.

I sobbed, not wanting to, but I sobbed nevertheless. Will drove on as we both sank into silence.

We took an elevator to the sixth floor, found the "C" wing, and walked down a marble hallway to room 101. Will knocked. The sign on the door read "Narcotics." Will knocked again, waited, and then tried the door. The room had three empty desks. Almost immediately a man dressed in casual clothing came in behind us, asking if we were Mr. and Mrs. McKenzie. Sergeant Breaux introduced himself and motioned us to have a seat beside a large metal desk. I immediately asked where David was.

The Sergeant said he was downstairs in a holding room, but not in the jail pen with other detainees. "We really don't like to target students. We would much rather finger those who are higher up the line, but your son was just in the wrong place at the wrong time. We thought we had the leader, but we got your son and a middleman instead. By then, the officer had no choice except to bring him in." He went over the details of the encounter.

When he finished, Will asked, "What do we need to do, Sergeant? What are his options?"

He outlined the normal procedures for ten agonizing minutes. We sat tense and nervous, trying to absorb a new world of legal and criminal matters. David now had a misdemeanor charge against him, and a court appearance scheduled in about two months.

After everything had been explained to us, David was released to our custody. When he came into the room he was pale and had been crying. He repeated over and over, "I'm sorry Mom. I'm sorry Dad." Will put his arm around David's shoulder, and we walked down the hall toward the elevator. David was clearly shaken. Will was shaken too, and worried. I was too. I thought of the numerous times Will had ministered to people in trouble with the law. Never once did I ever think this might happen to David.

I felt like a total failure as a mother. I sat limply in the back seat as Will drove us home. Part of me felt angry that Will wasn't lecturing David, yet a better part of me realized that was the last thing David needed right now. I mainly wanted to find a hole and crawl into it.

My stomach felt completely gutted. What will people in the church think about David? About Will? About me? What will David's teachers think? I wanted to hide, to run, to vanish ... to die.

+++++

Once home we talked at length. By now, Will was dealing with this situation much better than I was. Several times in the conversation he used the phrase "what you have done to yourself." I felt like "what he had done to us." I knew Will was right, that David had gotten into trouble, not us, but his arrest felt like a family indictment to me, a parental indictment, a certificate of failure as a mother.

David kept saying he was sorry. I knew he was, but I got tired of hearing him say that. Will assured David that we forgave him and that God forgave him.

David overflowed with regret. He claimed he just wanted to try marijuana once, insisting that this was his first time. He promised never to go near drugs of any sort ever again. He all but promised to be a saint for the rest of his life. Perhaps David realized for the first time in his life that he was capable of doing something seriously wrong and illegal.

After a while the three of us agreed David should go on to school rather than miss a whole day. I wrote him a note saying he was "unavoidably detained." I didn't feel completely right about the note, but I wrote it anyway.

As we neared the school, Will slowed the car and turned to David, "Remember that guy who was baptized in 'O Brother Where Art Thou?' Ulysses told him his sins were forgiven as far as God was concerned, but that he still had to contend with the State of Mississippi. Well, it's the State of Louisiana you have to worry about now."

David got out of the car and headed toward the school building, shuffling his feet as he went.

WILL McKENZIE

I decided to call the Assistant D.A., Ralph LaFouché, who served on our Board of Deacons. We were on friendly terms, and I felt relieved when he agreed to see me. If I had been the one arrested, I'd bite the bullet, appear in court, and take the consequences like a good Marine. But this was my son. That's different.

Later in the day I sat nervously in Ralph's office. He listened without comment from behind his paper-cluttered desk. He kept a poker face with no discernable expression; I bet he was practiced at that. I was thankful he had his own office with a door that shut.

I offered no excuses for David's actions, but I did promise we would seek counseling for him and for the whole family. I volunteered David for however many hours of community service Ralph thought appropriate. I volunteered the church facilities for a series of drug-awareness programs. If I could have promised him a place in heaven, I would have done that too.

I finally took a deep breath and asked if David's arrest could be expunged from the record. Instantly I felt dirty and cheap. I felt like I had just lumped myself in with all those who made deals under the table and manipulated the system to their advantage. I had criticized such tactics on numerous occasions. My stomach knotted.

Ralph still didn't change his expression but asked to be excused for a few minutes. I slumped in my chair. My heart seemed to be beating hard, and I could feel the blood pulsing in my ears. I sat and waited. I needed to go to the bathroom, but I sat and waited.

Ralph returned with a smile on his face. "David is a very lucky young man, Rev. McKenzie. We reviewed his case and found that the detective failed to read David his rights properly. That, plus the fact he has no prior record of offenses all worked to his advantage. The charges will be dropped and his arrest will be expunged from our records. The DA will have to sign off on it, but he always backs up my recommendations. You can breathe easier now."

I sighed an audible sigh of relief and thanked Ralph profusely, probably too profusely. He continued, "Now all the things you mentioned earlier would still be good ideas, of course. Why don't I introduce you to Sergeant Evans on your way out? She's in charge of community programs, and I know she would welcome an opportunity to come to our church." We both stood, and he put his hand on my shoulder, being both supportive and also moving me toward the door. "Being a parent is tough. There're so many ways a kid can get in trouble today. A lot more than when you and I were kids. Believe me, a lot more."

He stopped at a desk we passed and asked the officer, "Joseph, would you escort Reverend McKenzie down to Sergeant Evans' office? He wants to get some drug education going in his church." Then he turned back to me. "Tell David to stay clean. Give Carol my best. See you all in church."

+++++

Carol and I went walking on the levee to talk without interruption. I stumbled on a partly buried rock, shuffled to regain my balance and make up the missed stride. "What if I'd been a nobody? What if I hadn't known Ralph? I still feel shady and dirty; but I'm also thankful and relieved Ralph decided to help David. I want David to call and thank him as soon as he gets home from school." I absently looked at the ships anchored on the river, awaiting port.

The Mississippi River's strong, muddy current swirled and eddied, and a huge plank of wood bobbed up and down as the water carried it swiftly downstream. The anchored ocean vessels seemed like sleeping giants from far-away lands. They seemed so distant from our concerns. Who on those ships cared about David or what happened in our lives? The world seemed terribly impersonal at one level and yet intimately personal at the same time. I asked myself where faith fit in all this. Is forgiveness mostly a matter of having connections with powerful people ... like the Assistant DA? ... or like God?

Carol seemed greatly relieved, and her attention now turned to David. I knew my focus should be there too, but I churned over the happy ending brought about by an injustice within the justice system. I thought about the fact I had to preach in two days. The sermon I had almost finished writing seemed shallow now, and feelings of inadequacy flooded over me.

"How about Lillian Donaldson for David?" Carol suggested. "She's good with adolescents, and she could help us as well. We've got to get that going right away while David's still receptive to it."

"Lillian would be fine." I agreed. "Would you call her since you know her well?"

"Sure. As soon as we get home," Carol replied.

I had been absent from the church all day, and I felt a need to get back to the office, even though Marie had cleared my schedule, without asking why again, bless her. However, I knew I was in no shape to be in the office yet, particularly if a pastoral crisis arose.

So Carol and I left the levee and walked along the fence at Jackson Square where the artists paint and sell their creations. We passed several painters, pausing to admire a carnival scene as the artist put finishing touches on it. We approached a Dixieland band, pausing briefly to hear their music, but our hearts weren't into the music. A man juggling bowling pins took a bow. A tarot card reader wearing a flamboyant, wide-brimmed hat concentrated on impressing her customer.

We approached a performer dressed in the kind of black clothes I associated with homeless people. He danced and smiled and gestured with flowing hands and arms. But we couldn't hear any music. He danced to the music of an iPod playing in his ears. I paused and watched him. How strange to dance to music no one else can hear. You find all kinds of people here in the Quarter.

But there was something about him that haunted me.

+++++

The "morning after" left me feeling paranoid, and I still reeled from David's arrest as I entered my office. I wondered who knew, who saw the arrest take place, who suspected David was in trouble because he arrived so late at school. I wondered what ramifications I would have to face as a minister ... and when.

Calling the therapist to make an appointment for David loomed large in my mind. Carol had tried yesterday, but the doctor had already left for the day. Now Carol had left it up to me, while she went to talk to David's teacher. I wanted a counselor who would be effective with David, would hit it off with him, would be, well ... perfect. I counted on Lillian being just that. While I mulled about these things, a knock came at my door.

"Hello, Will. May I come in."? I was surprised to see Peter standing in my office door unannounced. I was also nervous about why he came.

"I want to talk with you, Will. Do you have some time?" He knew I would always make time, if at all possible. I figured he knew about David, so I braced myself for what was to come. He came in my office with his usual syncopated walk mandated by his short leg.

"Have a seat, Peter. What can I do for you?" I gestured to a chair. My paranoia increased; I flushed and began to sweat under my arms.

"Will, I've known you for ten years now, so I'm going to shoot straight with you. As hard as it is for me to say this, I think it's time for you to move on. Time to find another church." Peter punctuated his statement with a definitive head nod.

I went pale and felt gutted. He knew about David, but this was a pretty radical reaction. I had the presence of mind to say to him, "Peter, if this is going to be the tenor of your visit, I want another set of ears to be in here with me. May I ask Brian to join us?"

He readily agreed, so I buzzed Brian's office. I felt greatly relieved to find him in, and I asked him to join us in my office.

"He's on his way, Peter. Do you mind waiting?"

Peter shook his head "no." "While he's coming," Peter said, "let me just mention to you that a couple of people, including my wife, have commented that Brian is showing too much attention to Lisa Steen. Nothing really out of order, mind you, but enough to cause some heads to turn. How about saying a word to him. You'll know the best way."

"Okay, I will. Thanks for the heads-up," I responded.

Brian came in and quickly sat in the other chair across from my desk after greeting Peter. "Thanks for coming, Brian; thanks for waiting, Peter. Now Peter, tell me again what you came to say."

"Well, as I was saying, I think it's time for you to move on."

I felt the exposé coming, and already I resented it. How dare he ask me to leave this church because my son got himself into trouble?

Peter took a breath and continued, "You've been here over ten years now. You've gotten complacent, Will, and, well, a bit stale." He paused. "I came to early church last Sunday so I could go to the Holy Spirit Church on Nashville Avenue later. Their minister had an enthusiasm I wish you had. I want our church to have that kind of excitement. That place is alive with energy, Will. I just don't find that here. Not from you, anyway, and you set the tone, my friend." He paused briefly, but he hadn't finished. "Now I've come to tell you this so you can find some other place while you are still respected by our people. Some other people feel the same way I do. I don't know how long it'll be before that feeling spreads. That could hurt both you and our church."

I shifted gears, scrambled, and sorted out thoughts and feelings as fast as I could. He wasn't talking about David at all. So far there was no connection. But I didn't fully trust that either. If I put up any resistance, would he mention David as back-up ammunition? I didn't know. At the same time I wanted to be sure I really grasped what Peter was saying so I could deal with it.

Peter rattled on in the same vein for several minutes more, and I became convinced he had no hidden agendas. But this agenda was big enough! Peter had dropped a bomb unexpectedly. My Clerk of Session wanted me to leave, for God's sake! I had trouble believing this, but Peter was sitting right here to make sure I did.

The more Peter talked, the more it became apparent to me he was no longer happy with mainstream Presbyterianism. The Holy Spirit Church, in contrast, was very Pentecostal. Nothing wrong with that, but they represented an entirely different tradition from ours with a different approach to many things.

"Well, Peter," I ventured, "I'm getting the impression you may no longer be happy in a main-line Presbyterian Church. I know I'm the minister here and you're not happy with me, but I think your issue is deeper than just me, Peter." He listened politely and seemed to be hearing me.

"You could change ministers behind this desk," I continued, "but you'll end up with another Presbyterian, and I don't think that would satisfy you. I'm not sure 'Presbyterian' is where you are coming from anymore. You've compared us unfavorably with evangelistic congregations before, but this is the first time you have talked specifically about me. I think there's a bigger issue for you here." I was amazed at the candor that rolled out of me without special effort. Perhaps I was so relieved to know Peter wasn't talking about David that I felt free to confront him head on. At this juncture, dealing with questions about my competency seemed easier than dealing with David's difficulties.

We talked for a while longer, and our conversation remained civil and polite. Brian kept silent, but he was listening, and that was important. Finally Peter seemed to want to conclude the meeting. "Well, I want you to give it some thought, Will. There are plenty of places in God's Kingdom where you can serve. The change might give you a fresh start as well."

"I'll think about what you're saying, Peter. I hope you, in turn, will think about what I have suggested as well. God's church is filled with many rooms, and sometimes our spiritual needs shift." I stood up when he did and shook his hand. Brian did too. I felt no anger from Peter, but I certainly felt his strong resolve. He was a man with a mission and left without saying anything else.

"Wow, you sure did stand up to him," Brian volunteered after Peter left. "He's been after me too. He wants me to do more of what he calls 'Spirit-filled leading' with the young people. Even the youth don't want it." Brian shook his head.

I was so upset at what Peter's visit was about and also so relieved at what his visit was *not* about that I simply stood in the middle of my office staring at the open door through which he had left. I managed to thank Brian for dropping everything and coming to my office. "It was the kind of conversation I definitely wanted another set of ears to hear, both for my understanding and for my protection. I am grateful to you for being here, Brian."

"Well, I now understand how you got to be in charge of a platoon. Your skin's thick, and your feet are planted solidly on the ground."

Brian meant this as a compliment. I thanked him, but I assured him I was mush inside. I could tell he didn't believe me.

+++++

"Hey James. I'm in the Camellia Grill." I spun the empty stool next to mine. *"Wish you were here to have a seat, James. I'm going the whole nine yards today with one of their juicy cheeseburgers with thick-cut French fries and a chocolate malted milk. I'll bet you don't have such a fare in Paris.*

"Two years ago this week we all ate lunch here prior to the Iris Parade. God I miss Lanna, and I can only imagine how much you miss her. Remember how embarrassed she was when she spilled her water? We get concerned about the silliest things.

"None of it makes much sense to me. You and I killed people in Nam so that others could be free to die of cancer in America. Fill me in when you've figured out that connection."

I paused and looked around the café. The Camellia Grill hadn't changed in fifty years. The Southern Greek Revival building with its four white columns outside and fifties lunch-counter inside had held on to all of its traditions -- including nothing but black waiters, wearing white tuxedo shirts and black ties.

Customers often sat elbow-to-elbow at the counters while others waited their turn on benches near the entrance. The cashier shouted the number of free places as they became available, and those next in line knew to claim those stools. A young woman had already claimed the stool I had symbolically spun for James. The grill was always loud and crowded. Nevertheless, eating at the Camellia Grill was never rushed.

"Sometimes I wonder why I'm a minister, James." I wrote. My waiter slapped a fork, knife, and spoon onto the counter in front of me, then handed me the traditional large, white linen napkin. I continued typing on my laptop. *"I don't care if you're a doctor, lawyer, or Indian chief, what leads someone to do what he does for a living is terribly complex. Why did I join the Marines? Why did I decide to go to seminary? Why do I remain a minister? Ministers talk about being 'called,' but I think everybody is 'called' to do whatever fits them. Frankly, I'm not too fond of the word 'call.' It's a way of claiming to be special. The*

calling business is just a fancy way of talking about finding what fulfills us, what's rewarding and satisfying." The waiter put the milkshake in front of me with such gusto that I feared it'd spill into my laptop. The cheeseburgers and fries also arrived, and I dug in, blotting a tear with my huge linen napkin.

After taking a healthy bite, I typed, *"I understand why I went into the Marines far better than why I entered the ministry. For one thing, I had to work off the free ROTC ride to Tulane. I also had stars in my eyes. You know, the few, the proud. Vietnam snuffed out those stars, that's for sure.*

"I came out of the Marines eager to stop killing. I had a desire to work for some good cause. After much debate within myself, I decided to go to seminary.

"I know there must have been a lot of guilt involved in my becoming a minister -- guilt from Nam; guilt from college; hell, guilt from high school for that matter. I paused, drinking some of my malt.

"On the other hand, I really like the church family. It's a built-in, ready-made community that cares for one another. I always wanted to be a part of a large family. Now I've got a bunch of brothers and sisters around me. It's nice. I also really enjoy the children in the church, particularly the cute little ones that come to our nursery school. On the other end of the spectrum, I have caring parents among the older members, although the older I get the fewer parent-figures there are."

I knocked over my glass of water. I grabbed my computer as the waiter instantly cleaned up the mess. I thought of Lanna, and I was embarrassed too, particularly since I don't think of myself as being clumsy. The truth is that a lunch counter isn't such a great place to type e-mails while eating, and I did take note of the waiter's frown at my laptop.

"Let me tell you, James," I resumed. *"If you go into the ministry for prestige and respect, you're going to be real disappointed. I had a bit of that motivation in me, I must admit. It wasn't long before I realized that for every person who looks up to you there's one who looks down on you. Admiration of ministers is certainly not the operative phrase for people who don't belong to a church, and they are the majority in America, regardless of what the polls say.*

"When I first started believing in Jesus Christ, everything seemed real clear. I turned my life over to Him, and for a long time everything seemed

to fall into place. Of course Carol almost refused to marry me. She called me her 'religious nut' for a year or so. In time she became a believer too. She probably always was — she grew up that way, not like me. Nursing school had knocked religion out of her. Funny, one helping profession killed faith. Another helping profession instilled faith.

"It all seemed clear at first: turn to Jesus and follow Him as best you can. However, more recently I question the exclusiveness of Christianity. Not just because of my years in the Corps, but also because of all kinds of stuff that's happened in my church. Besides, there are several billion people out there who aren't Christians, and they all can't be lost. I still believe God loves us all, but everything after that is up for grabs. I do miss the certainty and authority I first found in religion."

I drank some milkshake and pushed the fries away. Between bites I wrote about Peter's visit to me. *"I was furious when he left my office, but his questions have haunted me. How long should I stay here? Maybe I really have outlived my usefulness. Maybe I really am turning into a complacent minister like he says. Sometimes I feel like I'm knocking myself out 24/7, and no one's benefiting from it. It gets discouraging, like writing the words to a sermon no one will hear."*

I looked at my watch and blanched at the time. It was much later than I thought. I quickly ended the e-mail and hit the "send" button. I grabbed my check, hopped off the stool, and reached for my wallet. I heard the cashier shout "One!" as the door closed behind me.

+++++

The dinner plates were mostly empty, and we had all finished eating. Carol's shrimp Creole always tasted great -- one of the few meals where I don't leave anything on my plate. Even though I rarely eat as much as either Carol or David, I still have to watch my weight. I complimented Carol on the dinner, puckering a kiss toward her across the table. But Carol cleared her throat. She had an agenda.

"Okay, Will, tell me exactly how this works; this business of Pops' bed. Take your time. Run it past me nice and slowly so I can understand." Carol put her coffee down, looked at me, and waited.

David asked to be excused from the table. He could tell something was up. As he left, I heard him mumble something and Carol snapped a stare toward him.

I waited until David was out of earshot before responding to Carol. "Okay." I took a deep breath. "We needed a hospital bed for my father, right? Well, the church could also use one to add to the supply of walkers, crutches, and wheelchairs we loan out to people when they need it. So I bought a bed for the church. Pops will be the first one to use it, that's all."

"And how did you pay for it?" Carol asked, rattling her spoon against the inside of her coffee cup as she stirred it.

"I wrote a check to the church, and the church bought the bed. Same thing as my giving it. Big deal."

"So your father gets a hospital bed *you* so graciously decided the church needed, and you just happen to walk away with a nice tax deduction. Right?" She stirred her coffee so hard some sloshed over onto the table, and she left it there.

"What's so wrong with that?" I answered. "The bed benefits the church and the tax deduction benefits us. All perfectly legal. Nothing out of the ordinary about that."

"Except that you, The Reverend William Blake McKenzie, are the one who single-handedly decided the church needed a hospital bed … and you, William Blake McKenzie, are also the one benefiting with a tax deduction from a personal expense our family would have to incur anyway. That's about as shady as you can get, Will, even if it's legal." She paused, taking a deep breath before continuing. "What happens if you decide the church needs a home theatre system and the only place the church can store it is in our family room? Would that be okay too?" She grabbed a paper napkin and vigorously blotted up her spilt coffee.

"That's quite different, damn it. That's not a fair comparison," I puffed, offended by her analogy. "What do you want me to do, Carol, blow off a tax deduction just because we're the first ones to benefit from the bed? I just don't understand what the problem is. Pops likes the bed, and I already told him it was on loan from the church. The motorized adjustments are just what he needs."

"Leave Pops' views out of this. No, as a matter of fact, don't leave Pops out of this. He's the helpless old man that allows you to be nice and benevolent, isn't he? Poor ole Mr. Pops could sure use a hospital bed, particularly the totally motorized variety. If only the church had one, we'd be delighted to let him use it. We really ought to try to get one for the church for folks like Pops. Come on, Will." Carol clearly mimicked my earlier puff, which made me seethe inside.

"Carol, I'm not ashamed that I gave the money to buy it. The church could also use several more of those high toilet seats. Right now we have one more person requesting the use of one than we have toilet seats. They're waiting in line, if you'll pardon the phrase, and Pops doesn't have a thing to do with that need which will provide a tax deduction for the donor."

"Now this all makes sense. I sure am glad you clarified it for me. The church is short on toilet seats, so you donated a bed? Very logical. And I wonder why. Why don't you just spell it all out in the church newsletter? Let the congregation applaud your high ethical standards."

"Damn it, Carol, what do you want me to do? I can return the bed if you want. It comes with a thirty-day guarantee. Is that what you want me to do? Do you want me to return the bed from the church and then go out and buy the same one again for Pops?"

"I want us to pay for your father's bed the same way we pay for his clothes, for his food, for the heat in his room, for the detective books he enjoys reading. That's what I want. Or maybe we need more mystery books in the church library."

"Carol. Get off of it and join the real world, will you?"

"Oh, I see. Poor stupid wife just can't comprehend the nuances of high finance. Well what about old fashioned right and wrong?" Carol paused, but not long enough to let me respond.

"You ask me what I want. I'll tell you what I want. I want you to promise me you won't claim the cost of that hospital bed as a benevolent gift on our income taxes, that's what." She and I were in a no-blink staring match by now. "And it's close enough to April 15th I won't forget about it. You do want my signature on that joint return, don't you?"

Carol fell silent. She stood and walked her still-filled coffee cup to the kitchen sink and poured it down the drain. I waited for her to leave the room before I got up from the table and reached in the cabinet for some relief to my heartburn.

+++++

Friday afternoon I watched the city skyline sink into the horizon as Thomas Gaubert and I headed to the Bridge City catfish festival. He had invited me earlier in the week, and I always enjoyed local Cajun festivals, which featured good food and good music. Within fifteen minutes we were out of the city and surrounded on both sides by heavy vegetation intermingled with swamp. A pair of snowy egrets flew across the road. The cleared field to our left was speckled with cattle egrets riding on the backs of cows. As our car settled into a long curve, scores of white ibis flying in formation filled the sky. The black tips on their brilliant white wings added an air of dignity to their flight. Nutria munched on water lilies in the marsh. I scanned the swamp for alligators but didn't see one. They were there.

Thomas and I enjoyed the wonderful display of nature at the close of the day. "What a rich heritage of birds and wild life we have down here," I commented.

"I like the laid-back Cajun atmosphere," Thomas added. "I can already taste good filet of fried catfish and fresh coleslaw washed down with a cold Dixie beer, all done in rhythm to a Cajun two-step led by a spirited accordion player. That's living." I nodded, indicating my agreement.

Once we parked, we followed the Cajun music to the food area. Soon we were carrying our plates to a table near the band. The succulent catfish filets were cooked with a crisp batter, and the cocktail sauce spiced with a generous shake of Tabasco smelled heftily of cayenne pepper. I couldn't resist a link of their rich andouille sausage. Thomas's plate was heaped to overflowing with twice as much as I had taken. I felt quietly proud of my restraint. The aroma of seafood gumbo tempted me to choose a bowlful as well, but I decided to go back for that … if I had room. So much good food!

The band played a waltz, and the accordion player sang in a high-pitched lament characteristic of slow Cajun songs. He wore bright red suspenders over his rumpled white shirt. The violin player had a colorful wood-duck feather stuck in the brim of his black Stetson hat. The fiddler held a cigarette between his two last fingers and still made music with the bow held between his thumb and first two fingers. When he reached a pause in the music, he took a deep puff, bow sticking high in the air, and then resumed playing. Fascinated, I slowed down my eating to sit back and listen to the music. The accordion player swayed back and forth as he squeezed out the Cajun melody. With all the members of the band enjoying themselves, their mood was contagious.

"Thomas," I asked as we ate our meal, "You said something about another event we might want to take in while we were down here. What was that?"

"Well, it's something I would really like to do. I think it'd be an education for both of us. Something you don't get to do just any day. It'd be an adventure, for sure, but I think it would be worth going to."

"Ok, you want to go, but what is it? One-handed alligator wrestling?"

"Close. I saw a sign when I did some business down this way last week." He smiled broadly. "There's a Klan rally tonight at eight, and it's open to the public."

"The Ku Klux Klan!?"

"Right. I've never been to a KKK rally, have you?"

"You have got to be kidding. I didn't even know they still existed, and if they do, I'm not sure I want to endorse them with my presence."

"The way I look at it, this is a perfect occasion to see those devils in action. They'll be meeting in a clearing in the woods in the middle of nowhere on Highway 90. Nobody will know who we are. It ought to be interesting." He looked hopefully at me before continuing. "One sign advertised that David Duke would be the main speaker. I know you've heard of him. You know, the Grand Wizard who ran for governor and has been written up in the magazines."

"Come on, Thomas, get serious." I hesitated.

"We don't have to stay long -- just long enough to get a flavor of it. We might not have a chance like this again. What do you say?"

I really was curious and interested in what the rally would be like. I thought about raising the appropriateness of a Presbyterian minister attending a KKK Rally, but I knew Thomas would ridicule that concern. So I raised my other concern. "Are you sure we'll be safe?"

"Lieutenant McKenzie, this isn't Hanoi. Of course, if you're so narrow you don't want to hear what they have to say, well ..." He smiled in his sarcastic way.

"Ok. I'll admit I'm really curious. I may live to regret this, but let's stay for only a little while. I don't want to spend the night there."

"Neither do I. Meanwhile this band's getting really warmed up, isn't it?"

We sat back and listened until it started getting dark.

+++++

A series of signs posted along the highway advertised various aspects of the rally. They reminded me of the Burma Shave road signs I had seen as a child. "KKK: The Imperial Wizard Speaks." "KKK: The Truth About The White Race." The last of several signs read, "KKK Rally - 1000 feet on the left."

"Look!" Thomas said. We're in good hands." Thomas sounded relieved. "Policemen are directing traffic at the entrance to the field. We'll be perfectly safe."

I added, "We also just passed a sign saying 'No Cameras. No Audio. No Video.' So maybe our picture won't be in the *Times-Picayune* tomorrow morning."

"Well, there are cars behind us now," Thomas observed. "It's too late to turn back. We're committed." We drove a hundred yards or so into the cleared field.

I saw uniformed policemen just ahead, and that did comfort me. They stopped each vehicle and spoke to the driver, then pointed the way to parking. More men in the field outlined a runway to parking places with their flashlights. By now there were several cars ahead of us and behind us awaiting parking instructions from the officers.

When we stopped beside the armed policeman I saw his arm patch: "KKK Security." A silver badge bearing the same label became visible as he looked at us and examined the interior of our car. A chill ran down my spine. They've got their own police, for God's sake!

This "security" guard sported an enormous potbelly, obscuring his belt from view. As he talked to us, he scratched his right cheek and rubbed his nose. You would think he had been invaded by a swarm of gnats. "No pictures, no camcorders, no cell phones," he repeated in a monotone, then indicated there were plenty of parking spaces in the field on the right. Thomas drove slowly in that direction. I was glad it was Thomas's car, not mine. This field was no airplane runway, and almost all the other vehicles were trucks built to take the uneven terrain.

"I guess they're screening for counter-terrorists," Thomas sarcastically sneered.

"And for anyone who isn't lily white," I added.

"You're probably right," Thomas agreed as he edged toward a parking spot where the policeman had indicated. We were going slowly over the bumps and held up a truck behind us. The driver revved his motor as an angry hint.

Only when we turned left as directed did we see the yellow flickering light from a burning cross shining through an opening in the pines. I felt myself take a sudden deep breath, and I held on to it for a second. I could see a stage beside the fiery cross, and I could hear someone speaking, but we were still too far away to make out any words. I felt an uneasy nervousness in my stomach and a bit of a chill. Mainly I felt unclean and paranoid, as if I had entered the notoriously sleazy Black Cat Bar on the Industrial Canal.

I took perverse comfort in the thought that anyone who used a camera would never leave with the images. What an irony. KKK Security guards were protecting me from my biggest fear of the moment: exposure.

Thomas whispered, "This is quite a different crowd than we have at Central Church, isn't it? I wonder what rock these folks crawled out from under."

"Shhh," I quickly sounded over his words. I hoped no one had heard his remark.

We tried to blend in with the crowd, although our city-casual clothes looked very urban in this setting. The man on my left was tall and unshaven, perhaps in his early sixties. He had a wooden kitchen match in his mouth with its red head sticking out. He managed to shift the match from one corner of his mouth to the other and back again. Then I saw the patch on his jacket pocket: "The Walking Dead; 1st Battalion, 9th Marines." He was a marine. Vietnam. Served in the same area I did. I flushed. Confusing emotions ran through me. But I really didn't want to say anything to him. What a can of worms that would open up.

I looked at the man to our right. He showed no acknowledgment of me. His face was acne-pocked and his cheek puffed with a healthy chew; he spit a mouthful of tobacco juice on the ground about two feet in front of him. He hadn't always been so accurate, as the front of his jumper overalls clearly showed. Someone nearby farted.

The crowd was almost all men, with just a handful of women scattered here and there. I tried to get a feel for how many people were present. I guessed about two hundred -- the size of an average wedding at church. My comparison struck me as humorous, and I chuckled. Then I had to explain to Thomas what was funny.

The KKK speaker wore a white sheet, but he didn't have on a hood. A handful of men stood attentively on the edge of the stage. They too were suited out, but wore no hoods. That didn't fit my image of the incognito KKK. Maybe a law prohibited them from masking at a public rally.

The cross burned like a huge torch. It appeared to be made of four-by-fours wrapped in some sort of cloth soaked in fuel oil. The fire was going strong and looked like it could burn for a long time.

In spite of his earlier bravado, Thomas fell silent and looked cautiously around. Another dozen or so people had arrived and were now standing beside us and behind us. If we tried to leave now, we would be very conspicuous. So here we were. Carol would hit the ceiling if she knew where I was, and David might ask what was so bad about "just trying" marijuana. Meanwhile the speaker rattled on. The word "nigger" punctuated his fiery rhetoric like buckshot fired at a sitting rabbit. The crowd seemed to get turned on by the word and shouted their support at every sentence. I had trouble believing this was actually happening.

"Now let's hear it for our Imperial Wizard, David Duke!" the speaker shouted. Clapping and cheering rose all about us as the mike was turned over to David Duke. A large red cross was sewn onto the front of his robe, the badge of the Imperial Wizard. Young, tall, with blue-eyes visible even from a distance, Duke assumed command and began to speak with authority.

David Duke spoke eloquently patriotic words about our "great country, America," and cleverly twisted his verbiage so that "America" became equivalent to "white." Everyone around us seemed to swallow the transformation and confirmed their acceptance of it with applause and shouting. Duke was a smooth, calm, convincing orator who quickly had the audience in the palm of his hand.

Then he asked us to join in the pledge of allegiance to the flag. Another Klansman marched onto the stage with a flag, holding it high. Everybody joined in the pledge, including Thomas and me, which struck me as horribly ironic and wrong. Here we stood, side by side with the KKK, pledging allegiance to our flag. I felt strangely deceptive repeating the pledge in this setting with these people. But who was more hypocritical, the Klan for using it to their ends, or us for repeating it with them?

Together we recited the same pledge used to open the church's Boy Scout meetings, the same pledge kids recite in school each morning, the same pledge we used in the Marines. As I recited the familiar words I wanted to think I meant something very different than "they" did, particularly when we got to "under God, with liberty and justice for all." My anger started to grow, and I began to hate the whole crowd.

Then David Duke launched into his main speech. I listened to his words underlined by spoken and mumbled comments around about us. "That's right"; "Say it, David"; "Un-huh." I even heard a distinct "Amen, brother" shouted by someone to my far right. The atmosphere reminded me of an old-fashioned revival service, and the liturgy had a diabolically religious fervor about it, except hatred had replaced love. But I began to realize that I was really hating these hateful people.

The crowd continued to respond. "Tell it like it is, David"; "Gotta hold the standard"; "No doubt about it"; "Fuck the damn niggers"; "Speak the truth"; "Screw the nigger lovers"; "Damn those liberal clergymen."

The last comment from an elderly man behind me caused me to freeze. I felt the hair twinge on the back of my neck. With some relief, I realized he had simply embellished on a phrase David Duke just used, but I felt like "liberal clergyman" was written on my forehead and stamped on my back.

Thomas leaned into my ear and mumbled, "Sure glad you don't have your collar on, Rev." I elbowed him in the ribs and whispered "Shut up!" The people nearby looked at me, but their heads quickly swiveled back to David Duke.

I was ready to leave. Now. I couldn't stand these people. But Duke continued for a total of twenty minutes, or just about the same length as my sermons. What irony! When Duke finished speaking, I urged

Thomas, "Let's head for the car." He nodded, and we walked away from the crowd.

Nobody cared. The man next to me burped loudly.

We searched for our car in the weedy lot. It was hard to find tucked in among the larger pickup trucks. "Part of a liberal education, I guess," Thomas said shaking his head. "Actually more of an education than I bargained on. Did you hear Duke spew out all that crap about genetics and race? Flies against everything we know on the subject. I'm mighty glad my company is privately owned and doesn't use any state or federal money. Otherwise I think that Duke fellow would fight against every dime of my salary."

I didn't say anything. I was just glad to be on our way.

The KKK police stopped us again on our way out. "Night fellas. Oh by the way, I noticed the Meadows Research sticker on your bumper. I hope you listened good, so you can straighten out those bastards you work for."

Even in the dimly lit car I could see Thomas go pale.

We drove off in silence.

Several miles down the highway, I spoke. "I don't believe it, Thomas. I don't believe we went. I don't believe we stood there and listened to that crap. So damn much evil gathered in one place. How do you forgive people like them? So irrational, so stupid, so evil, so destructive." Thomas didn't respond. "But you know, if I can't forgive them, why should I be forgiven for a lot worse stuff I've done?"

"Who said whatever you did was worse, Will? I take it you're talking about Vietnam, right?"

"Yeah. But what have African Americans done to these Klan people? How did these people develop such hatred? How do they perpetuate such prejudice? Why do they hate blacks so much?"

"Why do Irish Catholics hate Irish Protestants, Will? Why did Marines hate the Viet Cong?" He paused. "Why did Alice hate Stan?" he ruthlessly continued.

"Your examples aren't parallel," I replied with irritation. "Besides, how do I forgive folks like these KKK?"

"Well, think about it. Then tell me what ever happened to 'Father forgive them for they know not what they do.'"

+++++

Carol and David were in the family room watching Jay Leno. Each mumbled a brief "Hi," obviously not wanting to be interrupted. I stood for a moment watching them and caught a little Leno over their shoulders. They were laughing. Such a peaceful scene, quite different from the KKK rally with its studied hatred. Quite different from Nam with its senseless hatred.

I wandered into the kitchen, opened the refrigerator, and looked on the shelves. Then I closed the refrigerator. I paused, reached down to the bottom cabinet next to the sink, and picked up Ellis's bottle of bourbon. I read the label carefully as though it might have answers I was looking for. Then I poured myself a drink … straight … neat.

I took my drink out on the porch and sat in the cold night air. I thought, I mulled, and I remembered. I remembered Vietnam with its angry killings, with its dispassionate killings, with its logical killings, with its senseless killings. However motivated, however described, the killings were real and the dead remained dead -- who knows how many by my hand. Scores. Maybe hundreds. No, probably scores. Definitely scores. The whole thing caused my mind to spin with sickening confusion. I shivered from the cold.

I soon went back in the kitchen to pour another drink. The late night show rattled on, and laughter continued. Back to the porch. I sat for a while longer seeing … seeing my buddies, my dead buddies. I saw them one at a time parading before me. I saw them all at once, bombarding me with their deaths. Some called my name; some called my rank; some simply called out. Then they were silent. Gone. Where? No longer here. Dead. Not coming back. Ever. I found myself standing with an empty glass in my hand, and I went back to the kitchen. Then back to the porch that didn't feel as cold now.

Memories came flooding in as the bourbon flooded into me. Ugly memories. Of cruelty. Of slaughter. Of Bodies. Of Stench. Rot. Decay. Half-blown-off faces and dismembered bodies. A shadowy figure emerged from behind a thick patch of jungle shrubbery. I'm sure I saw him holding a gun. He put his hands above his head as I shot him. Then a crowded street in Da Nang pulling a buddy out of a doorway. He overdosed on something, and I carried him to my jeep. He slumped dead in the seat next to me as I drove him to a hospital. I kept driving anyway. Suddenly I saw a little girl running after a ball. Soon she was lying dead in a pool of blood. I saw a buddy get stabbed by an enemy soldier. I shot the enemy in the head and then dragged my buddy back to camp. He died anyway.

But I survived and so many others didn't. I survived the whole damn war … and I've felt guilty ever since.

My trips to the kitchen continued. The memories continued. Some vivid, some vague, but all chilling, all haunting. Would I ever find forgiveness? The Klan flashed before me again. The fiery cross. The savage barking of "nigger." My black buddy Washington's face materialized before me just before he was blown in half. Could I forgive those Vietnamese Nationals? Could I forgive the Klan? My buddy James and his wife Lanna filled my mind. Somehow forgiveness had to be all or nothing, and there the agony resided unresolved.

Little by little, drink-by-drink, the memories became fuzzy, the fury ceased, the rush came to a halt, and everything seemed to be all right. I found peace at last.

I woke up sitting in the broken deck chair. I moved clumsily to a sturdy one, bottle in hand. I had stopped using a glass some time back. I put the bottle down beside my chair, and it fell over when I set it down on the deck. Slowly I grabbed the bottle and set it upright, chuckling quietly at the pool of bourbon that drained through the spaces between the boards. Then I fell asleep again on the now warm, cozy deck overlooking the darkness.

+++++

I couldn't remember how I got to bed, but I was embarrassed to wake up there. Carol soon reminded me in no uncertain terms what had happened, "Like leading a damn zombie up the stairs. Fortunately David went straight to his room when Leno was over, so he didn't see how sloshed you were. It was not a pretty sight, Will." She shook her head. "So how's your head this morning?"

"Pretty bad," I confessed. My head throbbed and my stomach was queasy. "What time is it anyway?"

"Nine thirty. What the hell got into you?"

"Nine thirty! Damn." Things still spun now and then. "This is bad. "

"Yes it is," Carol agreed. I couldn't look her in the eye. She told me, "I called in sick for you." Carol paused briefly, then continued. "Now.

What's going on with you anyway? What did you and Thomas do last night that brought all this on? Ellis's bottle of bourbon is completely empty, and it was almost full. It's still on the floor next to the rocker. I want *you* to throw it away." Carol fell silent, straightening things on her dresser as she turned her back to me.

I swung my feet over the side of the bed and stared at the floor. "Where to start?" I rolled my neck. "Okay. Look. Thomas and I went to a KKK rally after the catfish festival."

"A what?" Carol stared angrily at me in baffled disbelief.

"I know. I know. There were signs on the highway near Breaux Bridge, and we both got curious." Carol, speechless, continued to stare at me. "Anyhow, the meeting was filled with hatred as you can imagine -- mostly at 'niggers.'"

"God. What did you expect? I don't believe you did this."

"I barely do either. I'll tell you about the rally some other time. The point is I got so angry with them I realized I couldn't forgive them. That triggered my agony over Vietnam and whether I can ever forgive and accept forgiveness for all of the hatred there."

"I don't follow you. What's one got to do with the other?" Carol showed no compassion whatsoever. I had rarely seen her this pissed, but I couldn't blame her.

"If I can't forgive those red necks standing in that field, how can I expect to be forgiven for all the stuff that happened in Nam?"

"That's a stretch if ever I heard one."

"Well, you asked what's going on with me, and I've told you. You can believe it or not, but that's cutting to the heart of the matter." Now I was getting pissed. I felt like a little boy being talked to by his mother. I felt like a sinner confessing to a priest who didn't understand. I felt guilty. A lot … and not just for getting drunk.

I told Carol some more about the Klan rally, but I again debated how much to tell her about Vietnam. I'd wrestled with that question for years. How much did she need to know? What difference would talking about Nam make anyway? It would be cruel to tell her a lot of things that happened there. What good would telling her do? I felt physically weak from the booze and fell back on the bed.

"Sleep it off or something." Carol left the room, closing the bedroom door with some force as she left.

Grief about lost buddies flooded over me again. Named buddies. Unnamed buddies. Guys who saved my life and then got slaughtered themselves. I tried hard to stop thinking about it. I told myself every Nam veteran had to deal with stuff like this; maybe the vets of every war did. I'm not unusual, I reassured myself. But so many guys, with so few returning. So few returning intact. Am I intact?

As I closed my eyes, scores of people I had killed flashed through my mind. Men and women and children. Those I killed couldn't forgive me. The dead can't forgive the living. The living have to forgive themselves ... and there's the rub.

+++++

By evening I felt almost normal again physically but was filled with regret and remorse. I felt like hiding, and New Orleans always offers ample opportunities to hide. The Krewe of Bacchus paraded tonight, one of the most spectacular parades of the carnival season. The parade attracted large crowds, a living fantasy for escape.

David went with a friend, and Carol and I met several of our friends at a location we have enjoyed for years. Our spot on Napoleon Avenue was in front of a mansion belonging to Anne Rice, the popular author. Brian and Blanche were joining us along with two of their friends named Spud and Sissy. Miriam and Ashley, and Thomas and Ann would be there too. When we arrived, I was surprised to see Lisa and Tony Steen there as well.

Thomas greeted me with a poker face, and I tried to respond in kind. I reminded myself he didn't know about my trip into the bourbon bottle after we parted last night.

Carol cordially greeted everyone. Then, looking at Lisa, she whispered in my ear, "Who invited her to meet us at this spot?"

I shrugged my shoulders.

Lisa wore a white angora sweater that was at least one size too small. I couldn't help noticing that she appeared to be braless. Carol had noticed too, as the disgusted expression on her face revealed. Tony was blasé as usual, acting as though Lisa were dressed for tea at the Orleans Club. I made a point not to glance again, much less stare, at her breasts. That took discipline.

Brian had dyed his hair a bright yellow, and everyone made some comment about it. Brian had a wild streak in him. I kidded him about blondes having more fun and chalked his dyed hair off to carnival madness. I certainly hoped the yellow could be washed out by Sunday.

Lisa walked over to where Brian and Blanche were standing. Tony occupied himself with organizing their igloo filled with food and drinks and, as usual, paid little attention to his wife.

Lisa moved close to Brian. She slowly ran her hand through his yellow hair while gazing warmly into his baby blue eyes. She took her time about the gesture, as though they were completely alone. Brian was eating it up. Blanche looked flushed with embarrassment, but didn't say or do anything. Then Lisa patted Brian on the cheek, and slid her hand down his face while saying a casual hello to Blanche.

What was that all about, I wondered? Lisa saw me watching and smiled broadly, pleased she had been noticed. Several people had already noticed Lisa tonight.

Carol stepped between Lisa and me. "I see you wore your bead-catching sweater, Lisa," Carol brazenly observed, a direct reference to the well-known carnival fact that a braless woman who raised her sweater as a float passed usually got bombarded with beads. Strands of long white pearls were reserved for particularly attractive women. Lisa just tilted her head toward Carol and smiled. Tony didn't notice. He never noticed anything Lisa did, or at least he gave that impression. Maybe that was the only way he could cope with her.

We were all spared further antics from Lisa because the first float of the parade came into sight. There would be 27 floats tonight, not counting the maids' floats and the King's float. The King of Bacchus was always a national celebrity, this year Marlon Brando. Aged and obese, he sat on a throne towering above the cheering crowd. He threw scores of special necklaces with his profile on one side of the plastic medallion and the profile of Bacchus, the god of wine, on the other side. The beads strung to the medallion were in the traditional green, purple, and yellow colors of Mardi Gras. Ashley caught one and proudly showed it to us.

As I got wrapped up in the parade, I realized I had forgotten about last night's drunken escapade. It didn't bother me anymore. Is that the same as forgiveness? Is it all in the eye of the offender? I didn't really care to think the matter through, but I finally felt good again.

I saw a Bacchus cup on the ground and picked it up. Carol and I hoped to collect a dozen plastic cups this year. We used them year-round for drinks of all kinds. Water, cokes, or iced tea. I used one last night … for a short while anyway.

The roar of the crowd never stopped, and the beads continued to rain down upon us. After almost two hours, the last float passed, and the crowd started dispersing.

We bid a brief goodbye to everyone in our group and joined the mobs of people heading to their cars. Lisa strutted in front of us, fingering a set of long white beads draped around her neck.

The KKK, the bottle of bourbon, the hangover, and the shame – all seemed like another world in another time. Or was this the other world? This City always keeps twisting realities, so you are never sure what's real and what's not. No wonder so many tourists come to the Big Easy to forget, to relax, to play, and to find new realities to replace older, painful ones … or just to dream about possibilities.

+++++

Saturday passed quickly, and I didn't get much accomplished. After supper I gathered my sermon notes and got in my car. I always went to the church on Saturday night to practice my sermon. Sometimes it helped, and if it didn't I could still feel like I'd given it my best shot. Tonight, without thinking, I took my daytime short cut to get there, even though I knew that the neighborhood was too dangerous to drive through at night. As I came to a stop sign, I watched a drug deal go down not ten yards away. I kept going, rolling through the stop sign after making sure no cars were coming on the cross street. I didn't want to stop anywhere in this neighborhood if possible.

The next corner had a stoplight. Red, unfortunately. I had hoped to run it, but I had to wait while several cars crossed in front of me. A big Mercury stopped next to me. Even with my windows closed, the bass speakers shook my chest. I didn't want to make eye contact with the driver, so I looked the other way.

As I turned my head, I found myself looking at an "Adults Only" place on the corner. I read its outlandish signs, but didn't think much about them … until the front door opened and a familiar man walked out.

Peter Bernard! For God's sake!

I looked twice, but there was no doubt about it. It was Peter. He even wore the same red and blue jacket he had worn at the Wednesday night church supper. I'll be damned. Our Clerk of Session! The righteous, lay-leader of our church. The man who had asked me to leave.

He walked quickly to the corner and turned down the side street, hurrying in spite of his characteristic limp. I chuckled out loud as I absorbed this happenstance discovery. I'll be damned. Peter Bernard.

A prolonged horn-blast from behind startled me, and I realized that the light had turned green. I crossed the intersection, wanting to drive slowly to see if I could see Peter again, but the car behind me followed too closely.

The initial surprise and shock passed. I became amused, curious, saddened, speculative, but above all angry. My anger increased by the second. I became more pissed than ever at his asking me to leave the church.

"The dirty old man!" I heard myself say out loud. "How many masks does he wear?" Did he really think he could compartmentalize his life like that? Go to a brothel on Saturday; go to church on Sunday. Work up guilt on Saturday; get forgiveness on Sunday. A sad, vicious cycle.

I shook my head as I got out of my car and walked to the door of the church.

I entered the dark, empty space we called "sanctuary."

+++++

Mardi Gras ravished the city like a friendly plague. Early birds got to the Avenue before dawn to stake out a spot on the front row. Carol and I didn't care about being up front, so we enjoyed a second cup of coffee at home and waited until later to head to Grits' office, our headquarters for the day. Pops felt particularly good this morning, so we folded his wheelchair into the trunk and brought him with us.

We were soon staking out our territory on the neutral ground of St. Charles Avenue. The streetcars weren't running today. Nothing was running today. Almost every business was closed. It was Fat Tuesday in the Big Easy. The only real holdout remained the post office. You would get your mail today since Uncle Sam doesn't recognize Mardi Gras.

David pushed Pops, while Carol and I carried the food, drinks, and folding chairs. After we got settled on the blanket we'd used to stake out our territory, David stayed with Pops while Carol and I went to say hello to Grits and Gail. They were sitting on the large front porch of a beautiful antebellum home he had converted into his office. It was our bathroom and our resting place, two very important commodities on Carnival Day.

People-watching constituted a big part of the day's fun. The closer you got to the French Quarter the more outlandish and skimpy the costumes became. The Quarter on Mardi Gras was not a place for minors, or the prudish. We were in the Garden District, a family area filled with children, and the costumes here were fun, interesting, and rarely offensive.

The air was filled with the smell of roasting onions and sausages, coming from a small barbeque grill set up by a family behind us. I was surprised that they fired-up in the midst of this crowd, but so far there was no harm done. A woman in a bright red cocktail dress passed by, reeking with enough perfume for ten people. I noticed that not many people were letting her get too close. I wondered if that was what she intended, or had she hoped for the opposite reaction? So goes Mardi Gras.

Carol was dressed as a nurse, because she still had her full white uniform, complete with starched hat. She wore too much ultra-bright red lipstick, and she had her own IV pole and bag filled with iced tea.

David wanted me to be a devil, but I remained a minister instead, but with a twist. My clergy garb was complete with black shirt and white collar, but I hung a twelve-inch cross on an extra long chain around my neck. The chain was so long the cross dragged the street and clanged as I walked. I wasn't sure why I had made such a cross; but I did, and wore it anyway. It's Mardi Gras.

The comments people made to me were fascinating. "Forgive me, father, for I'm about to sin," was my favorite so far this morning. A woman dressed like a little girl threw herself at me, wrapped her arms around my neck, and exclaimed, "Father! My dear Father! Where have you been all these years?" Carol belly-laughed as the woman grabbed her baby bottle, started drinking from it, and skipped away. Who knows what was in that bottle. Not ten minutes later a "nun" passed by. She looked at me and muttered, "Unh. You priests and your candy bars." Then she walked away with a disgusted air. Another man started singing, "The old draggy cross …." Mardi Gras was in full swing.

Mary Beth Stewart came up to me and wished us all a happy Mardi Gras. I introduced her to Carol and asked her how she'd been getting along. I was aware that I hadn't seen her in church lately. She indicated that she'd been traveling for the law school and had been wiped out on weekends now that she was so pregnant. I found her costume amusing – she was a pumpkin, orange and round and big. During Mardi Gras everything gets wacky.

As Mary Beth left, she indicated that she would be calling me for an appointment to talk about something that was on her mind. I told her to call Marie in the morning and set something up. She nodded and turned to three friends who were standing nearby waiting for her.

A young couple pushing a grocery cart filled with beer called out to me, "Spankings. Spankings. Father, do you need a spanking?" A sign on their cart read, "The Spanking Machine." In smaller letters was scribbled, "Get a free spanking for the sins you have committed today." The couple waved a large Styrofoam paddle in the air. They were dressed in khaki and had a sheriff's star pinned on their shirt pockets.

A witch ran up to the cart. "I'd like to get my spanking now and get it over with so I can enjoy the rest of the day." They told her to hold on to the handle of the grocery cart and bend forward. From inside the cart a taped song began to play, and the couple sang along, "Spank, spank, spank your butt, gently for your sin. Merrily, merrily, merrily, merrily, life may now begin." They slapped the witch's rear once with the paddle and then presented her with a certificate reading "Your spanking is good until midnight …" They pushed their Spanking Machine through the crowd looking for another sinner.

"How did you get out of that one, Will?" Carol asked with a big grin.

"Beats me."

Blanche and Brian found us and greeted us warmly. Blanche had on a huge pink T-shirt that hung down past her knees. She had printed across the shirt, "Shhh. The baby is sleeping." An arrow pointed to her bulging middle. Brian also had on a large T-shirt. His shirt read, "My baby wasn't sleeping, and neither was I." We chatted for a minute before they walked down the street.

The crowd's attention shifted to a side street as the Krewe of Zulu's parade turned onto St. Charles Avenue. Zulu didn't throw beads; they "threw" coconuts. Years ago they literally threw the gold-painted coconuts from their floats, but injuries resulted. Now they leaned over the sides of the float and personally gave coconuts to lucky recipients.

Carol let go of my hand and squeezed to the front of the crowd. I stayed back and thought "lots of luck." Lo and behold, she emerged from the crush of people with a smile on her face and a golden coconut in her uplifted hand. She had secured one of the true prizes of Carnival.

It still wasn't quite ten o'clock, but we ate Carol's egg salad sandwiches anyway and sipped another cup of coffee. David wanted to roam in the crowd and have us watch Pops for a while. We felt safe letting him do that, which was a good thing, because there was no holding him back. The crowd was usually good-humored and friendly, particularly in this part of town.

However, two guys with wineskins were lying on a blanket next to where Pops sat. They were already three sheets to the wind and half asleep. One woke up long enough to squeeze a stream of wine into his mouth, dropped the wineskin, and rolled over, bumping Pops' wheelchair. Pops kept on eating his sandwich, looked down at the sleeping drunks, and said, "Now I understand why Lent lasts forty days!"

A little after ten we heard police sirens signaling the arrival of the parade. Patrol cars and mounted police paved the way, pushing people back to the curb.

Leading the parade came Rex, the King of Carnival. His arrival marked the beginning of nearly six hours of continuous floats. He waved his scepter to the shouting crowd. Rex was always a prominent citizen. This year Rex was Louis Pouché, the president of the city's leading bank and a member of our church. Today's *Times-Picayune* featured his picture and a story about him -- quite a history of accomplishments. His queen was one of this year's lovely debutantes.

The Krewe of Rex paraded about twenty floats. Each float stood fifteen to twenty feet tall and held fifteen to twenty riders, all costumed and masked and throwing beads and cups. I knew several members of the Rex Krewe, but could not pick them out because of the masks. Unlike the throws of other parades, Rex beads were all identical — purple, green, and gold plastic with a featured medallion about the size of a silver dollar. Their plastic drinking cups also were cast in the colors of Mardi Gras, sporting the emblem of Rex on the side. Both the beads and the cups of Rex were a favorite to collect. I scrambled to catch a strand of beads coming my way, but the man next to me caught part of the strand at the same time and the strand broke. We both laughed as the little beads scattered in a random pattern between us.

Following Rex were hundreds of individual floats made from elaborately decorated flatbed trucks. Every truck had a different theme, and the costumes and colors were vivid reds and yellows and greens and blues. Color was everywhere, splashing across our vision in continually changing patterns. Glorious.

The roar of the crowd soon became deafening. Almost everyone shouted the familiar "throw me something, mister," and the trucks kept their air-horns blowing to keep the crowd at a safe distance from their rolling wheels. After several hours you felt battered by the noise, but the noise wouldn't stop until the middle of the afternoon when the very last float had passed.

The crowd went into a bead-catching frenzy. Small children sat in wooden seats bolted to the top of stepladders, while their parents stood on the bottom step for stability. Awkward and dangerous at best, but there were thousands of ladders lining the parade route today. Older children scrambled between people's legs looking for dropped beads and trinkets. Beads were hard-fought-for, strenuously-jumped-for, elbowed-and-shoved-for, jewels of the Day. Later when we got home, we would wonder what to do with them.

I loved Mardi Gras! It was truly a day away from the demands of church, and short of a death in the congregation, members would not call me, since they, too, were enjoying this day of misrule. I enjoyed the costumes and the loosening of normal social rules just a bit. Most of the Carnival festivities were fun and decent, even if bizarre at times. I liked that. I did go to the French Quarter one year and found the costumes, or lack of them, over-the-top and offensive, to say nothing about some of the behavior on the street. Not much is going to change all that except not supporting it with your presence, but the Quarter was always filled with shoulder-to-shoulder people on Carnival Day.

As the day wore on, egg-salad sandwiches yielded to fried chicken, and coffee converted to sodas, beer, or wine, or hard liquor in Pops' case. We always put our trash into a plastic bag, but many people threw chicken bones and empty bottles on the ground. By the time the parades were over, the ground would be covered with garbage, and our famous St. Charles Avenue would look like an extension of the city dump.

Street washers and clean-up crews went to work immediately after the parades passed. By tomorrow morning St. Charles Avenue would be raked clean, and all the trash would be gone. Each year the city estimates the size of the Mardi Gras crowd by how many tons of garbage they collect. Unfortunately, though, New Orleans had adopted a Mardi Gras mentality all year round. "Someone else will clean it up" seemed to be the prevailing attitude every day in the Big Easy.

By three-thirty all the floats and trucks had passed our spot on the Avenue. We packed our gear, folded our blanket and chairs, and headed back to the car.

As we rounded the corner onto Prytania Street, I was startled to see Margaret, dressed in her usual black, sleeping on the hood of my car. I wondered how on earth she found my car today. There were over a million people on the streets. I also wondered how long she had been waiting for me. I dropped behind David and Pops and joined Carol, who was bringing up the rear.

"Carol, tell Margaret I'm not with you. Make up something. I'm going back to Grits' place. Send David to get me when she's gone. I just don't want to deal with Margaret today."

"Why don't you go get Grits and lock her up in a mental hospital where she belongs?" Carol retorted with irritation.

I returned to Grits' house and shared my plight. He repeated his thought that we might have to swear out a coroner's committal after all. Trouble was, Grits reminded me, the committal would only last seventy-two hours. Then she would be free to go, unless three psychiatrists declared her insane and a threat to herself or to others -- which she wasn't. You can't institutionalize someone for being a pain in the neck.

David came to get me in no time at all. "It wasn't that Margaret woman after all, Dad. It was just some woman who had too much to drink. I guess our car's hood looked softer than some others. Come on, let's go home."

+++++

Later Carol and I snuggled on the sofa in front of the television, watching the final two Carnival balls wind down. The Krewe of Rex and the Mystick Krewe of Comus were being televised, and the camera alternated between the two balls as midnight drew near.

The band soon played the Mardi Gras theme song "If Ever I Cease to Love." Rex and his Queen rose from their throne, processed to the rear of the stage, and vanished from sight. The television showed them joining the Krewe of Comus on the other half of the Municipal Auditorium. Rex and his Queen bowed to the King and Queen of Comus since Comus was the older Krewe. The King of Comus didn't bow to Rex, however, but received his bow with a nod and a wave of his scepter. That gesture made it clear that he was the real king of Mardi Gras. Comus stayed masked and remained incognito. The ultimate mystery of Carnival was preserved.

Then the television shifted seamlessly to the streets of the French Quarter where mounted policemen formed a moving barricade clearing Bourbon Street. The riders broadcasted through foghorns, "The Mardi Gras is over. Go home. The Mardi Gras is over. Go home."

Midnight arrived and the day of fantasy ended. Lent had begun, and reality would return once again.

+++++

Ash Wednesday was gray and cold.

"I'm going to St. Thomas' to get my ashes," I told Carol who was still in her robe. "Want to come with me?" I smiled and waited for her negative answer.

"Ashes are for Catholics, Will. You go ahead and get greased up. Just don't get the ashes on your shirt this year, okay?" The ashes, made by burning last year's Palm Sunday palm-leaves, really were greasy.

Carol poured herself another cup of coffee. She was actually very open and accepting about various religious practices, but ashes on the forehead was one place that she drew the line. I think it was the greasy thing.

Father Ellis had made it clear that I was welcome to worship at his church anytime, but that I shouldn't come forward to receive the Eucharist, and I respected that. I saw the bread and wine as symbols. Roman Catholics believed the bread and wine actually became the body and blood of Christ. It still baffled me how anyone could believe that. "*Hoc est corpus*," "this is my body," had become "hocus pocus" for a lot of people.

Nevertheless, when it came to the Ash Wednesday worship service with ashes on the forehead, Ellis and I saw things the same way. The service was a stark reminder of our personal mortality and the continuing presence of that great common leveler: death.

At the proper time I went forward to get my ashes. Ellis took his thumb, rubbed it in a small silver container of ashes, and marked the sign of the cross on my forehead. "Remember you are dust and to dust you shall return."

I reflected on those words as I returned to my pew. Those words were true for me, were true for Ellis, for those who fought with us, and for those who fought against us. Those words were true for those who killed my buddies, and for those I killed, and for those I sent into battle who were killed – all dust to dust and ashes to ashes. Was there really any difference between any of us? What difference did our beliefs make? Those ashes were the great common denominator, and we all had ashes on our foreheads whether we knew it or not, whether we were living dust or dead dust. I wondered where any distinctions were to be found.

+++++

"I see you've been to Ellis's place," Marie observed as I walked into the church office.

"Yep. Do I have any calls?" I paused before opening the door to my office.

"Margaret called three times this morning. She wants you to bless her. She wants to meet you in the sanctuary at eleven for a blessing on Ash Wednesday."

"Then I think I'll leave to visit the hospitals at about ten-thirty. If she comes looking for me, tell her you don't know when I'll be back." I hated to be that way, but I had learned the need to put boundaries around Margaret, or she would dominate my ministry as well as my personal time. I let out a puff of air, stared at the floor for a moment, and then looked up and opened my office door.

"My God!" I blurted in surprise. Margaret was sitting on the sofa in my office. When she saw me, she smiled broadly and her eyes lit up. How on earth did she get past Marie? I could tell by Marie's gasp that she was as surprised as I was.

"Let's go to the sanctuary so you can bless me, Reverend McKenzie." Her black, shoulder-length hair was filthy. Her rumpled black blouse and tattered black skirt made her look like she had spent the night in the street. Her teeth, in contrast, were immaculately straight and white, but her huge grin was outlined with lipstick that overshot her lips.

"Margaret, you are a believer. God loves you. That's your blessing. You don't need any other blessings." I hoped she would agree and leave, but she didn't.

"You got a blessing this morning," she insisted while pointing to my forehead with her index finger, sighting my ashes with her right eye as though her finger were a gun. "You got your blessing. I want mine."

"The ashes are just a reminder that we are starting Lent, Margaret."

"It's a cross! It's a blessing!" she shouted. Marie became nervous and stepped away from Margaret. "Give me a blessing in the sanctuary. You got your blessing in a sanctuary, didn't you? Bless me now!" She was getting very loud and boisterous. I worried that she would become violent and I'd be forced to restrain her. I didn't want to have to do that.

"Okay, Margaret. Just sit down and relax." I paused. "Marie, would you page Mr. Mallroy and also call Judy Eller from the weekday school. Ask them if they can come to my office. Then we'll all go to the sanctuary for a time of prayer with Margaret."

"Not just a time of prayer," Margaret insisted. "A blessing. blessing like you got this morning. I don't need the black stuff, greasy; but I want you to bless me. Then we will both be bless together. We'll both be blessed. You and me. Don't you see?"

She became bubbly. "You and me. Don't you see?" she repeate moving her shoulders right and left to the rhythm. Then she bounc from my office to a chair in the waiting room and sat down with clumsy flop. She crossed her legs, folded her arms across her chest, a nodded her head in affirmation as she rocked herself back and forth the straight wooden chair.

+++++

At lunch Carol followed every word, wagging her head the wh time.

"She finally left," I concluded, "but only after I raised my han and pronounced the benediction over her. She was kneeling on t chancel steps by then."

"This kind of thing is only going to get worse, Will," Carol insiste "I've seen women at North Dallas Mental Hospital who thought th were the Virgin Mary and every man they met was Joseph. The blessi isn't the issue with Margaret. She's stalking you, Will."

I fell silent, looking into my coffee cup. The word "stalk" had been used before, and I was at a loss to soften it. The furnace kick on, blowing warm air from the vents. A bird squawked at the emp feeder outside the window. "You know, I can't seem to sort it all out looked in the hall mirror when I came in, and the ashes on my forehe are already smeared and faded. They looked blurred."

"So?" Carol wasn't in a philosophical mood; she was getti irritated.

"It struck me how fuzzily we all see things. 'Now in a mirror dim the passage reads. Nothing sharp and clear. Nothing cut and dried. blurred. I'm a blurred minister. Ellis is a blurred priest. Margaret i blurred …."

"Lover?" Carol emphatically interrupted.

"Yeah. Probably in her mind. But we're all alike. With fuzzy fai and blurred vision." I paused.

Carol didn't respond, but twisted her lips into a grimace.

"And you know what? I think Margaret's right. I think I was seeking a blessing this morning. Not just a reminder, but also a blessing. I could have rubbed some ashes on my face right here in our kitchen. But no. I had to go to St. Thomas Cathedral looking for a blessing of some kind." Carol remained silent and I rambled on.

"Why is everyone always looking for a blessing?" I continued. "Some in one way, some in another. Some spiritually. Some materially. Some socially. Some politically. Everybody's looking for a blessing, and we all keep adding formulas to our lives hoping to find that blessing. At church we add beliefs, doctrines, rituals, and creeds. Why is it so damn hard for us to believe that life itself *is* the blessing?" Carol still didn't say anything.

"After I pronounced Margaret's blessing, she jumped up from her kneeling position, reached above her head and grabbed the air with her hand as she shouted, 'Got it!' Then she skipped out of the sanctuary like a happy little girl."

CAROL McKENZIE

I'm glad that "The Muddlers" are back to full strength following the Carnival madness. Everybody seemed ready to do church again. Unfortunately, Grits had the flu, so the teaching fell onto Will. He claimed that Sunday school classes were harder to do than preaching because they went on longer, and unpredictable questions were usually thrown your way. Probably true.

Lesson twenty-one in our book was on "Authority," the authority of the Bible and the authority of Jesus. I found the chapter rather dull, but, still, I was surprised when Will sounded very unsure of himself as he started the class. He claimed that the Bible was the Word of God and that God inspired the Biblical writers. He affirmed that both the Bible and Jesus could be trusted as true and reliable. For the first time I can remember, however, he didn't say that Jesus was the only way to truth. I liked that omission, as I think there are many roads to truth.

Ellen asked about the authority of church tradition. Did what the church says rank up there with Jesus and the Bible?

Only if the Bible backs it up, Will replied. Then he admitted that the church had corrected its position from time to time as more light was discovered on a subject.

Thomas asked if Jesus were the only way to God. He knows how to bait Will, and I wondered if he too had noticed Will's omission of that concept.

Will quoted the Gospel of John: "I am the way and the truth and the life. No one enters into the father but by me" (John 14:6). But he also added Jesus' words saying that in his Father's house there are many rooms.

Will sounded more open to other views than he ever had before. Well, the class loved it. Will was changing, and I certainly liked the changes I saw. Something fresh and different was going on inside of him. I had seen it happening for a while, not just this morning. I bet his ferment had to do with some Buddhist monk whose name I'd heard him call out happily during dreams. I think his change had to do with God and with Vietnam. I think it had to do with forgiveness -- who got it and who didn't.

+++++

After lunch, Will and I drove to the French Quarter. We wanted to relax for a couple hours. Walking in the Quarter could be a wonderful break in the routine. There was always plenty to look at and listen to, and it was a completely different world than the one at church.

The weather was cool and sunny -- sweater-weather with no winter wind, a perfect day to roam the Quarter. I found myself praying, yes praying, that the afternoon would be relaxing for Will.

We parked in a lot beside the Moonwalk on the Mississippi River and watched the massive ocean liners glide through the strong, turbulent water with the ease of swans on a placid lake. The power and majesty of the ships never ceased to impress us, and no two looked exactly alike, which kept our interest going.

We ambled past a lone saxophone player improvising a slow, haunting melody. A brown pelican glided just over the water's surface and gracefully flapped his long wings twice to keep his course steady.

"How about coffee and beignets?" Will suggested.

That's always a treat, so we headed to Café Du Monde and found a table. The buzz of Decatur Street filled the open-air café with urban noise, but music from a jazz band on Jackson Square could be heard over the cars and buses.

Heavy white mugs filled with the best coffee in the world arrived at our little marble table. The waiter poured the coffee and hot milk into the cup simultaneously, that made the special difference. I've tried it at home several times, and the results are worth the wait while the milk heats up. Right behind the coffee came two plates piled high with beignets -- square, puffed "donuts" amply dusted with powdered sugar.

"Remember not to inhale as you eat the beignets," I reminded Will. He choked from inhaling the powered sugar about every second time we came here. Will nodded and commented that he wished he'd changed out of his black trousers and black clerical shirt. He had removed his white clerical collar, so he certainly was a man in black, a magnet for powdered sugar. We finished our coffee at leisure and got up to roam around Jackson Square. I felt Will relax for the first time in days. He actually whistled to himself now and then, and I felt good watching him loosen up.

We walked hand in hand to the St. Louis Cathedral. A mass had ended and people trickled out the small door of the huge eighteenth-century church. As we stood at the door and tried to look in, an older man with a blue ribbon on his lapel barked at Will: "Come in or stay out; but don't stand in the doorway. You're either in the Cathedral or you're out of the Cathedral." A coughing fit prevented him from continuing. We stepped back outside, not wanting to be a problem.

A small band played on the slate plaza in front of the Cathedral. A juggler performed at the other end of the block, and crowds gathered at each spot. We lingered in front of the jazz band and squinted into the winter sun as they played their rendition of "Didn't He Ramble." The whiskey-voiced tuba player sang while the band kept the beat without aid from his deep, punctuating notes. The man was as massive as his tuba, the clarinet player as thin as his woodwind. I asked Will if he had noticed. He glanced at each and chuckled. Sure enough, the trombone player was tall and had long arms.

Three songs later we left a tip in the hat, then moseyed toward the artists who displayed their paintings along the fence surrounding the Square. A clear, sunny Sunday afternoon like this was an artist's dream. One painter was putting the finishing touches on a bayou scene; a little girl was having her portrait drawn by another artist. One artist had etched sailing ships onto thin pieces of slate. The white lines against gray slate made striking images.

A mime covered with silver paint caught our attention. He held perfectly still until someone passed him. Then, behind their back, he mimicked their head motion or the way they walked. He froze again just before they turned back to see what people were laughing at.

As we walked up St. Ann's Street, Will stopped to watch a man trying to lock his bicycle to the fence with a chain. He couldn't seem to get the lock to work and threw the chain back into his bike's basket. I remembered this man from months ago -- the one who danced to music no one else heard. Will had shaken his head at the man when he saw him before, so I wondered what interested him now. I found the performer weird.

The man took off his hat and placed it on the slate sidewalk in front of him. He pulled a dollar from his pocket, tossing it into the hat. He hooked an iPod to his belt and put tiny earphones into his ears. His belt was far too long, leaving a foot-long tongue hanging down from his waist. He had on a black T-shirt, and his black pants were too long, but he bent over and rolled them halfway up his calf. His red socks contrasted brightly with his all-black outfit, calling attention to his feet.

Will froze in place and watched him prepare for his act, but the performer paid no attention to him. I stood there watching them both. The street performer reached into his bike basket again and pulled out a small plastic bag filled with rice, then scattered a handful on the slate at his feet. He checked the little earphones, shook his hands by his side to limber them up, pushed a button on the player, and paused.

Will, too, shook his hands by his sides. He arched his back slightly and stood at attention. Something about this made me nervous, so I pulled on his sleeve to leave, but he didn't budge.

"Come on, Will. Let's go," I urged, but he didn't respond. I started getting worried. Somehow this wasn't a normal scene. Something was happening to Will. I wasn't sure what, but I didn't like it. I felt distance from him, like he was almost in another world.

The performer's face snapped into a big smile as though someone had plugged him in. He raised his eyebrows, tilted his head slightly to the right, and started to sway back and forth. He raised and lowered his eyebrows. He bobbed his head from side to side and his smile broadened. He started dancing to whatever music he heard on his iPod.

Will started to smile too. He, too, started to rock his head rhythmically from side to side.

"Will, let's keep walking. Come on." I tried to divert him, to get his attention away from this ridiculous character, but it wasn't working. I finally stood directly in front of Will, looked him in the eyes, and implored him, "Will, we need to go now. This guy gives me the creeps."

Will raised his left arm and with a gentle, slow, yet deliberately strong and firm motion pushed me to the side with the back of his hand. My feet stuttered on the slate, and I scrambled to maintain my balance.

Then Will joined in the dance. He stepped to the right, and then slid to the left; he extended his arms and turned completely around. His smile became broad and toothy; his head continued to sway to and fro. He pointed his arms skyward to the left, then he pointed his arms to the ground on his right. Will was laughing now. He laughed loudly. Soon he laughed uncontrollably.

The street musician kept dancing but threw irritated glances at Will. The man started getting pissed.

"Don't you see, Carol? Don't you get it?" Will asked me between laughs. He doubled over for a moment he laughed so hard. But he stood back up, as though he had been remiss, and continued dancing. "Isn't this all absurd?" he asked as he danced in a complete circle. I was lost and was getting disturbed by Will's behavior.

The band on the corner started playing again. The tuba player sang "Eleanor Rigby." Will wasn't dancing to that song. He danced to another, unknown tune, a tune not even the street performer heard.

The street musician stopped and stood still. He grabbed his bag of rice, slung a handful at Will's feet, and then threw the bag back into his basket. The rice caused Will to slip at first, but he kept dancing and crushed the grains on the slate. Then the shuffling sound of old fashioned soft-shoe could be heard coming from Will's feet.

The musician picked up his hat, pulled his iPod off his belt, and put them in the basket. He grabbed his bike and walked away toward the River, turning intermittently as he left to scowl at Will.

Will looked at me as he continued dancing alone. "We dance to music only we can hear." He looked at me as though waiting for me to affirm what he had said, but he quickly continued. "Reverend McKenzie does," he blurted out between laughter and soft-shoe. "The church does. Christianity does. We dance to our own private music. It's crazy." He leaned to the left and turned in a circle. I stood quietly to the side.

The loud, deep gong of the Cathedral bell tolled throughout the Square. I glanced in that direction and saw a hearse parked in front. People in black were going in and out of the church's door. I thought again of what that old man at the door had said about being either in or out of the cathedral. Then my attention flashed back to Will.

I wanted Will to stop, to leave, to walk away with me; but I didn't seem to be getting anywhere. He kept dancing. I felt helpless ... and embarrassed ... and a bit scared.

"All this time we've been dancing to music no one else can hear, and we call it the only true tune." He laughed some more. "But many, many other people are dancing too."

Will was still dancing without music, without the street musician. He was still laughing. Several people paused to look at him, and Will turned to them. "Can't you hear? Come dance to the music. Come." He laughed some more.

Then he danced over to me and picked me up in his arms.

"Will!" was all I could say in my surprise.

I held my breath as he twirled me in a circle then swayed us back and forth. I wrapped my arms around him to hold on.

He set me gently back on my feet and let me go. "I'm beginning to see things more clearly now, Carol. It's a wonderful feeling."

I could feel his excitement and his energy. Maybe there was nothing to worry about after all. He reached down and held my hand. "Come on; let's go home. I want to get out of this black outfit."

He got no argument from me.

WILL McKENZIE

The appointment I had made with Grits was at noon. I came early and brought my laptop to catch up with James. His last e-mail disturbed me a lot. He had made several comments about how freely cocaine floated among the friends he had made in Paris, and I feared he might slide back into the addiction he brought back from Vietnam. My email expressed my fears, and hopes, for him, knowing full well his life was in his own hands. I erased a few phrases, figured I'd said enough, then feared I'd said too much – and finally paused, sat back in my chair and looked out the window.

A warm sun shone through the picture window, brightly lighting the room. The ancient live oak in the garden outside stood massive and majestic, with gracefully bent limbs. It stood beside a large lagoon where a great blue heron fished for his lunch. Spanish moss hung over the water from the oak. I could see a snowy egret on the other side of the lagoon. The scene was very pleasant, even if I was looking at it from inside the mental hospital where Grits worked.

I sat quietly in a wicker armchair staring at the great blue heron. The room was too warm for my flannel shirt and corduroy pants. I had dressed for the day, and it was cold outside. A woman walking beside the water was bundled in a bright yellow sweater and matching knit hat. She walked with her hands in her pockets, her elbows drawn tightly to her side, and her shoulders raised about her neck. She needed my heavy clothes.

I resumed my email, telling James about my epiphany in Jackson Square with the music and my dancing. *"I was in my own private world* for a while, I guess. Carol didn't seem to understand at first what I laughed at and mimicked with my dance. That sidewalk performer portrayed so accurately what I've felt lately. I probably got more carried away than I should have, but I didn't really care. Carol doesn't seem to hold the incident against me. She's gotten over her embarrassment and her fears, but she's also real pleased I've finally gotten into therapy."

I paused and wiped my brow with the palm of my hand, as I scooted my chair out of the sun.

"It still strikes me as symbolic, ironic, and even funny. For years now I've talked and taught and preached about Jesus. Jesus, the only way. I thought I was a true believer talking about true faith. The trouble is, only those who buy into it can make any sense out of it. Only those on the inside think they hear the music. The church has always tried to claim a corner on God and love and forgiveness. Come into the cathedral and you'll be forgiven and can dance. Stay out, and, well, that's just too bad. You're either in or out of the cathedral. Well, you know what? There are a lot of people outside the cathedral who are dancing too." I paused to watch as the heron caught a fish and lifted his beak to swallow it whole.

"It seems strange to be meeting Grits here in the mental hospital where I have visited people many times before. I offered hope and support to them until they could get right on the inside. Once they got right on the inside, they could be released to go back to the outside. That's ironic, isn't it? But it's true."

"Grits recommended that I attend a group as well as being in individual therapy. The group meets twice a week at twelve thirty. I usually take a lunch break then anyway, so nobody would miss me at church. Besides, I've been in all kinds of groups before. I've even led several groups, so I really don't mind if somebody knows I'm participating in one. Still, the fewer who know, the better. You know how the church can be." I shook my head at how provincial some church people were -- those who sneaked into their therapist's office – or drove across town to buy their booze.

"You know, James, I've made a great discovery in the middle of all of this. I finally realized things aren't true because Jesus said them. Rather, Jesus said things because they are true. That's a very important distinction; it opens things up. It keeps the music from being private. That's the important part.

"I have also come to realize that Jesus tells us we are forgiven because forgiveness is something that's always available. Forgiveness is a reality that's always there. Jesus simply pointed to it. He didn't create forgiveness, earn it for us, or dish it out like ice cream. Jesus simply tells people they are forgiven. Not, 'I've got some forgiveness I'll give you,' but 'Your sins are forgiven' -- a simple declaration of fact. There's a big difference in that distinction too. Forgiveness is part of life. It can be really hard to accept forgiveness, and I'm still struggling, but it's always there for all of us, even me.

"Well, time for me to go down the hall to Grits' office for my first appointment. Wish me luck, Bro."

+++++

Two weeks later I again joined others for group therapy in the large room that opened onto an inside atrium at the hospital. I was already getting tired of coming to these groups. They were messing with my schedule too much, but Grits asked me to hang in there a little longer, so I agreed.

Eight or nine chairs formed a circle. All group settings everywhere must look alike. I sighed as I sat down. Jeff wore a green blazer today and looked particularly young. Perhaps his light yellow tie added to that feeling. Somehow "Jeff" didn't strike me as a very professional name for a psychiatrist, but then, neither did "Grits." Jeff had actually proven himself to me during the previous sessions. He was a very sensitive listener and showed a great sense of timing in the remarks he made, or refrained from making.

All the regulars arrived on time, plus one new person. We went around the circle introducing ourselves to her. Everybody used only a first name, just like all of David's friends do. "I'm Will," I smiled at her. Not a very profound name for a minister either, I thought.

Jeff started the session by asking Ernie if he had anything to add to what he talked about on Friday ... I guess all group sessions must start alike too. Ernie affirmed that he was ready to let go of his beef with his boss and that he didn't want to spend any more energy on him. We affirmed Ernie with compliments and some clapping. Ernie was an outpatient member of the group. I still hadn't figured out who was an inpatient and who was an outpatient. Who was in and who was out of this cathedral? It didn't seem to matter.

Jeff asked if anyone had a pressing concern. When no one responded, he looked at me with warm and accepting eyes. In a soothing voice he asked me if I wanted to share anything today. I shrugged my shoulders.

Then I totally surprised myself. I started talking about the ears. The ears. I hadn't thought about the ears in a long time. Before I knew it, I was well into the story.

Shame filled me as I saw myself cut off an ear of a dead Vietnamese. That first time was innocent enough -- a convenient way to verify the body count after a battle. It was easier than lugging the body across the field. But then things changed and I started keeping ears like some of the other guys were doing. Soon the ears became a collection.

The eight-inch knife I kept strapped to my hip was sharp as a razor. Whenever I had free time, I'd hone it even sharper. Keeping that knife sharp had become a habit, like others would reach for a cigarette and light up. The first several ears I severed were awkward, but it soon became a quick and smooth action, a lot like filleting a fish. If the body had been dead a while, there was almost no blood flow, but if the killing was recent, I would sling the ear several times, removing any remaining blood. Soon they were pale and gristly.

I would punch a hole in the ear and string it onto a leather shoelace. The collection hung from my belt loop, and after a short time the ears would become firm. I was told that dogs really like to chew on these ears, and I even saw a mutt rip one off a buddy's belt and run away with it.

After a while I had so many ears dangling from my side they were getting in my way. One cold afternoon, while resting in a dry irrigation ditch, a natural foxhole, I counted up my major skirmishes and pruned the number of ears to one per mission. With a backhand flip I threw the excess ears into the tall weeds nearby. I shuddered as I recalled my reluctance to throw them away. Like notches on a cowboy's gun or scalps on an Indian's jacket, the ears gave me a perverted since of pride. Pride, mind you. Besides, those ears carried a magical sense of protection. I figured as long as I carried the ears, I was in charge of the killing and was somehow immune from that possibility myself. Crazy. But everything was crazy then.

A thin young woman in our group spoke up, saying how repulsive she found this whole story. She asked Jeff if we couldn't change the subject. Jeff was very gentle with her but firmly supported me telling my story. The woman physically turned her body away from me and stared at the floor. I could sense that Jeff was afraid I would back off as a result of her comment. However, with his encouragement, I went on.

I told how I stashed the ears in a zipped pocket when we weren't in the field, but dangled them visibly on my belt when in a combat zone. Once at base camp a chaplain discovered ears on Ralph's belt, read him the riot act, and made him toss them into the latrine. I winced when I saw Ralph do that. Most of us had a collection. Ralph just forgot to stash his out of sight, that's all.

Then one morning after a fierce nocturnal battle, we set out to recover the bodies of two men we'd lost, Roger Boudreaux and Henry Ivess. Roger was from New Iberia, Louisiana, part of the wonderful, carefree Cajun culture. I helped haul his body back to the staging area where the dust-off would land. Roger's body was exceptionally clean except for the blood on his shirt. He had bathed in a stream before the sun went down, washing this shirt and pants too. When the fighting started again, a single shot through his chest was all there was. Just like that. Dead.

Then I led the way over to where Henry Ivess' body lay. His right leg was gone from the knee down, and he was covered in blood and dirt. He lay there face-down. Drew and I turned him on his back, and I recoiled in shock.

"God damn! Who did this? What son-of-a-bitch did this to Henry?"

Henry's left ear had been cut off.

"Who knows anything about this? Did anyone see anything? Speak up!"

"Let it go, Lieutenant," I heard Sergeant say, but by then I had crumbled next to Henry's body, crying like a baby.

I grabbed the chain of ears on my belt and with a violent yank of force ripped it free from my belt loop and tossed it away from me, as far as I could.

"Fucking Charlie," was all I could say through my tears. "Fucking Charlie."

I chilled at the atrocity the ears represented. I came to see each ear as a person. A real person. Cutting off ears now seemed far worse than taking insignia off dead Nazi soldiers or a Lugar from a limp German hand. I now saw my ear collection as a desecration of the dead, a mocking of life, the reduction of a human being to a few ounces of gristle.

I looked at Jeff. I had never talked about this before, and the group remained silent. Most people were looking at their feet. One man was looking at me with tears in his eyes. I glanced quickly around the room and began to wonder if I could be arrested for committing an atrocity. Could I be tried as a war criminal? What was the statute of limitations for severing ears off dead men, for desecrating a corpse? As long as you've got a mind to remember it, was my guess.

The group was supposed to be confidential, but who knew what the real rules were? I waited to see if someone would say something, but everyone remained silent.

I felt drained, ashamed, and nervously distrustful, and I waited for the silence to be broken. Jeff, who was looking at me in a supportive, non-judgmental manner, ventured a simple, "That took a lot of courage, Will. Thank you for sharing it with us."

"You see, that's the kind of person I am." I paused. "Things like that are why it's been so hard for me to accept forgiveness, even though I'm a minister. Yes, would you believe that? I'm a minister." Now I knew I had exposed too much, for sure.

Jeff brought the session to a close, and I don't remember much of what happened next, except that he thanked me again for sharing. So did several other people.

I remain seated, and Jeff paused in front of me on his way out. "Will, I hope you can let go of some of that guilt now. You're on your way," he affirmed while putting his hand on my shoulder. He was almost young enough to be my son.

Shown forgiveness by a son. That thought rolled around in my head. It was Biblical.

An older man, probably in his seventies, walked past me on his way toward the door. He paused and stared down at me. Then he spat in my face.

+++++

"I'm beginning to feel more at one with creation," I began. Grits and I were meeting for a personal therapy session in his uptown office. "What I mean by that Native-American sounding statement is I know I'm filled with good and bad just like the world is, just like everyone else is, just like creation is ... and it's all right to be that way. At one with creation, not struggling to be different from it or better than it. That's a wonderful, freeing feeling. Is that what forgiveness is all about?"

"That's part of it, I'm sure," Grits commented.

"We usually feel like we have to earn forgiveness, which we just can't do," I ventured to Grits. "Or, in contrast, we think someone else has to earn it for us and give it to us ... like Jesus. But forgiveness is a free gift from God." I paused and checked out Grits' reactions, much in the same way I had checked out the group after my narrative about the ears. Then I realized, with a tinge of embarrassment, that I didn't need Grit's permission to feel the way I did.

"If we're dependent on someone else for forgiveness, even Jesus, then we're not taking full responsibility for our own actions. Maybe responsibility is what we'd like to avoid. As strange as it sounds, if we look to Jesus for forgiveness, we don't have to accept full responsibility for ourselves because Jesus is doing that for us -- but we also can't fully embrace the freedom forgiveness brings either."

I knew exactly what I was trying to say, but my ideas and feelings seemed to get tangled up in my words. Grits still listened quietly without judgment.

"When we accept both the bad and the good within us and realize there's still forgiveness for us, then we can also accept other people without provisional conditions. That's what Jesus did. He accepted Jews and Gentiles and Greeks and God knows who else. He told a tax collector, a prostitute, and a woman caught in adultery they were forgiven -- so why do we have trouble believing the same forgiveness is available to people of other faiths, or with other reasons for guilt? " Grits listened carefully to my monologue yet seemed quite relaxed and calm. He let me take the lead as usual.

"The living must forgive themselves ... and each other. That can happen only if forgiveness is freely given to everybody. Absolutely everyone. As long as there is one human from whom we withhold forgiveness, then there's not sufficient grace in us to forgive ourselves. It takes total grace given to receive grace totally." I paused for a moment of reflection, then continued. "If there's forgiveness for me, ears and all, then there's also forgiveness for my sending men into the slaughter, and for my Buddhist friends, and for those who killed my buddies, and for the murderer Alice Hendricks, and for sad, sick Peter Bernard."

I gasped audibly, realizing Grits knew nothing about the problems Peter had. I had badly over-spoken. I anxiously looked at Grits. "I'm sorry about using a name. Really." I was mortified.

"It happens. You can continue," was all Grits said. I looked intently at him, but he remained calm and showed no surprise. Did he know about Peter? Or maybe he assumed we all have our problems. At least I didn't say what Peter's difficulties were.

"I guess I'm starting to sound like a preacher, huh, Grits?" I laughed.

Grits smiled broadly. "My kind of preacher, Will. But probably not everybody's."

What did he mean by that, I thought. A long silence followed. "Does an appointment for the same time next week work on your schedule?" I asked. He nodded. "Good. Let's count on it. By the way, those group sessions are getting repetitive and stagnant. I'd like to drop that soon. What do you think?"

"That'd probably be all right. Jeff reported that you'd resolved some important issues and made some substantial progress."

His comment took me by surprise. I didn't know they had consulted each other. It was all right, I guess, even expected, now that I thought about it.

"You're doing fine, really," Grits said. "I wish everyone could have a road to Damascus experience like you had that Sunday afternoon in the French Quarter. You're sounding a lot less rigid and less legalistic – and a lot more human."

+++++

Alice was missing her children very much when I visited her in jail today. The authorities had arranged for her to spend an hour with them recently, and that only whetted her appetite for a full return to normality. I don't know what they can do about that. The whole thing was such a compounded mess.

Alice was getting visibly depressed, low on energy, and showing little interest in much of anything except her children. She was eager for her trial to get underway, and I could certainly empathize with that. She was standing by her plea of innocent by reason of temporary insanity. Surely the court docket would move in her direction soon.

I left my visit with her on a pending, somewhat unsatisfied note, but without any sense of how the visit could have been different. Ministry is like that sometimes.

+++++

The week between appointments with Grits passed quickly. I settled into the comfortable chair in his office. "I had the most interesting dream the other night. Do you do dreams? I told Carol about this dream, and she thought it might mean something."

"Tell me about it," Grits responded. "Dreams can often help us put our finger on issues that are going on inside of us." I watched Grits settle back into his 'listening' mode.

"Well, I was back in the service, and I was the captain of a big battleship, one of those huge World War II kinds, not one of those small boats we took up the rivers of Vietnam. Anyway, I was the captain. I was barking orders and people were hopping, and we were in the midst of a battle of some sort. I kept assessing the firepower and checking the ammunition reserves. Whatever we were after, we were fighting for all we were worth, and we were winning. All I know is I was in charge. The battle was in my hands. I can see and hear those big guns shooting even now.

"Then our ship entered a refreshing pocket of air, well …yeah, a pocket of air. You couldn't really see it, but you knew you were in it. Everyone breathed easily, and I did too. All the guns went silent, the smoke cleared, and the sea went calm. The day became sunny, bright, and peaceful.

"Then I realized I was no longer on a battleship, and I was no longer a military captain. A transformation had occurred. The ship had turned into the Love Boat. Remember that program on television?

Like that. I was still the captain, but everyone was happy, music was playing, and people were dining and dancing.

"That's all I remember of my dream, but it was very vivid. What do you make of it, Grits?" I paused, waiting for his answer.

"Sounds like some more changes are going on in you," Grits commented. He gave me time to think about that and then continued. "Have you always battled your way through life, Will?"

"Well …yeah … I guess I have. I had to. My folks argued all the time. Mom was an alcoholic. She dropped out of our life most of the time, and she finally left. Dad did the best he could, but growing up was tough.

"Still, I made my way to the top of everything I did. I was the star forward on our high school basketball team. I ran track too, hundred-yard dash. My senior year I was voted the most likely to succeed." Grits nodded with interest.

"College was more of the same. I hammered out straight A's in civil engineering, made the wrestling team, and helped organize a rugby team, the school's first. Top gun. That was me." My thoughts and feelings were flowing, so I kept talking.

"The Marines were certainly a battleship, and Nam was no picnic. Then came seminary. I pushed my way to the top there too. When I graduated, I got the biggest and best church assignment in the class. Look at me now. I'm at the helm of a large, prestigious church.

"Wow. I just remembered I've referred to the church as a battleship several times in the past. I sure like the Love Boat idea better." I stopped talking, remembering the image from my dream.

"Maybe you're moving beyond the battleground," I heard Grits say.

"What do you make of the fresh air I sailed into? That pocket of air was refreshing and freeing. I really liked that part of the dream. It wasn't a fog or a mist. There was something wonderful about that fresh air. Could it represent forgiveness?"

"Well, you just suggested love or forgiveness, and it was your dream, so that's probably on target," Grits affirmed. "Makes sense to me."

+++++

After Saturday breakfast I asked Carol if she would be willing to take a ferry ride with me.

"Usually if you want to ride the ferry you just say, "let's go ride the ferry." What's this "would I be willing to" business? What's up?" Carol doesn't miss much.

"I've got some unfinished business to tend to," I told her. "Something important to me. I'll tell you all about it when we get on the ferry. Don't worry; I won't try to walk on the water."

"Okay," came her reply. "It's a sunny day, so I'll go along with your little mystery."

We cleaned up the kitchen and started the dishwasher. It was Saturday and no telling how late David would sleep. Carol scribbled a note letting him know where we were; she posted it on the refrigerator door, our family bulletin board. We grabbed our heavy jackets. It could get cold on the Mississippi this time of year.

As I opened the back door, I gasped in surprise. Margaret was sitting on our back steps, and I nearly tripped over her. She remained seated and silent. "Hello Margaret." I said in a loud enough voice so Carol could hear me. "It's time for you to go home now, Margaret. Okay?" I said rather forcefully.

Margaret pulled her coat tightly around her, grumbled, and stomped off toward her old Chevy. I saw Carol watching from the kitchen window. Margaret soon drove off, and Carol joined me at the back door.

"This has got to stop," Carol asserted with renewed irritation.

"I wish I knew how." I was genuinely puzzled. "She's a total nuisance, and she's invading our privacy more and more. I agree it's got to stop, but how do you make that happen?"

"One of these days she'll catch you alone. I just hope she doesn't scream rape."

"You and me both," I earnestly agreed. "I started chronicling these incidents about a month ago. At least the Session will know what I … what we … have been up against. Marie is typing my log, and she's appalled. I've put the issue on the agenda for the next Session meeting. I'm going to share my log with them."

"Next week, isn't it?" I knew Carol had run out of patience and wanted something to be done.

I nodded, and we got in the car.

+++++

It was bitter cold as we drove onto the Canal Street Ferry. We got out of the car and walked to the rail at the water's edge. A fine mist filled the air, and a frigid wind went right through layer upon layer of our clothing. Carol and I leaned against the railing, and the River was only a few feet below us. The River was choppy, its currents highlighted with dangerous swirls discoloring the already muddy water as though someone had taken a giant spoon and stirred in just those places. We had often spent time riding the ferry, watching the River's activity, being hypnotized by the swirling water, letting the cobwebs clear from our minds. A ferry ride could be powerful therapy.

We could see barges sliding upstream pushed by tugboats. A Coast Guard cutter patrolled the wharf as though it were looking for something important. Sea gulls flew overhead, randomly landing in the turbulent, muddy water. The flag atop the ferry popped steadily in the wind.

After a few minutes of silence, I reached in my pocket and pulled out my key ring. "This is what the ride is all about," I told Carol. Without further explanation, I removed the keys from the ring, one by one, and handed them to Carol. She remained silent and was cooperative.

I held the empty ring to my eye, looking through it at the River as though it were a monocle. Then with a quick, backhand flip of my wrist, I flung the ring into the River. As soon as the ring touched the water, it disappeared. All evidence of its existence instantly disappeared.

I stared at the water as though I could see the place where the ring went in; but that place had vanished. Then I turned toward Carol. "That ring pulled the pin from the first grenade I tossed in Vietnam." I looked again at the water. "I don't think I ever told you that, have I?"

"No. You didn't." Carol affirmed, waiting for me to say more, but I fell silent for a while, and she let me.

I tried to focus on a middle distance on the water, but I found it impossible even to imagine where the key ring entered the River. There was never even a splash, at least nothing that could be seen. The ring simply became a part of the great body of water we call the Mississippi. Like alchemy, the ring may have turned liquid in the brown, churning, turbulent water flowing with unconscionable power and speed from somewhere preceding us to somewhere beyond our vision.

I couldn't imagine the ring falling to the mucky bottom two hundred feet down to stick there and remain stuck for eternity. Given the tremendous currents and the depth, the ring would probably never hit the bottom. Yet I also had trouble imagining it being carried, below the surface but above the bottom, for miles and miles until it dropped off the edge of the continental shelf into the Gulf of Mexico. What indeed might be happening to it?

A massive tree caught my attention. Stripped of its branches and bobbing above the surface, the tree looked like a huge telephone pole, only much bigger and maybe twice as long. It looked like it might breach the surface, but instead it suddenly submerged again, vanishing without a trace. I waited and watched, prepared to see the tree resurface like a playful dolphin or a cork on a fishing line. It never did. The muddy Mississippi had absorbed and incorporated the huge, defoliated tree as easily as it had swallowed and absorbed the little ring that once activated an instrument of death.

Carol and I continued to gaze at the vast expanse of powerful water. I was once again impressed with its mystery. The River covered a multitude of sins – like a huge, continuing confessional. The River didn't just wash sins away; it eradicated them by incorporating them into itself. Ongoing at-one-ment in constant action. Atonement.

The River represented one great act of absolution, leveling all things good and evil. No questions asked. No judgments made. No comparisons. No sifting of the evidence. No second thoughts or second guesses. The River took what it was offered and blended everything into one harmonious whole. Killer and killed could both be absorbed. Murderer and murdered equally engulfed. The victim had no need to forgive the perpetrator, and the perpetrator had no need to ask for forgiveness. Both were mingled in a common wash. A natural baptism. Alice and Stan; Viet Cong and Marines; Buddhist priests and Hindu peasants, and three nameless girls who became human skewers for a cause they didn't understand by people who didn't understand they were human – all of it … all of it … could be washed into Nirvana by the River. The grenades thrown, those who threw them, those upon whom they were thrown, and those who heard about them scores of years later are all absorbed like that firing ring that simply disappeared into a liquid oblivion. Christians and Jews and Muslims and Buddhists and Hindus all given equal status by the River. An instrument of eternity dwarfing our cycle of life with no recognizable entry point and no discernable terminus.

I shook myself, blinked, and became aware Carol was looking at me and waiting for me to rejoin her on this loudly vibrating ferry. I had been in a reverie.

"I don't need that ring anymore. Let the River have it and wash away its meaning in my life."

"Amen," was all Carol mustered. But that was sufficient.

The ferry bumped against the dock. Seeking hot coffee we left the River and drove toward a neon sign that flashed blue: "Laissez Les Bon Temps Rouler."

The café looked warm inside.

CAROL McKENZIE

Katie Morrison had choked on a piece of meat and died in the French Inn Restaurant. The sanctuary was packed for the funeral to overflowing in support of her husband and three small children. Will conducted a very meaningful service. I was surprised, however, when only a handful of people went to the cemetery for the burial.

A fine mist fell as we gathered at the gravesite. The casket had been placed in front of the marble door to the old family tomb. Marvin and his children stood facing the casket.

The oldest child, in second grade, was asking Marvin hard, painful questions. "Why is Mommy in that box? Why don't we let Mommy out of that box? Can she breathe in there?" Marvin answered as best he could, saying their mother had gone to be with God and we wouldn't see her anymore. "Why won't she come back to us?" I painfully realized Marvin had probably answered the same questions many times by now. The younger two, a boy and a girl, were very quiet. I choked up and tried to hold back my tears. Will, I noticed, forced back tears too.

The graveside service was a short liturgy, thank goodness. Then one by one the small gathering of friends and relatives spoke to Marvin and left. Katie's parents took the children home with them. Soon only Marvin and Will and I stood in the stinging mist, while the grave attendants stood impatiently to one side.

Marvin stared at the casket. He took several deep breaths, letting them out with long, heavy puffs. Stepping closer to the casket, he doubled his hands into fists and pounded ferociously on the coffin. He beat the casket unmercifully, and it resounded like a dampened drum.

"Damn you for leaving me, Katie," Marvin blurted out. "Damn you for dying." He started to shake with sobs, and Will put his arm around Marvin's shoulders.

I was crying openly now. I also realized that Marvin's outburst had embarrassed me. Then I was embarrassed that I was embarrassed. The whole scene left me paralyzed and deeply sad.

Will, however, calmly assured him, "It's all right to be mad at her for dying, Marvin. She's abandoned you and the kids." I thought about Will's words and agreed.

Little by little Marvin regained his composure. After a moment of silence, he turned to Will. "Katie never accepted Christ as her Savior, Will. What will happen to her? Is she saved?" Anxiety filled his eyes, and he looked desperate. I held my breath and looked at Will.

"Marvin, when God gives life, God gives it for all eternity. Katie is with God."

Will's broad, inclusive answer comforted me; I hoped it comforted Marvin. Will's arm stayed around Marvin's shoulder as they both focused on the casket.

"Well, where's that God now?" Marvin asked with numbed affect.

"Right here within us and among us, Marvin. We have to look within ourselves and within each other," Will answered.

Marvin was silent. He walked over to a spray of flowers, plucked a rose, and placed it on Katie's casket.

In silence, we quietly returned to the car as the mist turned into a steady downpour.

PETER BERNARD

"Can you get Will to move quickly through this meeting tonight?" Ben Farland asked me, half joking, half not, as he walked in the room for the Session meeting.

It's a short agenda, Ben," I responded. "If Will doesn't get carried away about something, we should be out of here within an hour." I was tired and ready to get this over with and go home.

The Elders were gathering quickly now, and I made sure my papers were in order. I considered myself to be a good Clerk of Session, but after ten years I was getting tired of the job. I wanted someone else to take over. I had docketed my request as an item under new business. Ten years tonight; it's a good time to bow out.

Besides, I was also increasingly nervous and scared. I constantly feared I was going to get caught entering or leaving one of those adult clubs. I also worried that the police might raid the place while I was there.

Why can't I stop going to those places? I've prayed and prayed about it, but I'm still driven by those passions. The trouble is, I enjoy the adult stores and clubs a lot. They are exciting and pleasurable, but I know going there is wrong. I've asked for forgiveness over and over again, but I keep going back as though some force beyond my control makes me.

If Betty ever found out, that would be the end of our marriage; I'm sure of that. She would have zero tolerance for that kind of thing. If I were ever spotted, I could never again hold my head up in this church, and New Orleans can be a very small town at times. What on earth will become of me?

"Good evening Peter," I heard Will say as he pulled up a chair beside me. "How 'bout the Green Wave last night? Tulane was pretty spectacular, huh?"

"Hello Will. Yeah, they sure were hot," I managed to answer, much more preoccupied with my own feelings.

I looked at the Elders gathered in front of me, wondering if any of them had seen me and not said anything. No one showed any unusual expression. All the Elders settled into their seats and got that familiar, dull stare on their faces as they read the agenda.

Will called the meeting to order. His opening devotional was short and to the point. It was about God's inclusive love. His brevity surprised and delighted me. His devotionals usually had to do with the so-called plan of salvation. That always baffled me -- the plan of salvation, as though it came out of an engineering book. I guess it doesn't turn me on because I don't feel certain about things myself. I wish I could find inspiration from Will, but thus far I can't.

Will read in the Bible where Jesus taught that in his Father's house there were many rooms and he went to prepare a place for us. Will emphasized there was room for everyone in God's house. I really wondered if there was still a room for me.

When the business of the evening got started, we moved through the agenda rapidly. The meeting might indeed be over in an hour. We soon came to new business, and I presented my request to be replaced as Clerk. I explained I had served for ten years, and the office needed to be passed on to somebody else. I asked the Elders to nominate another person to take my place.

Hal Johnson nominated me for reelection anyway. About half the room seconded the motion. Maurice called for the vote. It was unanimous except for my "nay," and Will declared me re-elected. They all smiled, pleased with themselves.

I started sweating and felt a knot tighten in my stomach. I managed to thank everyone for his or her kindness but insisted once again that I couldn't serve another term.

"You know you do a great job, Peter," Marcus asserted.

"You're our man," Josh insisted.

"Come on, Peter. You do it so well," Allison added.

"You're the rock, Peter. You can't say no," Maurice asserted.

"You're our rock, Peter!" several people chimed in.

Mary Standard called for adjournment.

"All in favor of adjourning please stand for the closing prayer," Will concluded. The shuffle of chairs made noise on the hardwood floor.

After the prayer, Will turned to me and smiled. "I guess they've spoken, Peter. You're the kind of rock the church is built on, do you realize that? If nothing else, the position will keep you humble." Will laughed and patted me on the shoulder.

You're damn right about that, Will. If only you knew. If only you knew.

WILL McKENZIE

"You'll never believe what happened this afternoon," I commented to Carol as I poured coke into a frosted glass from the freezer.

"Marie used a curse word?" Carol ventured with a smile.

"Never! But listen to this. A couple came to me for counseling; I'll call them Sally and Joe Jones. Sally looked down their pew on Sunday and saw John and Susie Brown. She told her husband she really wished their relationship could be like John and Susie's – happy, loving, and devoted to each other."

"Well, earlier this week John and Susie had been to see me. They had marriage troubles too. Susie said she wished her marriage could be as solid as the marriage of Sally and Joe Jones who sat on the same pew with them Sunday. Somehow I managed to keep a straight face at the irony. Each couple wanted what they projected on the other couple."

"I'll be darned," Carol commented through a broad grin. "They wanted to be like all those other perfect church-people, right?"

"Right. Something similar happened at the Session meeting Sunday night, but I can't go into that one. Isn't it amazing how we look at another person and project whatever we want onto him or her? At church, the projection seems to be piety, or joy, or faith. And of course everyone else has been forgiven."

+++++

When I went to the office the next morning, Marie told me of three appointments she had booked for me today and one for tomorrow.

"Mary Beth Stewart will come tomorrow," Marie indicated. "I worked her in at ten-thirty. You should be back from the Women's Shelter meeting by then. She works at Tulane Law School and can be free then. She's listed on our roll, joined when she was thirteen, but I don't place her."

"Oh yes. Mary Beth is being nominated as an Elder next month. She keeps a pretty low profile, but she's been a part of our singles group for a long time. She was president of that class a couple of years ago. Sits toward the back during worship and leaves during the last hymn. Never lingers. Actually, I haven't seen her since Mardi Gras when she wore a huge, ghastly pumpkin outfit. She's very pregnant." Marie frowned in puzzlement, and I guessed what she was thinking.

I went into my office, paused at my window and looked out at the overcast sky. A lone starling flew out of a narrow niche in the brick wall of the memorial garden and joined scores more feeding on the lawn.

+++++

Today's our anniversary, so Carol and I headed to the French Quarter for dinner. Galatoire's is our favorite restaurant in a city of fabulous restaurants. Serving superlative French Creole cuisine to the city's socially elite, Galatoire's accepts no reservations. Seating is strictly "first come, first served." Until just a few years ago, they didn't accepted credit cards. For its first ninety years, only cash was accepted. However, if you were an insider, you knew you could put your business card on top of the check, and they would mail a bill to your office for an extra tip.

Located on infamous Bourbon Street, the restaurant is an enigmatic contradiction to the honky-tonks, strip joints, and t-shirt shops that line this touristy street in the Quarter. Once inside, however, you entered a large room where white tablecloths, cane-bottom chairs, and fine silverware awaited the diner. The walls were lined with dozens of individual mirrors, and antique lighting fixtures hung in between. Chandeliers and old-fashioned ceiling fans filled the ceiling, creating a warm and inviting atmosphere. The mood was always festive and a bit raucous. It was casually taken for granted that you were one of the elite, even if you were in town from some other place, like Paris, or a small town in southern Mississippi.

As soon as we were seated, a waiter dressed in a tuxedo brought a baguette of hot French bread. Another waiter brought butter and a third brought a carafe of water. Yet another waiter brought the wine we had just ordered. The menu read like a catalogue of ageless New Orleans favorites: shrimp remoulade, oysters Rockefeller, Creole gumbo, crabmeat Maison, shrimp Clemenceau, pompano with sautéed crabmeat meuniere, banana bread pudding, crème brulée.

Carol and I split a Godchaux salad, which was topped with generous handfuls of lump white crabmeat. With an unrushed rhythm, the crumbs from the bread were scraped from the tablecloth, the water glasses refilled, the wine topped off, and the salads replaced by turtle soup enhanced with sherry. Our entrees were Poisson meuniere amandine and crabmeat Yvonne. Dessert followed, and we wondered if we could possibly eat another bite. But we did, splitting an order of bananas Foster and an order of crèpe maison.

The waiter's understudy poured cups of thick, pure, dark-roast coffee to finish off the meal. Only as he finished did I look up at his face. I did a double-take as he walked from our table.

"Carol, that last waiter is a spitting image of Matthew Cummings, one of my men who died in Nam." I paused, but without panic. "You've heard about how you're supposed to crouch down when leaving or entering a running helicopter? Well, Matthew didn't. The terrain was uneven and the wind was high, causing the swirling blades to bounce up and down. His head hit the chopper's blades. That was a horrible sight. We all watched helplessly. What a waste; what a tragedy."

"My God," Carol uttered as she reached across the table and touched my hand. My look at her let her know that the memory was sad, but it didn't tear me apart. I was surprised at how readily I could talk about that terrible event, and equally surprised at how I did not have to dwell on it.

I realized that my wounds were slowly becoming scars, and I no longer had to bleed with the memory. Carol, who continued to listen intently, let out a deep breath when I ended my comments by simply saying, "You know, Nam really did suck," and shook my head. I passed the cream to Carol after putting some in my own coffee and smiled at her to say, "It's all right." It was.

A few moments later Louis and Ella Pouché from the church saw us and walked over to our table. He was Rex this year, an honor that followed him wherever he went. They were both warm and gracious people, and not at all pretentious. We persuaded them to join us for a second cup of coffee. They quickly found out that it was our anniversary, and we compared numbers. They had quite a few years on us.

Ella was interested in Oriental art and told us about a tapestry from Beijing she had just purchased. They were having dinner to celebrate that find. Carol indicated that she would love to see the tapestry, and Ella promised to have us over when it arrived. Carol had seen her art collection several years ago and found it to be magnificent. At the time I had trouble with anything Oriental. Now, however, I really wanted to see her tapestry.

Louis, on the other hand, had become interested in Buddhism as a result of their travels. "One and a half billion Chinese can't all be wrong," was his frequent line. I found myself agreeing with him recently, even though I did wonder how many people in China were really Buddhist.

After a while they got up to leave, and we said our goodbyes. Carol excused herself to the ladies' room, and I started looking for our waiter to get the check. Carol returned and I still hadn't seen our waiter. At last he emerged from the kitchen, and I motioned to him.

When I asked for the check, he smiled, thanked us, and then added that Mr. and Mrs. Pouché wished us a very happy anniversary. We were both overwhelmed; it was a very generous gift.

+++++

The next morning Carol and I decided to go for a levee walk to burn off some of the calories from the night before. We headed for the West Bank where the levee continued for miles without interruption, but we ran into a detour turning us off Prytania Street onto Tchoupitoulas Street. Carol remembered that today was the Crescent City Classic, a 10 K race through the city streets. I suggested we park and watch some of the race. The lead runners would probably come past fairly soon.

As we joined other spectators lining the street, we found ourselves standing beside a grossly overweight woman tending an igloo filled with water and a washtub filled with little sponges. "Done this for years," she volunteered when she saw us looking at her. "You'd be amazed how many runners accept a water-filled sponge. Some drink it; some squeeze it over their head; some wipe their face with it. My son's up ahead with a sign pointing out the sponge return. We recycle." She grabbed a handful of the little sponges and squeezed them underwater to fill them up. I cringed at the sanitation issues. Carol suggested to me in not-too-soft a whisper, "Perhaps I should stand upstream holding a sign reading, 'Don't drink the sponge-water.'"

Of course the woman heard Carol and responded, "The way I figure it, honey, these runners don't have the flu or nothing. They're in good shape. This can't hurt nobody."

As we waited for the lead runners, I looked across the street and noticed a Roman Catholic priest dressed in his white collar standing beside a monk in a brown robe. At the sight of the monk I found myself drifting far away, halfway around the world.

Carol noticed my distraction. "World to Will. World to Will. Hellooo."

"Sorry. I was thinking about Trong Tri," I told her rather calmly.

"You've called out that name in your dreams. Who is he?" Then Carol pointed up the street. "Look, here come the lead runners."

"Trong Tri was a Buddhist monk who saved my life and nursed me back to health," I replied. The lead runners streamed past, and the cheers from the crowd grew louder. Hearing me respond, Carol turned her back on the runners and faced me with keen interest. I realized again she hadn't heard me talk much about Vietnam, at least not while I was awake.

"We were in the village of Hue on the Huong River. It was supposed to be a friendly place, so Daniel and I were playing tourist. We were looking for the Imperial City, remains of ancient structures that were centuries old. However, Daniel let himself be lured into a brothel, which left me standing alone on the street. I knew wandering around alone was a dangerous thing to do, but there was no telling how long Daniel intended to be in there, and I wasn't going to just stand around and wait.

"When I turned onto a narrow street in search of the Imperial City, three men with knives appeared from nowhere and surrounded me. One pushed me, yelling in Vietnamese. In the split second it took me to register my predicament, I felt a hot, sharp pain in my chest. My attacker pulled his arm back, and I saw the bloody knife. I fell to my knees. I knew this was the end. I held my chest with both hands and collapsed with excruciating pain, coughing blood.

"They grabbed my weapon, and I knew they would shoot me or stab me again. I wondered why they took so long. I coughed more blood and rolled onto my side. They kicked me several times in my back and on my head, but it was the pain in my chest was unbearable.

"One of them took my wallet, another took my camera, and the third untied and pulled off my boots, all in a matter of seconds. They were robbers. Robbers, for God's sake. I was being killed by robbers, not by Charlie. It didn't seem right; but it was happening. I remember feeling strangely insulted.

"I curled up in shock and barely remained conscious. They dragged me into an alley and dropped me by a pile of charcoal stacked against a wall, then vanished as quickly as they had appeared. I tried to get up, but the pain kept me on my knees. Even though I was quickly becoming very weak, I managed to crawl out of the alley back to the street before I collapsed again. But the street was deserted. I tried to yell, but I had no breath and inhaling hurt. I knew I was going to lie there until I died."

Carol followed my story with intense interest. The runners passed us like a scene from some other time and place. I took a deep breath and continued.

"The next thing I remembered was a man in a bright orange robe lifting my head and pouring water into my mouth. I gagged, but swallowed some. Then he left. He returned with two other men. They picked me up, carried me a long way to a house, and laid me on a pallet on its dirt floor. They helped me drink water again.

"I figured I was now a prisoner. I hurt so much I didn't care. They had captured an officer and were very humane in how they treated me. Surprisingly so.

"After a while a new face bent over me to examine my wound. "You lucky," he said in broken English. "Only lung." He smiled and applied a clear gel to my wound; the ointment was from a tube I recognized as an antibiotic issued to our troops. He sealed my wound shut with tape from a standard issue roll. Then he lifted my head and put a pill in my mouth, followed by some water. I remember coughing up more blood before I passed out again."

Runners continued to pass where we were standing. They were coming in larger groups now. The leaders had gone on ahead. Neither Carol nor I paid much attention.

"I was left alone most of the time. I figured out that the door wasn't locked, and I realized that I was in friendly hands. I was grateful for the care they gave me. In several days I no longer felt faint all the time, and I could stand up and walk a little. Base camp was probably about four miles away, but I still wasn't strong enough to make a go for it. The orange-robed man who found me checked on me daily, bringing soup, rice, or a meat dumpling.

"One time I pointed to myself and said "William." After several repetitions, he smiled, pointed at me, and tried. "Filliam." He then pointed to himself and said, "Trong Tri." He repeated his name several times. "Trong Tri," I tried to say. He laughed heartily repeating it again, "Trong Tri." We both laughed.

"I grabbed his sleeve and pointed to his robe with a questioning look on my face. He simply said, "Buddha," and bowed deeply.

"Not too many days after that, I left and made it back to camp. I discovered Daniel had organized searches for me, but they couldn't find me because I was inside that private house which was on the edge of town.

"I never saw Trong Tri again. I went back to Hue twice searching for him, but I never found him."

Only then did Carol speak. She put her hand on my cheek and kissed my other cheek. "Thank God for Trong Tri," she affirmed as runners grabbed little sponges from a big woman.

+++++

Back in the office the next morning, I buckled down to deal with the inevitable paper work and numerous e-mails that had piled up.

"Mary Beth Stewart is here to see you, Rev. McKenzie," Marie announced on my phone intercom. "Okay," I replied. "I'll be right with her."

I covered up a college recommendation I was working on and went to the door. "Come on in, Mary Beth." I motioned to the pair of comfortable green chairs that faced each other. She was very pregnant, but she carried herself very stately and with unusual charm.

"Well, you certainly are in a motherly way, Mary Beth. You're looking great. When are you due?" I glanced at her left hand and saw no ring.

"In about two weeks, if the doctor is correct."

I raised my eyebrows. "Any time, then."

"That's about right. My sister and I both came early, so I guess we'll see if genetics affects timing or not. It's a little girl, and I'm going to name her Grace." She broke into tears and cried for a moment. Then she stopped, wiped her eyes with the back of her hand. She smiled. "I'm sorry, it's just I miss Stan so much."

"Stan?"

"Yes, Hendricks. You already know a lot about him." She shifted in her chair to get more comfortable. "We were planning to get married, but Alice killed him." She paused to let her words sink in.

I swallowed and started to take in the larger picture and its details. This was a shock to me, and the complexity of the situation impressed me as being immense.

"We talked a lot about marriage. When he found out I was pregnant, he set a date to leave Alice."

She cried without restraint now. "I miss him so much. It's hard to grieve freely in front of other people because of the circumstances and all. Everyone thinks this baby is the result of in vitro fertilization." She paused. Raising her head high, she firmly stated, "You can't hide a baby, and I'm proud she's his. Stan was proud too. Most everyone thinks I got pregnant using in vitro fertilization. I never said that, but that's what's going around. But my closest friends know the truth." She was trying hard to stop crying, but her tears continued to flow.

My God, I thought, what kind of a mess are we getting into with this? I could already feel the complications and conflicts when church members found out, as they probably will.

"There's no way I can have my name put up for Elder, so I need to ask you to remove my name from the nominating committee's list. Tell them I've simply changed my mind." Her crying had stopped by now.

"Sure. That's the least of difficulties you face," I said.

Then my thoughts were cut short by Mary Beth's second request.

"Will, I want to have my baby baptized on the 24th. That's two weeks before Easter. By then I should have recovered somewhat from the delivery, and Alice should still be in jail. There's no chance that her trial could begin by then. I certainly don't want her at church during the baptism."

Mary Beth reasoned like the law professor she was. She had put things together very deliberately and carefully … and in a very determined manner. I tried to absorb all this as quickly as I could.

"Alice knows that I'm pregnant. Stan told her. But for her to admit that the baby Stan's child would make her look like a double loser and would greatly complicate things for her children. I'm sure Alice wants me and my child to vanish, which is exactly what I hope to do for a while. I know it's just a matter of time before everybody puts all the pieces together. It will all come out in the trial, I'm sure."

This is one tough bird, I thought, one determined woman. I watched her intense eyes shift about in the telling of her plans.

"Because Alice admitted killing Stan, I have been able to keep my name out of the papers so far. A few words of a legal nature to the news people took care of that, but it won't be possible for me to remain anonymous after the trial begins. I'm an eyewitness to the murder and will be called to the stand. I just want Grace baptized before my name and hers get plastered all over the news."

"Grace, what a fitting name. But isn't all this going to get terribly ugly?" I asked.

"I'll face all that music when it comes. By the time the trial begins, Grace and I will be in Franklin, Louisiana, living with my brother on his sugar cane farm until all the dust settles, however long that might take."

She had scripted her scenario down to its fine details. I looked at her and said, "My experience is that life never follows our plans as closely as we would like it to. I'm sure, for example, you didn't expect Alice to grab a butcher knife on Christmas Eve."

"You're right about that," she assented, "but just like that navigation system in my car, I'll re-adjust my course as needed." She raised her eyebrows and tilted her head just a bit in face of admitted uncertainties. "The main thing is to get my baby baptized before Alice can put a rude stop to it by running screaming down the aisles. She'll leave me alone in the long run, particularly when I make no demands on Stan's estate."

"Whew! This is really getting thick, Mary Beth," I said. "Let me think about the whole thing for a minute. It's hitting me out of the blue, as you can appreciate." I swirled my head to illustrate that it was spinning.

"Think about it as long as you need to, Rev. McKenzie. Just remember, as a life-long member of this church I have just as much right to have my child baptized as Stan had to be buried, or Alice has to receive your pastoral care. None of us are saints, you know." She rested her case and looked at me as she sat in the green chair that had witnessed such a variety of confessions over the years.

I got up, touched her arm and walked to the window, looking out over the church gardens. A starling in early spring plumage strutted across the grass. A gray squirrel tried to rob the bird feeder. Behind me I heard one, slowly spoken word: "Well?"

"You're right," I concluded resolutely. "You're absolutely right, Mary Beth. You and your baby should not be denied the sacrament of grace and the blessing of the church. Let's count on the 24th. We can work out the details later," I indicated as I turned around. "I want us to talk some more between now and then."

"Thank you. Thank you so very much, Rev. McKenzie ... I mean Will." She paused. "Thank you ..."

She held her stomach, then burst into tears and threw herself into my arms.

BRIAN DAWSON

"I think it's time," Blanche announced nervously.

I felt a wave of panic. She wasn't due for another week, so I hadn't expected the baby to come tonight. I had just undressed for bed, but I quickly reached for my clothes. Blanche grabbed her robe and checked the hospital case she had prepared days ago.

"We'd better hurry, Brian," Blanche insisted. "The pains are really frequent now. I'm scared, honey." I hugged her tight and promised that everything would be all right.

I grabbed my keys, and we headed out the door. I helped Blanche into the car and started worrying that the baby might be born in our car as we drove to the hospital. I realized I hadn't locked the house, but I decided to forget it, hoping no thief would try to get in using the front door. I paused as we were halfway out the driveway. Maybe I should go back and lock up. Blanche winced with pain, and I again decided to leave the house unlocked.

Blanche held her stomach with both hands and squirmed restlessly in the passenger seat. She groaned. I slowed down, thinking maybe I should stop and help her get into the back seat where she'd have more room, but getting to the hospital seemed more important, so I sped up once again.

I felt helpless and nervous and as I wove in and out of lanes. Other cars seemed like obstacles, and my anger flared at them if they slowed me down. Maybe I should hold a white handkerchief out the window to let people know this was an emergency. I'd seen other cars do that, but I thought I'd better keep two hands on the wheel instead. I wallowed in uncertainties.

+++++

I stretched and looked at the clock on the birthing room wall. It had been six hours since we arrived. Part of me wanted to run down the hall to the waiting room until Blanche's labor was over. Yet I didn't want to miss a second of the birth. The prenatal class taught me to be Blanche's coach, but at this moment I didn't even feel like a water boy.

Blanche held my hand and squeezed tightly every time she had a contraction, which came almost all the time now. My fingers were beginning to hurt from being crushed together. I had been standing the whole time, taking only bathroom breaks and a moment to grab a cup of coffee that sat cold on a nearby table.

How on earth was Blanche enduring all this? I cringed at her pain. She rolled her head, eyes closed, face covered with sweat. I mopped her brow with a cool washcloth as she continued to squeeze my other hand. I marveled at her courage and stamina. I had no idea birthing our child was going to be so hard on her.

I tried to push aside my fears, but I couldn't. Will Blanche be all right? Will the baby be all right? I figured all expectant fathers had fears, but mine were fueled by guilt and fear that now surfaced like a bubble that had been held underwater. My guilt centered on a steamy evening with Lisa two years ago. That unfaithful transgression was rolling back on me now as though it had happened yesterday.

Lisa's car wouldn't start after the little league soccer game. I tried to jump the battery, but that didn't work. I couldn't get her car started, and soon everyone else had left. She had come by herself because Tony had gone to New York. I was also alone because Blanche had chills and fever all day and had gone to bed early. So there Lisa and I were standing beside her car on a deserted soccer field. We'd flirted frequently since I'd been at the church, and recently our exchanges had become more suggestive. I felt a rush of blood to my face as I considered the possibilities. "How about just locking your car and leaving it here. I'll give you a ride home, and you can deal with the car in the morning?"

"That would be wonderful," Lisa answered slowly, then smiled coyly. Her reply sounded encouraging to me.

I had barely gotten my own car started when Lisa reached over, put her hand on my leg, and warmly thanked me for the ride home. She went on to comment about how hard it must be to be a minister, always having to look out for so many people. "It's got to be draining," she suggested, rubbing my thigh in a sympathetic way. Her touch felt warming and exciting, and I hoped she'd continue. I knew she'd continue. I didn't know exactly how much to advance toward her, however. I surely didn't want to turn her off. I drove slowly out of the parking lot, being careful not to move my leg too much. I didn't want to discourage her gentle, soothing touch, but I knew I was walking a dangerous line. I wanted to help the action along, but I didn't want to overstep Lisa's intentions.

Lisa continued to speak in admiring and compassionate terms about me and my work. She was very understanding and I felt very supported. Then her hand moved from the top of my leg to inside my thigh, and she began a gentle massaging action. I felt a strong tickling sensation in my groin. Her words and her affection were powerfully enticing. I put my hand on her leg and was delighted to realize she wore no stockings, and she didn't flinch.

She unsnapped her seat belt and shifted toward me, lifting her hand from my thigh and starting to stroke my cheek and neck. Her right hand quickly replaced her left on my thigh, but higher than before. I half heard her say, "I just don't see how you take all the pressures. You're such a warm and loving man. I really admire that." I soon stopped listening to her smoky words and squirmed in my seat as her hand touched the growing lump in my trousers. I knew none of this was right, but she kept on, and I didn't want to stop her. She got more and more intimate. I enjoyed being the recipient, and my hand rubbed her firm, smooth thigh in return.

I was firm and aching by now. I didn't want this; I wanted this. I didn't like this; I loved this. I had to put a stop to this; I didn't want it to stop. I was driving slowly and trying to be careful, fearing someone would see us together in the car, yet a part of me didn't care. This was a fantasy coming true.

By the time I pulled into her driveway, Lisa had unbuttoned her blouse. Her white lace bra accented beautifully formed breasts. I reached over to caress her. She curled her shoulders so her bra was looser in front, making it easier for me. Her breasts were firm and ample, and exciting. Her massage of my swollen member was even more exciting. After a few more passionate minutes in the driveway she broke the silence. "We're here." She motioned to her house with her head.

As I got out of the car, my pants bulged and I was embarrassed, even though the street remained empty and dark. I also became a bit fearful. Tony really was in New York, wasn't he? Blanche really was sick in bed, wasn't she? Nothing seemed certain except the passionate possibilities of the moment. She led me into her house with her hand under my shirt against the small of my back, and then she moved her hand around to my stomach and lower as we walked in the door.

We had barely gotten inside when she dropped her blouse and bra to the floor. She unbuttoned my shirt as I caressed her breasts. We made it as far as the plush red carpet in the family room. She was firm and smooth and beautifully proportioned. We fit together quickly, easily, and perfectly. The moment was divine.

Soon we lay still and contented on the rug. Then Lisa kissed me once more and promised to be right back after freshening up a bit.

I lay naked on my back, catching my breath and barely believing what had happened. I pulled my shirt from the pile on the rug and covered myself. The pleasure of the moment lingered. Then I started to feel paranoid, and waves of guilt washed over me. Lisa returned, wrapping a pink silk robe about her shapely nude body. She sat on the arm of the nearby sofa, gently reaching under my shirt with her foot. She looked warmly at me, blew a kiss down to me, and told me what I yearned most at that moment to hear. "No one. No one, my dear, will ever know," she assured me.

Now, as I stood with Blanche in the labor room, I felt isolated with the secret. I still worried that Lisa would spill the beans in an impulsive moment. I was very uncomfortable trusting her to keep our affair confidential, but I had no choice. The knot in my stomach tightened as I thought about how much I was at Lisa's mercy.

Blanche moaned loudly, and I leaned over and kissed her. She was sweating profusely, and I wished I could take away her pain.

Why did all this stuff have to surface at a moment as important as this? I wondered if I'd ever be able to talk about the incident and get rid of my guilt once and for all -- with Blanche, or with someone like Will, with a therapist, with anyone. I just didn't know.

I also wondered if there would be a problem with the baby as a punishment for what I did. I looked at Blanche whose eyes were closed in grimacing pain. Would she and the baby be all right? I had often comforted others by assuring them God wouldn't punish them because they had done something bad. God doesn't work that way, I'd tell them. Now I had trouble believing it myself. The doctor had assured us everything was normal, but somehow that didn't comfort me right now.

I had hoped my fears would simply fade away. But now, during one of the most important moments in my life, half of me focused on Blanche and our baby, and another covert side of me burned with guilt over what I had done.

Blanche abruptly pushed my hand from her forehead with some irritation. Only then did I realize that I was probably being overly solicitous toward her. I was showing too much concern and too much sympathy, like I needed to make up to her. Or maybe I wasn't. I couldn't figure out how my guilt and shame were affecting me. With painful sadness I realized I didn't have a clue what it would be like to have normal thoughts and feelings at a time like this.

I remained a quagmire of uncertainty. Then I wondered if maybe that uncertainty was the punishment. Maybe I'd have to endure such feelings all my life. I even wondered if a deformity might be a convoluted way of removing my paralyzing guilt. If my daughter were born with a handicap, my guilt and shame would be externalized. I could then focus on concern for the baby as a way of making up for what I had done. My stomach tightened harder as I realized how sick these thoughts were. I gagged a little, but quickly swallowed the burning acid.

Blanche squeezed my hand again, really hard this time. She rolled her head in pain and I winced with her. I was a basket case as I stood in the room that held the promise of new life.

The doctor arrived and took charge, much to my relief. Grabbing my digital camera, I snapped picture after picture after picture. I hid behind the camera by watching life on a little monitor of reality. That realization was painful. Nobody knew or noticed; but I did, and it was killing my soul. God help me!

The baby started to emerge. Hair first, then a distinct pink head and neck. A miracle emerging. I watched what felt like a surreal drama, and I continued to take pictures. The next thing I knew, the doctor held up a messy red baby for me to see, then handed her to the nurse to clean her up. At the sight of our new little girl I started to cry at the beauty of it all.

I hugged Blanche, who was fatigued and drenched in sweat, but whose eyes were smiling brightly. She grabbed me by my neck, pulled me tightly to her, and kissed me. My guilt and shame melted into joy. I sobbed like a baby and dropped the camera on the bed. We watched the nurse wrap our newly cleaned baby girl in a blanket.

"Ruth!" I exclaimed. "Our Ruth. She's so beautiful!" I kissed Blanche again, as she glowed with a broad, exhausted smile. The nurse handed Ruth to me, and I was thrilled. The doctor picked up our camera from the bed and snapped our picture before he left the room. A nice touch. I handed the baby to Blanche, who smiled with joy and satisfaction.

Blanche commented on how brown her hair was -- just like mine. It was, and I was proud. Blanche then called attention to Ruth's hazel eyes. "Like mine," she smiled. We both stared in wonder at our newborn child. I smiled so broadly my jaws ached.

Blanche held Ruth to her breast. "Our girl!" Blanche sighed triumphantly, "Our perfect baby girl."

I hoped so.

CAROL McKENZIE

Will and I were busy talking as we walked back to the elevator from seeing Blanche and Brian's new baby. We nearly ran down a nurse carrying a tray full of meds. Stepping aside just in time, we apologized and pushed the "down" button for the elevator. I yawned. We had come as soon as Brian called us, and it was still very early in the morning. But what a treat to see and to hold little Ruth.

"Blanche and the baby are looking good," I mentioned to Will. "I'm excited for them. While you were talking with Brian, Blanche told me the baby is named after her grandmother Ruth. It's such a pretty name, and Biblical." We watched the elevator light move from 3 to 4. Will grew impatient and pushed the down button again. "Brian sure did look washed out," I added. "You'd think he'd been the one who had just been through seven hours of labor." I laughed at the image.

"He did look tired," Will replied. "Maybe everything will be all right now that little Ruth is here." We both fell silent as we stepped into the crowded elevator.

When the door opened to the ground floor, Will looked at his watch. "Say, it's only seven o'clock. I don't have to be in the office until nine. Let's eat breakfast in the Quarter. Game?"

I nodded and called home to let David know our plans before he left for school. I grabbed Will's arm and we started walking.

Then Will suggested that we go to "Le Croissant de Ville."

I stopped dead in my tracks. My jaw literally dropped. "Are you sure?" I emphatically asked.

"Yep. I can handle it. Having breakfast there has been rolling around in my mind for a while now. Let's do it."

"Well they do have the best croissant in town, and great French coffee and heavenly pastries. Best you can find anywhere, as you have heard me say many times." I hesitated, and then added, "But it's family-owned and operated by, well, you know … by a Vietnamese family." I looked at Will and waited.

"Yep. That's the one," Will agreed in a matter-of-fact way. "They were written up in *Gambit* several weeks ago. Two Vietnamese brothers started the French café. Their combined families now run it. When Saigon fell, they settled in New Orleans East, in the area they call Versailles. Who knows what side they were fighting for?"

I was amazed at Will's ability to talk so calmly and candidly.

"I trust they will let an old marine walk in without poisoning my coffee."

"You don't have your uniform on. Let's go."

+++++

Will opened the door for me, showing no hesitation as he entered. He nudged me toward the display case filled with pastries. He remained calm and peaceful.

Will ordered a butter croissant, and I ordered an apple turnover. I also got a Napoleon I intended to take home for our dessert tonight. We took our coffee and food to a table and sat down. Just as we did, an adorable little Vietnamese girl, probably the owner's daughter, ran up to Will, looked up at him, and loudly greeted him, "Hi!" Will stooped down to her level, responding "Hello!" She ran back to the pastry counter. Will beamed.

I was the nervous one, not him. I kept waiting for something to break loose, but nothing did. This was the first time in our married life Will had gone into an Asian restaurant, café, laundry, or any other kind of oriental establishment. Tears filled my eyes as I watched Will sip the dark roast French coffee. "It's all right," he assured me. He reached over, wiped away my tears with the back of his hand, and smiled.

His eyes were dry.

Come to think of it, his right eye had been dry all morning.

WILL McKENZIE

Sunday worship went well today, and I was pleased. I particularly enjoyed doing the children's sermon. I always do, because I really love children. Today over thirty children gathered on the steps of the chancel. My subject was God's love for us, and it went well.

Then came the regular sermon. For the first time ever, I illustrated my presentation with a story from Vietnam. It fit right in with the text, and the story made my point emphatically. It wasn't about ears or human skewers or something like that, but I did refer to the death and carnage that surrounded us and talked about the inner conflicts and the guilt that we experienced. I used the story to expand on the subject of forgiveness, talking about how it as a free gift from God. The congregation seemed more attentive than usual, and I could tell from their facial expressions that I was causing a lot of them to think. A few wrinkled brows told me that those people were trying to understand what I was saying, or perhaps trying to fit what I was saying into their current faith perspective. At the end of the sermon I felt particularly good about how it went, and I felt like I had broken into a new and more meaningful approach to my preaching. Carol's beaming face certainly confirmed that for me.

I always checked my weekend phone messages after worship before going home. In addition to several pieces of information people had left on the machine, Marie said that Paul Gravois had called and wanted an appointment for counseling with me. She had set it up for next Tuesday morning when he would be coming into town from Chicago. Marie added that Paul wanted the appointment to be strictly confidential. She also noted that he was not a member. I wonder why she always looks that up. It doesn't matter to me.

Paul had to be Grits' son, the one who left home years ago. I had heard Grits and Gail make references to Paul from time to time, but they never talked at length about him. The most they had revealed was that things fell apart when he was a teenager and have never mended since. I knew the broken relationship brought a deep sadness into their lives.

Paul's coming to town certainly piqued my curiosity, and I found myself a bit nervous in anticipation of the appointment. I wondered if Grits knew he was coming to town, if they would meet and talk, if my time with Paul would be catalytic one way or the other. My anxiety increased as I thought about that. Of course I could in no way indicate to Grits that Paul had made contact with me, much less say that he was coming to see me. But because of my personal and therapeutic relationship with Grits, this one was tough for me.

+++++

When I walked in the house, the phone was ringing, so I answered it. "That was Emily Richardson," I told Carol who came into the room as I hung up. "The Richardsons were our next door neighbors growing up. They moved to Boston when I was still small. I bet I haven't seen her in about twenty-five years. Anyway, she's in town for an Elderhostel convention of some sort, and I invited her over for coffee at two this afternoon. I hope that's okay."

"Sure, as long as she doesn't want a tour of the bedrooms."

+++++

The doorbell rang a little after two. It was Mrs. Richardson all right, complete with the toothy smile I remembered from my childhood. I didn't really know her well since she was my mother's age, but she was frequently in our house. However, she was much smaller than I remembered her.

We were soon sitting on the sun porch talking. She reminisced about life and people when we lived next to each other on Second Street. I was amazed at what I remembered and equally amazed at what

I didn't remember. I certainly knew that none of our houses had air conditioning back then, but I had no clue that the man across the street was an alcoholic or that the man we called "Uncle Henry" was deeply involved in local politics. Emily also told about the time I ran away from home by taking a bag of Oreos and camping out in her car. Carol absorbed every detail about a part of my early life that I simply hadn't talked about. Who does?

We found out that Emily's husband died three years ago and she had recently sold their house in Boston and moved into a condo, a high-rise overlooking the Boston harbor. I bet the view was spectacular.

"When did you all move to Boston? I forget."

"Not long after Karen was killed by that car," she replied. "Dan had an opportunity to start his own agency, and I was eager to get away from the things that reminded me of Karen's death. For him our move was advancement; for me it was escape. It seemed to help at the time. The irony was that I soon started missing all the familiar surroundings, even the ones associated with Karen's death. It takes a long, long time to get over the death of a child. I think I finally have."

As we talked, I suddenly saw an image of black hair matted with blood. I tried to concentrate on Emily and push the image aside. "Did you go back to teaching in Boston?" I asked.

My conversation with Emily Richardson went onto automatic pilot, and I fell into silence broken with occasional nods. Yet the images kept coming. Blood and hair and people screaming. Mommies and daddies running into the street. A lot of loud screams.

Mrs. Richardson was the first to get to Karen. She was lying in the street just beyond a gap between two parked cars. Blood pooled on the asphalt. Her long, black hair was bathed in blood that looked thick and sticky. Her arms were smeared with blood as well.

Carol now carried the conversation. "How is Boston this time of year?" I heard Carol ask while she repeatedly glanced at me with a worried look.

Carrying Karen limp in her arms, Mrs. Richardson ran screaming into the house. An ambulance with a red light arrived. My mother and father took me inside. Then my mother went next door to Karen's house. I remember the ambulance leaving. I watched it go and heard its siren fade into the distance.

I saw myself playing doctor with Karen. A red and yellow Jacks' ball was the baby. We were sitting on the ground facing each other. Her dress was up. She was sitting on the ground in her panties. I put the ball into her panties and called it a baby. Karen took the ball out. "Look a baby," and then put it back into her panties. We laughed. It was fun. We did that several times. Then I threw the ball away saying the baby was gone. She jumped up and ran to get the ball ... to get the baby. Tires squealed, a horn blared. I heard a thump. Her mother carried her into their house with her limp bloodied arm dangling down. I threw the ball away saying the baby was gone, and Karen went after it. I didn't know where I threw the ball. I just threw it. She jumped up and ran after the ball yelling, "My baby. My baby." It bounced and bounced and bounced. She ran after it.

Emily Richardson was standing now, and she gathered her purse and coat to leave. She thanked us for the coffee and added how good it was to see me. We thanked her for the visit.

My daddy told me that a car had hurt Karen. He never asked me what happened. I never told. I just became quiet and crawled into bed. It was the middle of the day.

I never heard about Karen again. She never came back from that ambulance. Her mother cried a lot whenever she saw the rest of us playing in the yard. She never asked what happened. Her child innocently ran into the street between two parked cars. No one talked about it. They accepted Karen's death as a tragic accident.

As soon as the door was closed behind Emily, I sat down on the sofa and looked at my feet. Carol sat down beside me. She put her hand on top of mine and looked at me with concern, waiting for me to say something.

"My God. It was Karen's hair. It was Karen's hair I've seen all these years. I thought those memories had something to do with Vietnam, but it was Karen. I was involved in her death. I caused her death." Tears filled my eyes and rolled down my cheeks.

I cried freely, but I didn't sob. Somehow the time for sobbing had long since passed. I felt profoundly sad. Sad for Karen. Sad for Emily and her deceased husband. Sad that Karen was taken away. Sad that my impulsively thrown red-and-yellow ball from a Jacks' set had caused such tragedy. Sad there was nothing I or anyone could do about it.

I went through the memories with Carol, ending, not in guilt and shame, but in a keen sense of a tragic death played out between two very young children.

"I didn't have the heart to tell Mrs. Richardson, Carol.' I paused. "I wasn't trying to protect myself. I just couldn't bring myself to shed a whole different light on Karen's death than what Emily had already come to terms with." I paused. "If I'm wrong, let me know. I can still tell her the whole thing if you think I should. She'll be in town for two more days. But I don't see what good it would do half a century later. It would certainly stir up her emotions again. I don't see the point."

Carol nodded in agreement.

After a silence, Carol gently asked, "Do you need to tell Emily for your own sake?"

"No. I'm all right. I'm not into the guilt. I think there's forgiveness for this, just like there is for Vietnam."

+++++

However, I made another appointment with Grits to talk about Karen's death. As I walked into his office I thought of Paul, not Karen, and started speculating again about his coming to town. With some discipline, I shifted back to myself and my childhood incident and told my story to Grits.

"I thought Nam was the end of my bad memories," I pondered as I concluded my story. I had used up most of the therapy hour dealing with it.

"Vietnam was a real problem for you all right, and it probably will still bubble up from time to time," Grits replied. "But often coming to terms with one set of painful emotions can free us up to deal with pains of a different nature. My hunch is you would have remembered your childhood friend sooner or later anyway, even if her mother hadn't visited you."

I fell silent for a second then asked, "Is there no end to our need for forgiveness?"

"Probably not. It's like peeling an onion. We're made up of layer covering layer covering layer. The good news is that forgiveness covers all the layers."

"Forgiveness even for layers we're not aware of?"

"Sure," Grits confirmed, "and you're now probably wondering what else is going to pop up, right?"

"Yeah, I was wondering that. I don't know how much more I can take."

"You're doing all right so far. There's no need to be anxious about other stuff that may or may not surface. No need to go poking around for something, but no need to worry about it either. There's also forgiveness for whatever else is there." Grits fell silent and looked at his hands in his lap.

"Then there also has to be forgiveness for those who don't even know about forgiveness." I paused and thought about what I had just uttered. "Yeah, there has to be."

"I think so too," Grits agreed. "Where there's life there's love; and where there's love there's forgiveness. Without the two there's no healing and no real living." Grits smiled coyly. "Now I'm sounding like the preacher, huh?"

He paused and our eyes met. We were both somewhat tearful, but there was no embarrassment, only acceptance.

As I left, my thoughts returned to Paul. I still wondered if Grits or Gail knew he was coming into town. It's strange ... no; it's beautiful ... to counsel the son of the one who counsels me. Full circle.

+++++

Blanche and Brian had made an appointment with me to talk about baptizing their daughter Ruth. They were seated in my green office chairs.

"Sure. The 24th will be great for the baptism of little Ruth. She's precious. Anytime you need a baby-sitter, Carol and I are always ready. Seriously."

"Great," Brian thanked me. "That's the only date both Blanche's folks and my folks can come at the same time. Ruth will be well-supported by family that day.'

"I know you won't mind having another church member sharing the space with you that morning," I told him. "Mary Beth Stewart has scheduled her daughter Grace to be baptized that same day. She was born just a few days ago in Memorial Hospital, remember." I waited for Brian and Blanche's response, watching them carefully.

"That's fine," Blanche volunteered after a moment of silence. "Tell me about Mary Beth Stewart. Who's her husband? I don't think I know them."

"The baby's father is dead; unfortunately Mary Beth wasn't married to him. So Mary Beth will be by herself with little Grace."

"How sad. What did he die from?" Blanche innocently asked.

"Well, Blanche ... Brian ... Grace is the daughter of Stan Hendricks of Alice and Stan fame."

"Oh my goodness," Brian blurted.

A long silence followed.

Brian spoke at last. "Well, she needs all the support she can get, is the way I see it."

"I feel so fortunate there're two of us," Blanche added. "Is there anything we can do to help?"

I silently let out a lung-full of air and felt tremendously relieved. "Just keep being yourselves," I told them.

+++++

We had a long, free weekend at last. I was off from Friday noon until Monday morning. Brian was holding down the fort and preaching on Sunday. I turned off my cell phone and Carol and I drove west toward Lafayette. Cajun country here we come!

After a few hours, we pulled into the gravel parking lot of the *Bois des Chenes* in the heart of Lafayette. This bed and breakfast was a plantation dating from the 1820s. We checked in and were escorted to our room. Our host told us a glass of wine waited for us on the front porch, so we were soon sitting in rockers overlooking the garden, sipping the special wine they made on the premises. We relaxed into the unique pleasures of Louisiana's Cajun country.

Our main goal for the trip was to spend an evening at Mulate's. This famous Cajun dancehall in nearby Breaux Bridge featured good food and exceptionally good Cajun music. So, shortly after dark we parked our car beside a row of pickup trucks and went into the small, windowless building. Its ceiling was held up by cypress logs that were skinned and shiny. The modest dance floor was in the center of the room, surrounded on three sides by tables with red-and-white checkered cloths. On the fourth side was a place for the band. *Soufflé* was playing tonight, a group that I had enjoyed when they came to the Jazz and Heritage Festival in New Orleans two years ago. I can still see and feel the unceasing energy of the red-vested accordion player as he pushed out the fast moving Cajun music.

Finding a table next to the dance floor was a real coup. We ordered two Jolie Blonde beers, a house favorite. The beer's label pictured a melancholy maid wearing a large white hat accenting her long golden ringlets of hair. The picture was originally oil on canvas by the Cajun artist Rodrigue.

After an excellent dinner of flounder stuffed with generous portions of crabmeat, we pushed back from the table as the band started to play. They began with a fast two-step that brought the best dancers to the floor. The Cajun two-step was too aerobic for me, although Carol tried to get me to dance it with her. Rather, we enjoyed watching the younger folks dance this one. The accordion and fiddle vigorously pumped out the melody, and the drummer sang in Cajun French. I understood very few of the words, even though I spoke a fair amount of French. The patois was unique; you almost had to be Cajun to understand it.

Next came a slow number, so Carol and I ventured onto the dance floor, and numerous people of all ages joined us. We bumped elbows with a mother who was dancing with her daughter. To our left a tall, white-mustached man, standing a lean six foot three or four was dancing with a thin little girl about ten years old -- probably his granddaughter. Her proud parents smiled from ear to ear at a nearby table. A baby was sleeping in a 'sugar-scoop' on the table next to ours. The mother and father had joined in the dance, leaving the baby on the table in that carrying seat. No one seemed concerned about the baby's safety, and the baby slept soundly. Carol and I kept an eagle's eye on that baby – but sure enough, he remained securely in the middle of the table until the happy parents finished dancing.

Two young lovers danced affectionately as though they were alone on the floor. An ancient woman two tables over followed their every move with a satisfied, confident look on her face. No one else paid them much attention.

The dance floor was now packed. The band played smoothly, and the drummer had stopped singing. A boy of about fourteen walked onto the floor with a girl about his age. He danced with his head held high, unashamedly proud that he had landed a dance with this particular girl. She, in turn, stared into his eyes like a moon-stricken maiden. Everybody in the room seemed to be relaxed and at peace. It was family night out on the town, and all were having a wonderful time.

People wandered from table to table, talking, sitting down to enjoy a beer, or asking someone to dance. Everyone appeared to know each other, and if there were a care in the world, it wasn't in Mulate's tonight. It was Friday night in Breaux Bridge, and everyone had gathered to "pass a good time." Carol and I loved the ambiance. Mulate's atmosphere and all of its patrons embodied the freeing "joie de vivre" the bayou people exuded. It was a gift, and we shared in it.

I was surprised when the leader of the band announced the next number would be the last dance of the evening. The time had flown by. I glanced at my watch and was surprised again. It was only eleven o'clock. In New Orleans, entertainment spots stayed open into the wee hours of the morning. I looked again at all the children and elderly people present, and I realized eleven was late enough. There was always next Friday night to dance some more.

The fiddler announced in English that the last dance would be a waltz. He gave its title in Cajun, and half the room headed to the dance floor. Carol and I joined in. We all started waltzing to the introductory strains of music. It felt good to waltz again. Everyone danced in a large circular motion around the floor as though the dancing had been carefully choreographed. The band played smooth, soothing music, and the accordion emphasized the romantic three-quarter-time tempo.

After a long period of improvisation, the fiddler started playing the melody, and the drummer began to sing. "La Grâce du Ciel est descendue," came the pleading falsetto. "Me sauver de l'enfer. J'étais perdue, je suis retrouvée."

I smiled from ear to ear and whispered into Carol's ear. She was also smiling broadly. We both laughed out loud as we continued to dance. We kept laughing and smiling and dancing. Others were smiling pleasantly. Everyone seemed to have a peaceful look. As Carol and I gazed into each other's eyes, our delight quickly overflowed into tears of joy. I kissed her cheek.

We both had trouble believing what was happening, but we loved it. We were waltzing, yes waltzing, to the hymn "Amazing Grace." I never realized this hymn was a waltz. I would never have thought of dancing to it. Yet how fitting it was to dance to it. If you can't dance to God's grace, what can you dance to? It was a beautiful experience. A joyful experience. The dance was unbelievably freeing.

"Aveugle, et je vois clair," the fiddler sang with soul-felt passion. "Was blind but now I see."

+++++

Back home from Breaux Bridge, I had trouble realizing that another Sunday had arrived, and that Easter was only three weeks away. I wanted to be back in Mulate's waltzing to "Amazing Grace." In contrast, our choir director had chosen "A Mighty Fortress is Our God" as our opening hymn. Somehow it reminded me of that battleship in my dream. This hymn certainly wasn't talking about a Love Boat. I made a mental note to choose the hymns for Easter myself.

I was eager to preach my sermon today. After a word of introduction, I read my text from the seventeenth chapter of Luke. "Once Jesus was asked by the Pharisees when the kingdom of God was coming. Jesus answered, The kingdom of God is not coming with things that can be observed; nor will they say, Look, here it is! or There it is! For, in fact, the kingdom of God is within you and among you" (Luke 17:20-21).

I looked out over the congregation and saw the same hopeful eyes I saw every Sunday. I launched into my sermon. "The kingdom of God is within us all and among us all, among and within ordinary people like you and me." I received no particular reaction to this introduction, but I continued. "We each need to dig down deep within and claim that kingdom." A few people started paying closer attention. I asserted that "The kingdom of God is not found exclusively within any single denomination or faith group." Some people wrinkled their brows; most listened carefully by now. "We need to see God in ourselves and in each other; that's right -- God in me and God in you!" By now the congregation was involved with my message.

I spoke for the first time from the pulpit about my struggle with guilt over all the killings in Vietnam. I talked about my guilt. I talked about survival guilt. I told how only recently I had reached deep within myself to find the forgiveness I needed to put that guilt to rest. My autobiographical illustration seemed to capture the congregation's interest and engage their thinking. But maybe it wasn't because my sermon was about me personally, but because it was universal -- or maybe both. In any case, everyone was listening and continuing to listen until I finished speaking.

The service ended with time to spare. Everyone always likes that. Thomas stopped on his way out. "Where have those verses been all my life? They sure sum up where I'm coming from. Luke 17, huh?"

Agnes and Howard Benson, whose brows remained wrinkled throughout the sermon, gave me a polite but cool "hello" as they left. Howard commented, "I'll have to think some more about your sermon this morning. It raises a lot of questions for me."

Peter Bernard, our Clerk, asked for an appointment to talk about my sermon. I agreed to call him and wrote "Peter" on my pocket notepad. I figured he would spend the time straightening me out as best as he could.

But Peter surprised me. He stopped in front of me, and a lull in the exiting crowd gave him a moment. He looked me very directly in the eye and said, "The ultimate survival guilt, Will, comes from not going at all. Try living with that one. I have for years."

I fixed in amazement, the meaning of his words sinking in.

"My leg," he continued. "My leg kept me from serving. I've been limping in a lot of ways ever since. Give me a call when you can. I guess I need to talk." He shook my hand and stepped forward to leave. Then he paused, turned around, and warmly added, "I'm glad you're here, Will." I watched him limp down the steps to the sidewalk, marveling at his transformation.

Martin Hebert, who worked for the District Attorney, had obviously waited to be the last person out of the church. He shook my hand strongly, and while he continued to shake it told me, "Alice Hendricks' case goes to trial one month from tomorrow in Judge Bordeaux's court. It'll be in Room C on the main floor of the courthouse. Nine o'clock."

He waited for his words to register. "It'll probably take a week to select a jury. She's sticking with her plea of not guilty by reason of insanity. The whole thing could get ugly and sticky. Alice's parents and children will need all the support you can give them. The *Times-Picayune* is going to give this trial front-page coverage, and that'll make it hard on everybody involved."

"Thanks for telling me, Martin. I assume it's all right for me to attend."

"Sure. I think you might have trouble getting a seat when it first starts, but the crowd usually thins down after a few days. By the way, I'm glad you declined to be a character witness for her. I don't think it would have done any good, and it could have backfired on you as well as on her. Ministers are hard to believe as character witnesses about their own parishioners."

"I didn't decline, Martin. Alice's defens ...," but he had already turned to leave and didn't hear me. Alice's defense attorney had thought better of the idea and withdrew his request. I wondered how Martin found out I had been asked and "declined." I guess he knew everything that goes on down there.

I made a mental note of the trial's date and another note to visit Alice's parents. I was sure they'd try to shield the children from as much as they could. So young. So sad. When on earth would they be old enough to hear how their daddy died? Ever?

I was preoccupied as I walked to my car. Alice's trial was going to shake up a lot of people in this city. A killing. A violent murder with a butcher knife by a person of "good standing." I thought about how many ways killing happens. A knife through the heart. A bullet through the chest. Shrapnel from a grenade. Fire from a flame-thrower. An incendiary bomb dropped on an anonymous enemy, sometimes including civilians.

But I realized there are other ways to kill people too. A word of condemnation to someone looking desperately for hope. The poison of neglect for those crying out for love. A back turned in an hour of need.

What about a strong judgment toward someone's beliefs? Or chalking off a person because he or she follows a different religion. Or burning a cross of hatred because some people have darker skin. Sometimes we also eradicate people by making them invisible, rendering them of no importance to us whatever. Sometimes we discount the souls of those who are strangers and neglect the people closest to us.

We're all killers and need forgiveness. All of us. Often death lacks a fresh corpse; but the death is still real. We humans eat up each other all the time. We are not vegetarians.

+++++

"Well, James, I feel more at peace lately than I have in a long time. I feel lighter and freer. I feel less defensive and unapologetically alive." I paused to think about James. His acceptance and understanding freed me to be exactly who I am without editing. Best friends are like that: maximum acceptance demanding minimum forgiveness.

"If God accepts us the way we are, warts and all, then God doesn't need to forgive us, right?" I typed. *"Understanding and acceptance pre-empt the need for forgiveness."* For several minutes I thought about what I'd written. "Yes," I finally affirmed out loud to a deaf, busy street.

I was eating a po-boy sandwich on Magazine Street. The sidewalk table allowed me to enjoy the early spring sun, but it did get a bit noisy as cars and busses passed by. As I concentrated on my letter to James, the noise seemed to fade into the background.

"Am I losing my faith or finding it? Am I losing my sanity, or finding true sanity? I ask myself those questions often. But you know, the way I answer isn't critical anymore. Life's always a mixture of sanity and insanity, of faith and doubt, of good and of evil. I have stopped worrying about where it will all come out. The good news is I don't have to maneuver the results. I can let life be, and that's all right." I glanced at my watch and realized it was getting late. *"I gotta run. Ciao."*

I finished my roast beef po-boy. The sandwich was sloppy with gravy, and my fingers were sticky from the delicious mess. So was my computer keyboard. I chuckled to myself as I remembered that I used to measure how good a roast beef po-boy was by the number of napkins needed to eat it. That hasn't changed much at all over the years.

I was about to shut down my laptop when the inbox registered a message. I instantly flushed and felt my heart pound when I saw that my e-mail to James had come flying back to me, "addressee unknown."

With trembling hands I went back to my message. His address was the same as always on his Blackberry. I sent the e-mail again. "Addressee unknown" came the quick return.

I didn't know what to do. I hoped he had changed servers and e-mail addresses. The cocaine issue loomed large in my heart. I quickly checked his last message to me, and the properties were the same. I thought about his last message again; he told me he'd "moved past" the girl he'd been dating. Maybe he'd moved, started over once more time. But where? I didn't even want to think about other reasons for the returned mail. Cocaine. Overdose. Suicide. Somewhere at home I had his street address in Paris, but he had no landline to call.

With a growing knot in my stomach, I tried to push my speculation, fears, and frustrations to the side. I took a deep breath and blew it out. "Let me hear from you, James! Let me hear from you!" I heard myself say out loud as I closed my laptop and headed toward the church.

+++++

I entered the sacristy to put on my robe. The door to the parlor was open, so I could hear everyone talking. I heard Peter arrive and greet everyone. Carol's cooing at the babies floated into the sacristy; I heard her saying sweet things about both babies. I was delighted she was enjoying the gathering. After all, children incarnate the hope that keeps us all going.

While I adjusted my robe, I noticed a strip of masking tape on the windowpane hadn't been removed after last year's hurricane threat. We dodged that bullet one more time, and Mr. Mallroy had to spend days scraping tape off the windows. He obviously missed a piece. I made a mental note to stock up on masking tape to avoid the rush once the season began again this year. This year's supposed to be particularly bad for hurricanes -- but they always say that.

I put a white baptismal stole over my black robe and entered the sanctuary to start the worship service. The baptismal parties also entered and sat on the front pew.

When the time for the baptisms came, I called the families forward and we all gathered around the font. I faced a side window that opened onto the patio garden. There I saw Margaret looking in at us from behind an azalea bush. I smiled to myself.

Smiles, in turn, greeted me from every angle as we stood around the font. The godparents stood beside the parents. Mary Beth held Grace, and Miriam and Ashley stood warmly close to them. Mary Beth's eyes showed a lot of anxiety. Today was a good day for Mary Beth, but also a tough one. She and I had met several times during the past weeks to deal with her feelings and the complexity of her situation. She was ready for today, but not steady. I reached over and put my hand on her shoulder. She looked at me warmly, and tears came to her eyes. I then reached out and touched Blanche's shoulder too.

Blanche held Ruth, and Brian had his arm around Blanche's waist. Both babies wore white -- Grace with a long, flowing gown and Ruth with a shorter, more tailored dress. Both babies slept soundly.

I always marveled at the beauty of this sacrament. I knew the service by heart. As I began, familiar words flowed freely. Some of what I said came from the *Book of Common Worship*, and some were my own words that I had used over the years.

"A sign and a seal of God's covenant of grace." "A welcome into the household of faith." Mary Beth rocked Grace who was now stirring a bit.

"Celebrating God's love for us long before we are aware of it." "Celebrating God's love for us long before we can articulate any beliefs about God." Little Ruth sneezed suddenly, then fell immediately back to sleep. Brian chuckled.

"The sacrament of infant baptism is filled with grace. It proclaims God's amazing love for us regardless of our age or stage in life. This sacrament declares God's love for us regardless of our knowledge, regardless of our institutional alignments, regardless what we say we believe, regardless of the worthiness of our own life." I saw tears come into Brian's eyes, and he pulled Blanche closer. "This sacrament celebrates love freely given and freely received long before we ourselves are capable of loving."

Peter stepped forward. He lifted the wooden lid off the baptismal font, uncovering the silver bowl inside holding the water.

"What is the name you have given your child?" I asked Blanche and Brian.

"Ruth Elizabeth Dawson" Blanche replied. I baptized her with three handfuls of water on her head. "In the name of the Father, the Son, and the Holy Spirit." She barely moved, but continued to sleep peacefully.

Turning to Mary Beth, I asked for her child's name.

"Grace," she answered.

As I put the third handful of water on Grace's head, she woke up with a start. She had the most beautiful, pale-blue eyes you could imagine. I rubbed her soft cheek with the back of my first two fingers.

She cried once, then smiled an endearing infant's smile before falling back to sleep.

Blanche, Brian, and Mary Beth all smiled with joy and satisfaction. The godparents looked on with pride. Peter stepped forward and covered the font once again.

As the ancient ritual ended, we stood silently around the font of grace. Bright rays of sunlight suddenly flooded upon us through the patio window, and we all basked for a moment in the unexpected warmth and light.

I raised my hands to give the blessing.

In the middle of the blessing I turned slightly toward Margaret to include her. She watched intensely, smiling along with everyone else.

Unnoticed by the others, Margaret reached above her head and grabbed the blessing with her hand. Then she skipped away like a happy little girl.

+++++

Acknowledgments

Nancy, my wife of 45 years, has remained steadfast in her love, support, and encouragement during this project; without her continuing optimism and "can do" attitude, this novel would have died on the hard drive. To her I dedicate the finished product.

Friends offered early and ongoing support. I am most grateful for Martha Stevenson's encouragement after an early reading of a very rough draft; likewise to Jewel Deane Suddath, a very early editor.

Then there were the seven members of my bi-monthly writers group, which changed membership over the past four years but maintained high standards for us all. I am grateful to Jan Ross who did a thorough editing job on my completed manuscript, as did Anne and Richard Gowdy – all were gifted professors of college English.

Roy Cooper, North Carolina's Attorney General, gave his valuable time to advise me on the crime-processing scenes, and Bill Brawley, a Silver Star Vietnam Lieutenant, was most helpful on the war scenes. Scores and scores of war veterans shared their stories in my counseling office over the years, and hundreds of church members opened their lives to me during my parish years. No one in the book is an actual person, but all the characters are compilations of numerous real people. To them all I am most grateful for helping me to see the true nature of forgiveness.

Printed in the United States
140501LV00002B/114/P

9 780595 533244